"I know you're not good for me, but I can't seem to stop wanting you."

That was fine. She'd decided he was bad for her too, hadn't she? That was why she hadn't texted him, because she was cutting out things that hurt her.

So why did hearing him say those words hurt so much?

"It's never been like this before. Every year I'd come back from our . . . meetings, and I'd eventually get back to my life. I'd sleep and eat and socialize and be normal. But you being here, so close . . ."

"I can't leave," she cut in.

"I didn't say you should."

He was pummeling her with feelings. Giving her bursts of pleasure and a hit of pain.

But didn't that basically sum up their whole relationship?

By Alisha Rai

Hate TO WANT You

Forbidden Hearts

ALISHA RAI

AVONBOOKS

An Imprint of HarperCollinsPublishers

HarperCollins
PUBLISHERS
Since 1817

This is a work of fiction. Names, characters, places, and incidents are products of the author's imagination or are used fictitiously and are not to be construed as real. Any resemblance to actual events, locales, organizations, or persons, living or dead, is entirely coincidental.

First Avon Books mass market printing: August 2017

Print Edition ISBN: 978-0-06-256673-7
Digital Edition ISBN: 978-0-06-256671-3

Avon, Avon & logo, and Avon Books & logo are registered trademarks of HarperCollins Publishers in the United States of America and other countries.
HarperCollins is a registered trademark of HarperCollins Publishers in the United States of America and other countries.

FIRST EDITION

17 18 19 20 21   QGM   10 9 8 7 6 5 4 3 2 1

*For the heroines
who raised me.
Aai & Aaji.
I love you.*

Acknowledgments

WRITING A book is never an easy thing, but having the right people in your corner can make all the difference.

Thank you to my agent, Steve Axelrod, and editor, Erika Tsang, as well as the entire team at Avon Books. Your genuine enthusiasm for this series has made this whole experience so amazing!

A special thanks to Sasha, Corey, and Allie for invaluable input on drafts of this book; Bree, Donna, Courtney, Alyssa, and Beks for raptor-ishness; my family for being generally fantastic and lovely; and you.

Yes, you, reader. If this is the first book of mine you're picking up, whoa. If it's the second or the fifth or eleventh, whoa. I'm thrilled and so grateful. Thank you for giving me your time, because I honestly don't know what I'd do if I couldn't write romances for you. I'd probably be herding goats.

And I don't know a thing about goats.

I hope you enjoy.

Chapter 1

O<small>NE NIGHT.</small> *No one will know.*

Those were the rules.

They weren't romantic rules, but nobody had called Nicholas Chandler a romantic in a very long time. Love rarely conquered all, the true villains almost always went unpunished, and happily ever afters? Ha. Sometimes all you could hope for were secret stolen moments with one messy, royally bad girl.

Nicholas shut off the engine of his sedan. He preferred using terms that were clearly defined, so he shied away from adjectives like *bad*. *Bad*, especially when used to describe a woman, could mean too many things.

In this case, though, it meant she was bad for *him*.

The Open sign flashed in the window of the tattoo parlor. Dusk had settled, and the other businesses in the strip mall had already closed. He sat in one of the only two cars in the parking lot, the other a fourteen-year-old rusted yellow sports car. How the Mustang was still functioning, Nicholas had no idea. Given how far its owner had run, he was certain that car had hit the upper limit of mileage a long time ago.

He kept his hand on the keys. If he left right now, he would still have time to squeeze in his usual after-work run before he sat down at his kitchen table with a nutritionally balanced dinner for one. Plus, he could avoid the risk of someone spying him and rumors spreading about his suspicious presence in this firmly blue-collar neighborhood of Rockville.

A shadow moved in the brightly lit storefront. Every muscle in his body seized. Part of him had hoped the gossip was false, even after he'd identified her car, but he supposed his life could never be that easy.

Livvy Kane had come home.

He leaned forward, but he was too far away to see her clearly. It didn't matter. The restless energy in that body as she walked, the curve of her hip, the whip of her dark hair. All of it was imprinted on his brain.

Livvy paused in profile, backlit by fluorescent lights, and gathered the mass of her hair up on top of her head. Her back arched, full breasts lifting. He knew exactly how those firm globes felt in his hands, the point where her light brown skin faded into a paler color untouched by the sun, the taste of her small, tight nipples in his mouth. He'd sucked them, bit them, rolled them between his thumb and forefinger. He knew how much pressure to exert to make her sigh, and how to lick her to make her scream.

Livvy's arms slowly lowered. She pivoted and walked away, out of view.

He breathed deep and sat back, the odd spell broken. Livvy was *home.* His home, and technically hers, though she hadn't called it that in a decade.

He curled his hands into fists. He wanted to march in there and demand answers almost as much as he wanted to go home and forget she was breathing the same air as him. Two contrary, irreconcilable desires.

His phone buzzed, and his head jerked toward the dashboard where it was mounted. It took him a second to process the message that had popped up. The number was unfamiliar, but the attitude was not.

Can I help you?

In terms of pure pleasure and relief, he imagined the feeling he got when he received a text from Livvy was similar to what an addict felt when they got a hit of whatever drug they craved.

This time, though, a beat after the surge of excitement came mortification. If running a corporation didn't work out for him, he wasn't going to be able to count on a backup career as a spy.

His phone buzzed again. **Quit creeping.**

Nicholas scowled. He was not *creeping.* He was sitting in a dark parking lot, watching a woman through a window—

His face heated. Okay, point taken. Nicholas

picked up the phone, thumbs poised on the screen. He hesitated, unsure of what to say.

He'd gotten exactly nine texts from her over the years, like clockwork. With the exception of that first message, they'd been sparing on words, containing only a time, a room number, and the latitude and longitude of wherever she happened to be in the country. None of them had required a response.

His phone vibrated against his fingers, a reminder and a rebuke. **If you want a tattoo, you'll have to come inside.**

He didn't want a tattoo. He wanted her. He couldn't have her. *Bad for you.* Like his weakness for sweets.

He was not unaware of the parallels between his sugar addiction and his Livvy addiction. He ruthlessly controlled himself around the white stuff, bypassing the bakery at Chandler's entirely for long stretches of time. Until he couldn't help himself anymore, and he found himself eyeing the cannoli in the refrigerated display case.

He only ever allowed himself to purchase two. He ate one in his car, wolfing down the treat in greedy bites. The other he took home and ate slowly, savoring every second of the flaky fried shell encasing sweet ricotta, letting the creamy, rich filling linger on his tongue in a fit of self-indulgent need.

Nicholas shook his head, hating the uncharacteristically flowery thoughts that had invaded his brain. *Today's not a day for hedonism.* Which was why he could not go inside.

He could not go inside, he repeated, as he snatched his keys and got out of the car.

He could not go inside, he told himself, as he mounted the steps to the brick building.

He could not—

The bell above the door to the establishment jingled cheerfully as it opened. He stepped inside and closed the door firmly but quietly behind him, the bell cutting off.

His shoes squeaked on clean tile as he took a few steps into the deserted reception area. The shop was small but tidy, warm and brightly lit, with a colorful seating area crammed full of mismatched comfortable chairs. There were magazines spread out on the coffee table, ranging from *Better Homes and Gardens* to *Car and Driver*.

A curtain separated the rest of the business from the front. It rippled like someone had disturbed it recently. She knew he'd entered, no doubt. She hadn't seen him yet, though. He could still leave.

Chandlers aren't quitters.

He adjusted the cuffs on his shirt, though they didn't need adjusting. Team See Her had destroyed Team Avoid Her at All Costs. He was committed to this now. There was no turning back.

It was fine. He wouldn't gorge himself on her. He'd simply . . . gather information. As president of Chandler's, it was his duty to evaluate any issue which could affect their company.

Cold. Formal. It's business. In no way, shape, or form could he let the careful barrier he'd constructed to keep her at a distance slip.

Firm objective in mind, he squared his shoulders and walked to the curtain. As he parted it, that firm objective promptly turned into an objective that was roughly the consistency of tapioca pudding.

Livvy sat on a stool in profile to him, bent over a worktable, doodling on a scrap of paper, seemingly oblivious to his entrance. Her foot tapped, striking the concrete floor in rhythm with his pounding heart.

She decorated her sweetly rounded body like a canvas and framed it with tiny scraps of fabric: today, a red bustier and black leather pants. On another woman, he might wonder if she were in costume. On her, he didn't care. He only wanted to rip the clothes off her.

He remembered her natural hair color from when they were young, a perfectly lovely midnight black. Her parents had grounded her for a week the first time she'd used drug-store peroxide and dye to turn it some shade of the rainbow. They gave up by the third or fourth color.

Now it was almost subdued, pulled up in a messy knot on top of her head, dark brown shot through with burgundy highlights. He failed the struggle to not think about what those waist-length waves looked like spread across a pillow. Or licking his body like flames as she slid down his chest.

She bent over her drawing, her bare midriff pooching over the waistband of her pants. She didn't look at him, but she did speak. "I see you decided to quit lurking."

The last time he'd heard that voice, he'd been driving into her, her snug pussy gripping his cock, toned legs locked tight around his waist, her fingernails drawing blood on his shoulders. *Don't stop*, she'd whispered in his ear. *Fuck me harder.*

He didn't know what he'd said in reply. Their encounters were usually a haze of sweat and pleasure and filthy words and filthier actions. Nicholas assumed he'd complied, because he'd ached the next day. He didn't know if she'd been similarly affected. He'd always left before dawn, before she woke up.

Those were the rules. One night, wherever in the country she might be. After nine years of illicit sex, he'd learned them well.

He had to swallow twice in order to speak, but he was gratified he didn't sound like he'd been punched in the stomach. "I was not lurking."

"I didn't realize there was a threshold for how long a guy needed to loiter in a parking lot in order to be classified a lurker." She placed the pencil neatly next to the pad and stood. Her black, laced, knee-high boots added about three inches to her five-foot-nothing height. She crossed her arms over her chest. A tattoo decorated her shoulder and arm, highlighting her toned muscles, a twining vine of prickly black flowers. It was new.

He wanted to touch it, but *that* wasn't new. He always wanted to touch her.

They stared at each other in silence for a long moment. The corner of her lips curled up. "Hello, Nicholas."

He grasped on to the polite, meaningless greeting like a man grabbing the handiest lifeline. "Livvy. You're looking well." An understatement.

Her kohl-lined eyes dipped over his body, from his head to his feet, leaving fire in their wake. He found himself straightening. *Asshole. You're two seconds from flexing your muscles for her.*

"You too. New tie?" She batted her lashes.

He automatically smoothed his hand over his tie, but then stopped. Last time they'd seen each other, she'd grabbed the strip of fabric and hauled him close to press her mouth against his. Did she remember? "Perhaps. I don't recall."

"Nice. It brings out the blue in your blood."

Her attitude wasn't new either. "My blood isn't any more blue than yours is," he pointed out. Both of their grandfathers had been the first generations in their families to be born on American soil. It had been one more commonality that had made the two men such good friends and business partners.

"Hmm. Must be the Scrooge McDuck vault of gold you swim in every morning that gives it that bluish tinge." She leaned back against the table. "Who told you I was here?"

"A cousin. She saw you at a gas station." It had taken a second to google Livvy and discover she was working at this place. Nicholas was mildly ashamed of the level of familiarity he had with her social media profiles. Far more than an ex should have.

She didn't ask him which cousin, probably because she realized it didn't matter much. He barely knew everyone in his clan. His vast extended family shared two things in common: one, they were amiable and bright but not terribly self-sufficient, and two, they were all employed by the corporation. *Family first.*

"I didn't think gossip would spread this quick. I've only been here a week."

"You've been gone too long if you think that was quick." Even without taking his network of family into account, their corporation was the single largest employer in Rockville, New York. There were more than a few people, related to him or not, who figured they had a vested interest in the personal lives of the Chandlers.

As far as he could tell, no one had told his father. Yet. He'd know the second the old man learned.

"I guess so." She spread her hands in front of her, a mocking smile crossing her blood-red lips. "Well, now you've seen it with your own eyes. Ding-dong, the witch is back."

"I've never thought you were a witch." With her mischievous eyes and delicate features, Nicholas would say she resembled a rather naughty punk fairy. That is, he would say that if he were a fanciful sort of man—and he wasn't, not in the slightest.

"No? Don't tell anyone. I have a reputation to maintain, friend."

"I'm not your friend." The protest was automatic, one he couldn't stop himself from uttering.

Her eyes hardened to onyx chips. "Figure of speech. Blood enemies doesn't sound nearly as polite. And we both know how much you like to be polite."

"I'm not your enemy either." Not technically. He had no idea what he and Livvy were. There was no word to encompass their relationship.

"Depends on who you ask, I guess."

Yes. If he asked their respective families, there would be no hesitation. Criminals or cheats, depending on who was talking about whom.

Livvy examined her nails. "Gotta say, though, it's strange for a guy who's not my friend or my enemy to come running over here to creep on me the second he finds out I'm in town."

He straightened. It was time for him to take control of this meeting. "First, I was not creeping. Second, I did not come running here." He'd had to sit through two meetings. "Third, it's not strange at all for me to be curious as to why you're back after so many years. Working, no less." Working implied a long-term commitment, didn't it? He'd mulled that over during every minute of those two long, unnecessary meetings, and decided it did.

She held up her fingers. "One, I'm guest spotting."

He wasn't entirely sure what that meant, but it sounded more temporary. Good. He was relieved. Definitely.

"Two, you were absolutely creeping. Three, it's not the first time I've been back in years. I was here for Paul's funeral."

Nicholas wasn't sure if she'd mentioned her dead brother so matter-of-factly solely to rattle him, but mission accomplished. He shifted his weight and turned his head to study the bulletin board closest to him, taking a beat to collect himself. A number of pieces of paper had been stuck to the bottom haphazardly, pages torn from a sketchbook and cheap glossy prints of anonymous people's adorned body parts. The designs were rich and bold, popping with bright colors, some of them looking more like watercolor paintings than something you would put on skin.

"I meant for a longer stay," he finally replied. Of course she'd come home for the funeral. Jackson too, probably. Nicholas had done his best to avoid thinking about it too much, even scheduling a site inspection in another state that weekend.

His ex–best friend's tragic death in a hiking accident a little over a year ago had been well publicized, all of the old dirty laundry dug up, everyone watching to see what he'd do. The gossip mill would have gone berserk if Nicholas had so much as shown his face in a five-mile vicinity of the church.

Paul and Nicholas were being groomed to run the C&O together, but then, you know, the accident happened, and Brendan Chandler swindled Tani Oka-Kane out of her half of the grocery store chain, and the Kanes were left with nothing. Poor Paul.

Or:

Paul and Nicholas would have run the C&O together, but then, you know, the tragedy happened, Tani Oka-Kane sold her half of the company to Brendan, and Paul's little brother Jackson grew so enraged he burned down the first store the company ever built. Poor Nicholas.

It didn't matter which way the gossip slanted. His and Livvy's former relationship might be mentioned somewhere in there, but to outsiders, their breakup was probably the least exciting and most predictable part of the saga.

A particular crooked sketch caught his eye. A flighty hummingbird in blues and greens flew against a splash of pink, the initials L.K. scrawled on the bottom. He righted the angle of the drawing, adjusting it so it hung properly.

Despite dreading the subject and his feelings about it, he'd imagined what he would say to Livvy when they met up for her most recent birthday, months after Paul's death. Though it would have been a sharp departure from their usual script, he'd rehearsed a few simple sentences. "I'm sorry about Paul." He sounded stiff and wooden, but he couldn't help that. He was out of practice when it came to consolation.

"Little late, isn't it?" Her voice was quiet, subdued. Unlike her.

"Should I have contacted you earlier to offer my condolences?" What would that conversation have been like?

Her heels tapped on the tile. Nicholas concentrated on the feathers of the bird as if they held all the mysteries of life.

"I didn't expect it. We don't have that kind of relationship, right?" Her soft arm almost brushed the front of his suit jacket, and he glanced at her sharply. She was so close he could count the freckles scattered over her cleavage. She'd hated those freckles as a young woman, comparing herself to her blemish-free mother. He hadn't been able to understand her dislike. How many times had he dragged his tongue from one freckle to another, playing connect the dots and creating a perfect pattern in his head? Too many, and not enough.

His body tensed and hardened, readying for her. God, he was always so ready for her.

She placed her finger on the drawing, exactly where his had been, and adjusted it so it was crooked again. Clear eyes locked on his, daring and tough, not a single vulnerability visible. "Right, Nick?"

He was Nicholas to everyone. She was the only one who'd shortened his name, but not to Nick. She'd always called him something else.

He made sure his tone was well modulated and even. She was correct. The only relationship they had was one based on lust. "Right, Olivia."

Her frown was barely there, but he knew he'd scored a hit with her full name. He knew, and he hated himself for it.

She lifted her bare wrist and studied it. "My, look at the time. As much as I have loved this awkward visit, I really do have so much to do. So if you only came here to offer your belated condolences . . ."

"I didn't." He might have gotten sidetracked, but his initial objective seemed more imperative now. How long would he have to deal with this interruption in his perfectly ordered life? "I came to talk to you."

Her sardonic smile called attention to the tiny

scar next to her lips. A souvenir from her adventurous childhood. "To talk to me?"

He edged closer because he couldn't not take advantage of this opportunity to inhale the scent of vanilla and sugar. "Yes."

"Talking's not usually what we do when we're together. And last time I checked, my birthday isn't for another eight months, so . . ."

He flinched, unprepared for her to speak so bluntly about their odd arrangement, though he should have been—she was a blunt woman.

"I know exactly when your birthday is," he said, sharper than he intended. "I suppose I ought to give you belated felicitations as well. I missed your thirtieth."

Her stubborn chin lifted. "Oh, were you expecting to see me?"

Of course he'd been expecting to see her. That was how they worked. For the past ten years.

For the past nine years, he corrected himself. The last year had come and gone without their annual sexual marathon. "I assumed. We'd established a pattern." Another small step and he could get a tiny bit closer to her. How did she smell so good? Like every delicious thing he craved and couldn't have.

Livvy had to tilt her head back to meet his gaze. If he moved his hand, he could touch her. Lord, how he wanted to touch her.

"We both know I hate being predictable," she breathed. "Sorry if I kept you waiting."

Her apology rang hollow. A ripple of repressed

anger swirled under his careful icy calm, and he squelched it. If it were anyone else, he'd assume Livvy was playing a game, but she was far too straightforward to bother with games. Or at least she had been. "No apologies necessary," he said. "I moved on."

"Did you?"

"I had to." He'd told himself her absence had been understandable, only a few months following the death of her brother. The eagerness with which he'd waited for her text . . . when he realized he'd blocked that day off on his calendar . . . that hadn't been acceptable.

Darkness touched her expression, and she glanced away. "Right. Great. Well, I'm honored Rockville's golden prince spared me a fleeting thought."

He wanted to laugh, but there was no humor in his body. A fleeting thought? She honestly believed that was all she'd been worth over the years?

"I'm not a prince," he reminded her. Both of them.

She turned and walked away, and his gaze dropped to her bottom. She'd gained weight since he'd seen her last, and it looked good on her, making her ass even more clutchable. He curled his fingers, remembering how those round globes felt when she was riding him.

"Whatever you say. If you want to talk to me, text me," she said over her shoulder, breezy and careless once again. "You have my number now."

"Or we can talk here." There was no guarantee that number wouldn't change tomorrow. The first few years, he'd saved the phone numbers that popped up on his screen with her message. In moments of weakness, more times than he'd like to admit, he'd call them. Thank God, they were always disconnected. She changed phone numbers like she changed cities.

"No, thanks."

"I insist."

"Just like a Chandler," she said coldly, not looking at him. His last name dropped into the conversation with the weight of a thousand pounds of baggage. "Selfishly taking whatever you want."

There it was. Only a few feet separated them, but the battle lines had been drawn, creating a gulf the size of an ocean.

Her harsh words stabbed straight into his heart. Electricity zipped through him, the rush of fierce blood pumping in his veins a foreign and heady sensation. Sugar rushes had nothing on this. She always made him feel alive in a way no one else did. Like he was a wind-up man resting in a case, waiting for her to apply the key.

"Just like a Kane," he replied with devastating calm, hating himself for every word that fell from his lips, not believing a single one of them. "Running away."

She spun around. The air crackled. "Fuck off," she said, her soft whisper more threatening than any scream. "Like I said, I'm working. So unless you want a tattoo, you can get the hell out."

He stared at her, took in every perfect, enraged

line of her body. *I dare you to kiss me*, she'd smirked that first time they'd gone out. Poking and prodding and demanding and taunting him until he'd pressed her up against her front door.

The scratches on his back faded every year, but he'd always carry her marks. And he'd take any reason to steal a few more minutes in her presence, to take a few more hits of these unwise emotions.

"Fine," he heard himself say. "Then give me a tattoo."

Chapter 2

LIVVY HAD never been good at maintaining rage, which had turned out to be quite the problem when it came to staying away from *certain* people she was supposed to despise with all her might.

She cracked out a laugh, her anger giving way to genuine amusement. "Shut the front door, Nicholas. Behind you, on your way out, I mean."

He grew still when she laughed, but his dark blue eyes were expressionless. She supposed some people would call him cold, but she knew him too well for that. For all that he was three years older than her, they'd essentially grown up together. She'd seen him happy, devastated, grief-stricken, and angry.

Not since they'd broken up, though. Since then, she'd only seen him cool and controlled. Or hot, his face twisted in savage pleasure as he fucked her. Those were his default modes when it came to her. And she'd never let on how much she missed those other emotions.

"You don't think I'm serious?" he asked.

She rolled her eyes and paced back to her table,

unable to stand being so close to him. "You mean about my inking you? Yeah, no, I don't think you're serious." She knew exactly why he was here, had figured it out the second she'd spotted him in his car, his features shadowy but unmistakable. The man might be brilliant when it came to business, but covert he wasn't. He'd parked right under a streetlight.

Nicholas had always liked order. Black and white. And above all else, he was loyal to his family and C&O—or Chandler's, as it was called now.

When something unexpected happened, when the patterns in his life were interrupted, his immediate instinct was to circle his wagons and make sure those two things were protected. And he was trained to see a Kane—even her, maybe especially her—as a threat.

She could never let him see how much that hurt her. Let him think she wanted nothing from him, except his body . . . and maybe not even that anymore.

A muscle in his square jaw twitched. His features were too blunt and harsh to be called pretty, but he was beautifully compelling in the same way a blade was. Sharp. Lethal. Devastating.

His fingers went to the knot of his tie. It took her a second to realize what he was doing.

Oh no. She tensed. No, no, no, not his *tie.* Goddamn it.

Did he know? Could he possibly have any idea how much she loved watching him unfasten the Windsor knot at his throat?

Livvy traced her tongue under the edge of her upper teeth as the expensive silk whisked against Egyptian cotton. He carefully folded it around his hand, and she had to fight not to press her hand over her belly at the jump of excitement there. That deliberate, neat gesture always did something to her.

The times they'd come together over the years, he started the night like this. Tidy. Then she eroded every ounce of his control, until he was a naked, stripped animal, hungry for her.

She remembered the first time she'd taken notice of him in a charcoal-gray suit. She'd been fifteen, and he'd walked into her house with her brother, still wearing the corporate uniform he'd donned for his summer job at the family company. His lanky frame in the finely tailored dress slacks and jacket had made her look twice, then a third time.

He'd been wearing a red tie that day. She remembered, because it was the first time she'd imagined grabbing the thing and dragging his lips to hers. He'd gone from a family friend to the object of her teenage lust in a few seconds.

Bastard had imprinted on her. Now she was helpless against his formally clad figure.

Oh, he knew she was affected. He couldn't be so dense. He must know because he was standing there all *hot*. And *suited*. And, and, and . . . rubbing his thumb over his tie like he knew exactly how she wanted him to drag it over her body. Or wrap her up in the silken bindings.

Stop. Drooling.

Nicholas neatly placed his tie in his pocket and pushed the sides of his jacket away, his hands on his hips. Asshole! What kind of sexy show-off power pose was that? And *why* did she find it so sexy?

News at ten. Area woman finds powerful, confident man sexy. In other top stories, water is wet and puppies are goddamn adorable.

She averted her eyes from the way the jacket framed his white shirt stretched over his flat belly. Disciplined guy that he was, she bet he still woke up daily at five in the morning to work out. Every year she hoped she'd find him less attractive, but when she peeled that fucking delicious suit off him, he was all tight, lean, muscular flesh. All hers. For a night, at least.

"Where do you want me?"

Everywhere. That's the problem. I want you every-where, and I always will.

"It's a bad idea to play chicken with me. We both know I'm not afraid of jack." Lies. She was deathly afraid of the things he made her feel. But if she kept saying how courageous she was, maybe she could make everyone believe it?

"I'm not playing chicken."

"Neither am I. I will pierce your skin, kiddo." More lies.

He shrugged, cool as a cucumber. "I have to begin somewhere. You've got a head start."

Definitely, compared to him. She'd gotten her first tattoo when she was seventeen, a tiny pot of gold on her hip she'd been delighted to show off in a bikini as soon as possible. Mostly to show off to Nicholas, who had stared for a long time before he'd realized she was watching him. Then he'd flushed a dark red, before making his excuses and disappearing inside his family's lake house.

They'd started dating a week later, and the first time his hands had coasted over her body in the backseat of his car, he'd gone straight for the gold, fingers and lips and tongue tracing it reverently. She owed that lucky charm a lot.

Like years and years of heartache, dummy. She pursed her lips, trying to think past her inconvenient lust long enough to get out of this.

She'd known keeping off his radar would be difficult, but she'd thought she'd have more time. She'd kept a low profile, only traveled back and forth between home and work, hadn't looked up any old friends or acquaintances. What a naive, silly idea. Clearly, all it took was one person who spotted and recognized her to get the phone trees ringing. This town literally wasn't big enough for the both of them.

You came home to move forward.

There was nothing to discuss here, nothing that would help them move forward. Only a repetitive cycle of pain and desire she had resolved to break this year. If she hadn't had to come home, it might have worked too. "You've got a ways to go if you're planning on catching up."

She played with a lock of her hair, draping it over her left shoulder, letting it cover her heart. She'd done a shitty job of protecting that foolish organ her whole life. That needed to change.

Nicholas's gaze dropped to that lock of hair. When she'd caught sight of him sitting in his car, she couldn't deny she'd felt a spark of joy.

That same spark tingled to life as he walked toward her now. But then she noted how his steps were hesitant, reluctant, and that spark died a swift, fierce death.

Because he didn't *want* to walk toward her. He might crave her body, but that was all he wanted. And he hated himself for it, the same way she hated herself for being unable to control her feelings for him.

Every muscle tensed when he raised his hand, but it only hovered over her bare arm before dropping back to his side. "This is new."

Her skin was hot and tingly, like the ink on the vine was fresh. "Got it a few months ago," she managed. Because a clinging vine the color of her eyes served as a good reminder of what she didn't ever want to be.

"Hmm." His gaze dipped to her cleavage and grew heavy-lidded. They never lingered when they were in bed together, and the lights were usually off, so he hadn't seen the details of the rest of the ink on her body. Part of that was by design. Each dot of pigment meant something to her, something she wasn't sure she could share with him and be okay.

But in her fantasies, they played a wonderful game called Inspect Livvy's Body Thoroughly. It was a good game.

But you're not playing it anymore, in your mind or

reality. Because you're taking charge of your life and your future and heavenly God, he smells so good, like cinnamon and . . .

"It's pretty. What does it mean?"

She faltered. "It means I like pretty things," she lied.

Deep lines etched his forehead. "Why . . . ?" There went that muscle in his jaw again. "Why are you here?"

More reluctance. He hated he'd had to ask that. She bet the only son of a family on *Forbes*'s richest must generally know everything going on in his world.

Did he not know about her mother's accident? She'd simply assumed he would hear of it. Or . . . A sharp pain lanced her chest. Maybe he did know, and he hadn't expected her to show up.

If that was the case, then it only underscored how much they'd changed. The woman he'd known all those years ago would have dropped everything to come home if her mother'd broken her hip. No, that wasn't right. That woman would have never left to begin with.

Ugh. The last thing she wanted to do was talk about her mom with him. "I told you. I don't have time to talk. I'm working."

He leaned closer, giving her another delightful hint of aftershave. "And I told you. I'll get a tattoo, if that's what it takes to have you answer my questions."

Her lips firmed, her temper crackling. *Yes, good,*

get mad. A solid show of messy drama will chase him out just as well as anything else. "Fine." She reached behind her, grabbed the clipboard holding blank forms and a pen. "Here."

He accepted the board when she shoved it at him. "What is it?"

"A health and safety acknowledgment and a disclaimer. Says you're not drunk and you understand I could screw up and completely destroy your body, turning you into a hideous monster that makes all those hordes of women panting after you run screaming from your bedroom." She smiled sweetly.

He raised an arrogant brow, but he didn't dispute the part about the hordes of women. "Do you do that often? Disfigure men?"

"Twice on Tuesdays."

"I wouldn't sue you."

"That's good," she said flippantly. "I don't have anything worth suing for."

She waited for him to fumble his way out at the reminder of her diminished fortunes. The Chandlers had wound up with everything, and the Kanes with nothing, after all.

Because the Chandlers are opportunistic, greedy, soulless bastards, came Paul's voice in her head.

Nicholas looked down at the clipboard and quickly signed it without reading it.

"You should read the things you sign," she snapped, genuinely annoyed with his carelessness. "I could have stuck a blank check on there."

"Do you need money, Livvy?"

Not from him, thanks. "Only what you'll pay for your tattoo. Spoiler alert: I'm fucking expensive."

"I know." He shrugged when she met his gaze. "You can get a lot of information on the Internet."

He'd googled her? *No, heart, don't you dare go pitter-pat over that! Googling is hardly a sign of caring. Do you know who casually googles exes? Everyone with a stinkin' Internet connection.*

She yanked the clipboard from him and ripped off the last page of the carbon copy. "Your after-care instructions are on the back of this. Might wanna keep them." She gestured to the seat. She'd done the guest-artist deal in a ton of shops over the years, some better than others. This place was on the small side, but scrupulously hygienic, her biggest requirement.

He peeled off his jacket and draped it neatly over the plain plastic chair in the corner that was reserved for guests of customers before settling into the leather padded seat. He looked far too good in her chair. "Where do you want to do it?"

Her step faltered. To cover her reaction, she went to the sink and washed her hands. The *it* was a tattoo. He meant where did she want to tattoo him on his body, not where did she want to have wild animal sex. "Usually the customer decides that."

Not in this case. Livvy knew exactly what she'd put on him, and where. She'd scribbled it on a cock-tail napkin years ago, around three a.m., when he'd been sleeping soundly next to her, his naked back bared.

She'd like to say she'd thrown that napkin away, that she hadn't visualized that design getting more elaborate and perfect, but that would be a complete lie.

It was art, she told herself defensively. She didn't throw away any of her designs.

She dried her hands and turned to catch him undoing the right cuff of his shirt. Ohhh, she liked watching him do that too. Usually by the time he was done unfastening his tie and the cuffs, she was in a frenzy of lust. Not today, though. Today she'd be all adult and shit. In full command of herself.

Nicholas rolled up the sleeve of his shirt, baring his muscular forearm, and rested it on the arm of the chair. She hooked her stool with her ankle and shoved it closer so she could sit next to him, contemplating his arm like it held all the secrets of the universe.

She could do it. She could totally touch him and control her pesky base desires. Livvy pressed her fingers against the skin of his wrist.

Her stomach clenched. Okay, maybe she couldn't. "There?"

"Fine."

She slid her fingers higher, up to the middle of his forearm, because those base desires demanded to be fed a nibble of pleasure. His late mother had been Greek, and his heritage was apparent in the olive tone in his skin. She swallowed. "Or here?"

He cleared his throat. His hand had become a fist, she noted. "Whatever you want."

"What am I putting on you?"

He released his fist, and his arm jumped. "I told you. You decide."

Livvy slid her finger down again, and that damn muscle responded. She kept her head bent. "You're permanently altering your body," she began, about to launch into the speech she'd had to give to intoxicated college students for the past year in Boston.

"I don't care."

Lies. He cared about his body. He treated it like a goddamn temple. Yet another thing for him to control. "Oh, goodie. I haven't done any naked women in a while."

"You wouldn't do that."

Always so confident. "How do you know?"

"I know you."

The three words had her swallowing around the lump in her throat. No, he didn't really know her. She was hardly the same pigtailed kid who'd tagged along behind him and Paul, eager to play with them. Or the young woman he'd swept off her feet, whose virginity he'd taken in a luxurious hotel room a few towns over.

Everything had seemed so easy then. Perfect. They'd been a magical couple, young wealthy royalty destined to unite two powerful families.

Then it had been over.

"You don't know shit," she managed, then grabbed a Sharpie from her workbench.

He was silent for a bit. "You're probably right."

She uncapped the green Sharpie and bent over

his arm. A blank canvas. A tingle of excitement ran through her, the same tingle any artist would feel if they'd theoretically been given carte blanche.

"What are you doing?"

"I draw my designs first," she lied. She tended to freehand most of her work, unless her client wanted to see it in advance. Then she used transfer paper, like a temporary tattoo.

There was no way she was actually piercing Nicholas's virgin skin with a needle, though. Otherwise she would have prepped the area properly by shaving and cleaning it.

"Naked lady it is," she said lightly, and bent her head to draw a woman's head on his inner wrist, making it deliberately big.

She didn't have to steady him—he was unmoving—but she kept her finger right on his pulse. Its regular tempo reminded her of all the times they'd lain curled up around each other, their heartbeats synchronized. Nothing frazzled him, not even his childhood sweetheart and former lover putting permanent marks on him.

Livvy bit her inner cheek when she sketched in huge boobs, waiting for his yelp of outrage. When she glanced up, though, his eyes were shut, head tilted back, thick lashes flaring against his cheeks. It wasn't fair for a man to have eyelashes like that when she had to wage a war with her mascara brush every morning to turn her short lashes into any kind of flirtatious arcs.

Was there anything she didn't like about his

face? Nope. It wasn't perfect, but she lusted after all of it, from his fierce eyebrows to his twice broken nose to his high cheekbones to those aforementioned lashes. She wanted to drown in his eyes and be revived by his cruel lips.

She drew the female's legs coyly bent to preserve some modesty—Livvy would happily draw a vagina, but she wasn't sure what level of detail she could manage in a hasty doodle on an arm, and she hated to half-ass a vagina—and continued sneaking peeks up at the man. There were new lines on his forehead and around his mouth, like he frowned a lot more now. He was thirty-three, hardly ancient, but silver threaded through the hair at his temples.

"Why are you really in town?"

She concentrated harder on her dumb drawing than she needed to. "My mom broke her hip. Where do you think I'd be?"

At his silence, she looked up. His lips were compressed tight. "I'm sorry. I didn't know. How is Tani?"

At least he could say her name. "She'll be fine. She just needs someone."

Not entirely true. Tani wasn't totally alone. She lived with her sister-in-law, and she had other people who could look out for her.

But Livvy wanted Tani to need her.

Livvy had managed to avoid spending more than twenty-four consecutive hours in this town or in her mother's company for longer than a decade, since her beloved father had died and everything had come crashing down around her. Her self-imposed exile had felt like protection back then. Not so much anymore.

In a fit of whimsy, Livvy added two large wings to the back of the voluptuous female.

"Did your brother come back too?"

Her hand jerked at the bite in the words, the first real, non-lusty emotion Nicholas had clearly betrayed.

She knew Nicholas probably had ten thousand unresolved feelings toward her late father but she didn't really think he actively hated her or her mother. She didn't even think he'd despised Paul, though Paul had been eaten up with bitterness toward anyone named Chandler. Nicholas probably considered them collateral damage in the sequence of events that had happened after the tragedy, people who were simply too painful to be around or think about.

But her twin? Yeah, the guy who'd been arrested for burning down the very first Chandler's was a pretty easy target for his anger. "No," she said shortly.

There was a beat of silence. "I'm happy to hear she's okay."

"Are you?"

Nicholas shifted, his heavy thigh brushing against hers. She scooted back a hair. Those thighs were dangerous. "Of course I am."

She hummed, wishing she'd kept the snarky question back. *Move on.* Ten years ago, she'd run away instead of staying in the dramatic role of spurned lover in this feud. She wasn't about to start now.

"Of course I am," he repeated more forcefully. "I wouldn't wish her ill."

She finished the outline of the woman's legs and leaned back on her stool. "Yeah. Fine."

"You can believe me or not, Livvy." His voice was downright frigid now. "I'm not a monster."

"My family would say differently." She roughly capped the Sharpie, rose to her feet, and threw it on her worktable.

"What would you say?"

I would say I've never been able to hate you the way I should. "I'd say nothing."

His eyes dropped to her hands, and she realized she was wringing them. She immediately turned to her table and started to arrange and rearrange the few supplies she kept out. Though she was messy in the rest of her life, she was a neat freak at work.

Leather creaked behind her as Nicholas came to his feet. She didn't hear him walking toward her, but she could sense his body behind her. "Livvy—"

"I do actually have a lot to do," she interrupted him. "You can go."

"I'm not done talking to you."

"Well, I'm done talking to *you.*"

Silence, for a long moment. "You didn't finish my tattoo."

She closed her eyes at the ridiculous statement. "For fuck's sake. There's not going to be any tattoo." He'd won this round of chicken. He'd won all the rounds of chicken, because she was the ultimate chicken, okay? Cluck, cluck. "We don't have anything more to talk about. I'm only here for a month, tops, until my mom's self-sufficient again. You can go back to your peaceful life and—" She broke off with a gasp when he grasped her shoulders and whirled her around.

Whoa.

He crowded her, big hands planted on the table on either side of her hips. Metal hit her ass, and his body pressed flush against her front. He should have looked ridiculous with the pinup fairy doodled on his arm, but it didn't detract from his attractiveness. He was too close, too big, too . . . *him.*

His chest was hard, and beneath her top, her nipples tightened with the friction. Without conscious thought, her legs widened, making space for him. Their clothes did nothing to disguise the thick bulge of his penis. It pressed tantalizingly against her softening core.

"You think I can have peace with you here?"

His rough whisper blew over her senses and her ear. Her head fell back submissively, baring her throat. "Yes."

His head lowered, lips hovering over the arch of her neck. "Why didn't you text me this year?" he asked.

She should have expected that question, as awkward as it was. Black and white. She'd ruined a precious pattern in his ordered brain.

She could bullshit him, but he'd only poke and poke. So she'd give him a snippet of truth. Enough to satisfy him. "I turned thirty."

"I know how old you are."

"Ten years." She licked her lips, wishing he was the one licking them. "It would have made it an even decade since we first started meeting like that." He'd called it quits with their relationship two months shy of her twentieth birthday, two weeks after the accident that had left them both grieving a parent, a day after his dad had swindled her mother out of her half of the C&O.

The threads that made up the timeline of their complicated past were basically a tangled knot.

I can't do this anymore. It's impossible for us to be together now, Nicholas had told her, stony-faced.

"I figured ten years is long enough for us to get each other out of our systems." *Ten years is long enough for me to be hung up on a man who hates to want me. Who I can't seem to hate enough to stop wanting.*

He lifted his head. "Did it work? Am I out of your system?"

"Am I out of yours?" she countered.

Instead of responding, his hand left the table and skimmed over her hip, barely touching her. Long, strong fingers pressed against the strip of flesh bared between her pants and her bustier. Unable to stop herself, she gave one shimmy of her hips, gasping at the burst of pleasure that ran through her as his cock dragged over her clit.

You were going to stop, she thought, with no small amount of despair. *Don't do this to yourself. This isn't healthy.*

She took his lust because it was all she could

have of him. She knew how this would end, and still, part of her brain wanted it.

"How is it still like this?" he muttered, incredulous. His index finger inched under her top, and she ground up against him again, their breaths coming faster. His head lowered, and she lifted hers, waiting for him to kiss her. Needing something to hold on to, she clasped his forearms, one bare, the other still covered by his shirt.

The second her skin touched his, he jerked like he'd been scalded. Nicholas straightened, separating their bodies so fast she had to grab the table for balance. "No. I can't."

What?

No.

"I can't do this." He took a giant step away. "We can't do this."

She was cold. Colder than she'd been in a while. "I'm not the one who sought you out."

"I know." He ran his hand through his ruthlessly clipped hair. She bet those thick brown strands never disobeyed him. Even in his agitation, they only appeared slightly mussed. "But this isn't what I came here for."

"Could have fooled me." She lifted a shoulder, pretending a blasé attitude she didn't feel. "You still clearly want me." And as much as she knew she shouldn't be happy about that, she couldn't prevent a trickle of joy.

His head moved slowly from side to side. "I'm seeing someone."

She stared at him, the words pushing through her brain one by one. They made no sense at first. Her body was still clamoring for attention and hungry for his touch.

Then, unfortunately, comprehension came. And with it, a new kind of pain. She opened her mouth, but no sound emerged.

She'd never assumed he was celibate when they were apart. She wasn't.

She was commitment shy. She didn't want to be tied down. A relationship would make her nomadic lifestyle difficult.

Those were the things she'd told herself for why she only sought out casual hookups with other men over the years, until even those lost interest.

The real, dysfunctional, fucked-up reason? It was hard to maintain a relationship when half your attention was on the few hours you might steal in another person's arms.

When they were together, they'd both been single. That had been part of the agreement, set that first time. *One night. No one will know.*

Don't bother coming if you're with someone.

Nausea roiled through her stomach. She hadn't contacted him because she'd decided she needed to move on with her life. Funny how she hadn't really thought about how that meant he'd be moving on too.

She had to clear her throat twice to speak. "Cool. Cool. Cool. Cool."

"Livvy—"

"It's cool." She had to find another word. "Great.

Awesome." No, that was going too far. "Like I said, I'll be leaving soon." She imagined the world beyond this shop. She wished she felt excitement instead of weariness at the thought of setting out into it again. "Forget I'm here. Don't get any tattoos."

Livvy couldn't watch as he moved away after a pregnant pause and gathered his jacket, or when he hesitated at that curtain. "It's not serious. Me and her."

The burst of joy she felt at that news terrified her, second only to the fear that she didn't know if it would matter if Nicholas was serious about this mysterious woman. Even if he told her he was engaged and then opened his arms to her, would she be able to resist him? "Don't care. None of my business. I'm fine."

"You don't look fine."

The blood in her veins turned to ice. Oh God. No. She couldn't let him see how not fine she was.

All those years ago, she'd lost her father to death, her mother to grief, her brothers to hate. And then she'd lost him. It had been her one measure of solace, when he'd smashed her already broken heart into smithereens, that he hadn't known the extent to which she hadn't been fine. Every year she put all her energy into proving to him how fine she was.

Get him out. She had to swallow twice to speak, and finally met his gaze across the floor of the shop. "I'm *fine*. And you need to leave."

"I—"

"You need to leave," she said, with a calm she

didn't feel. But if messy anger couldn't chase him out, calm was the only thing that would appeal to logical Nicholas. "Because the longer you stay, the more likely it is that someone will spot your car. And we both know you don't want to be seen with the daughter of the man who was responsible for your mother's death."

Chapter 3

Nᴜᴄʜᴏʟᴀs ʀᴀɴ his fingers over the curves of her breasts, along the delicate arch of her back, down her crossed legs.

Then he reminded himself he was fondling a fucking doodle on his arm.

He snatched his hand away, grateful the other occupants in the boardroom were too busy arguing to notice him stroking his shirtsleeve. Over the past three days, he'd picked up a washcloth no less than a dozen times, determined to eradicate the ridiculous naked fairy Livvy had drawn on him. Instead, he'd done his best to preserve the fading drawing. Last night, he'd even found himself absentmindedly tracing it as he closed his eyes and pretended he was back in that chair, calm as she ran her small hands over him.

It had been a tiny respite. He hadn't had calm moments like that in a long time with a woman, and especially not with her. He hadn't even realized he'd been missing that sort of intimacy until he'd had the barest taste of it.

Maybe you can pretend to have it with your pretend girlfriend, dumbass.

Nicholas picked up his fork and moved the lettuce around in his barely eaten salad. Masculine voices were gaining in volume around him, which meant he needed to forget Livvy and his past, and focus on the present.

Easier said than done.

Talking's not usually what we do when we're together. She was right. Aside from gasps and filthy words, they hadn't truly spoken in a decade. Had he really thought he could calmly ask her about her plans and they could both go on their ways? A fool, that's what he was.

From the second he'd walked in the door, his brain had taken a backseat to his impulses. She'd poked, he'd prodded. She'd demanded, and he'd reacted.

Reacted in probably the dumbest, most immature way when he realized how close he was to ripping off their clothes and fucking her on that rickety table. His only consolation was not giving his imaginary girlfriend a name or backstory, and that was a thin consolation.

He cringed inwardly. It wasn't his finest moment, and not only because it was the sort of thing a high school boy might do.

Her skin had turned ashen, her face stricken. He hadn't seen her display hurt in a long time—only physical pleasure and smirks and mocking smiles.

How would you feel if she'd told you she was seeing someone?

Not good. Nicholas speared an olive. He'd made a conscious decision after the first couple of years to not think about what Livvy might be doing on the 364 nights they weren't together. He didn't always stick to that resolution, but he'd done okay, probably because she'd always texted him, an implicit sign of her continuing singlehood. When her last birthday had come and gone, he'd spent more time than he'd cared to admit wondering whether she'd found someone.

He'd had sex and relationships with other women. He'd even stuck it out with one woman for a full ten months. But when Livvy's birthday had rolled around, he'd always been magically single.

Magically. Sure.

He consciously shelved that thought, because if he went down the rabbit hole of how he'd structured his life around one night a year for the past decade, he wasn't sure he'd be able to concentrate on anything else.

He should be grateful she'd launched that final grenade at him, or he might have spent more time embellishing his imaginary relationship with a nonexistent woman. There was no danger of any further conversation after she'd invoked their parents.

You don't want to be seen with the daughter of the man who was responsible for your mother's death.

Sometimes, when he was able to detach sufficiently from his emotions, he could marvel at how the ripples of a single accident could spread out and affect so many lives.

Nicholas swallowed the bitter taste in his mouth. Regret and sadness and recrimination ate at him, coupled with longing and lust and affection.

He really was a wind-up man in a case. She'd turned the key and ushered in a host of emotions he hadn't planned on dealing with.

"Nicholas."

He looked up from his salad and the olive he'd nearly pulverized with his fork. "I'm sorry?"

Brendan Chandler had two modes of looking at his children: icy disinterest and frustrated impatience. The latter stare was what Nicholas was getting treated to right now. "That's the second time you've zoned out."

"Are you okay, Nicholas?" The soft question came from across the table.

Nicholas neatly placed his fork down and forced a smile for his baby sister. Eve took after their mother, small and round, and in her old-fashioned white blouse and prim skirt and dwarfed by the massive oak table, she looked far younger than her twenty-three years. "I'm fine, sweetheart. I have a lot on my mind. Didn't sleep much last night."

Eve nodded, her glossy dark hair catching the light. She hadn't eaten much of her own meal either, but that wasn't unusual. These mandatory biweekly lunches weren't meant to be conducive to a good appetite.

Lunch with his family hadn't always been a dreaded event. Every Sunday, his mother would dismiss the help for the day and she'd putter around the kitchen. After Eve was born, she'd usually do it with his baby sister strapped to her back. His father would stick to his study, but at least he'd be around the house. More often than not, the Kanes would join them after church, and the place would ring with laughter and food and talk.

Then she was gone, and every day of the week changed, including Sundays. Now, the couple of hours he spent with his father and grandfather every other week were more interrogation and battle than anything else.

"Stress is a silent killer, Nicholas. Get more sleep," John Chandler advised, his normally boisterous voice somewhat muted by speakers. His face grew larger on the large computer monitor placed on the table as he leaned in to see them better. Nicholas's grandfather's hair was a messy shock of white, and he wore his usual plaid shirt. This was the second time this month that his grandfather had chosen to call into the meeting instead of coming to the office, citing fatigue.

Nicholas had no doubt his grandfather would have been happy to step down as CEO and retire entirely to play in his garden, were it not for the barely concealed decade-long power struggle he was engaged in against his son. "I will, Grandpa. Don't worry about me." To prove how okay he was, he choked down a cherry tomato, wishing it was an actual cherry. He could do with something sweet, and the untouched cookies on the platter in the center of the table looked way too tempting.

"Now that we've analyzed your sleeping habits, are you capable of answering the question?" Brendan checked his watch. Life had etched deep lines on Brendan's face, but his father had otherwise aged gracefully, his hair a distinguished gray, his body still fit. Nicholas imagined he'd look much like this in thirty years.

Like father, like son. He'd heard some variation of that his entire life. It never failed to make him feel slightly ill.

Nicholas set his fork down, trying to concentrate. Dealing with his father and grandfather was hard enough when Nicholas was in peak condition. "The question. Yes." What could they have been talking about? "I'll consider the matter and get back to you."

His father's eyes narrowed. "You'll consider whether you have a status update on the protest?"

Oh Jesus. The protest.

"I didn't realize the company was being protested. Did something happen?" Eve's brow furrowed.

Brendan scowled at Eve. "It's all over the news."

"It's not all over the news," Nicholas corrected his father. "It's been reported on one local news station. There were a few picketers at a Pennsylvania location yesterday. Activists claiming a couple of products we sell there are the byproduct of a prison-work program."

"A prison-work program?"

"Honey made from bees raised by a place that employs prison labor, that sort of thing. And no, Dad, I don't have a status update yet. We're checking the source on those products right now."

Eve looked between him and their dad. "But this is only at one store?"

"So far. I say we don't wait to see what the report says, we cull whatever products they've indicated and make sure we're not using such suppliers. If someone isn't being paid a fair living wage for a day's work, then their labor isn't voluntary," John said sternly. "And we shouldn't be subsidizing that. It's antithetical to our company's values. People. Quality. Fairness."

Three words Nicholas had had pounded into his skull from the time he was a baby. John and Sam Oka, Livvy's late grandfather, would have been considered progressive employers and businessmen by contemporary standards, let alone over half a century ago when they'd founded the company.

Brendan's lip curled. "I know the motto as well as you, Father. But we have eighty stores now, not eighteen. We can't personally check the provenance of every item we sell."

The words were both a reminder of their size and a reminder of Brendan's role in increasing it. If Nicholas were truly a dick, he'd remind his father that he was behind their recent boom of expansion in the past couple of years. But that would create more friction, and his main role here was to mitigate that.

Which was why he couldn't close his eyes, ignore their squabbling, and obsess over Livvy. He also couldn't scream about how this was a relatively minor issue that he could handle with his eyes closed.

The company had grown quickly, and sometimes Nicholas couldn't tell if the two equal shareholders of Chandler's really were micromanagers or if they were actively looking for ways to find every tiny detail to fight over. The latter, he assumed.

The company had once thrived under the control of dual CEOs, but Sam Oka and John Chandler had essentially been of one mind. After Sam had died, his shares had passed to his daughter, Tani. Livvy's mother had no interest in running things, but her husband, Robert, had been smart, eager, and charming, a vice-president in the company already, and had stepped into the vacated co-CEO position in proxy for his wife.

When Robert had died, though, and Brendan "acquired" the Oka-Kane shares, the strife had begun. The boardroom became the war room, the company a pawn in Brendan and John's battle for control.

Nicholas was aware every decision he made had to straddle two lines—pleasing his grandfather and his father. Following tradition while chasing expansion.

People. Quality. Fairness.

Money.

If he failed to maneuver and his dad and grandfather deadlocked, it wasn't just what was left of his family that suffered. It was every single person that owed their livelihood to them, a number that grew every time they broke ground on another store. All those managers and farmers and checkout clerks and chefs and bag boys and and and . . .

Every day, he had his assistant refresh the list of every person who worked for Chandler's in every capacity, no matter how small, and place it on his desk, in plain sight. A visible, tangible reminder of the small universe of people who were relying on him.

"I'm well aware of how many stores we have, boy," John sniped. "I'm old, but I can still read a spreadsheet."

Nicholas placed his hands on the table, making his tone firm. "We've issued a statement that we stand by our rigorous quality standards for all our suppliers and we'll investigate the charges. If it comes up that this is accurate, we can discuss how we'll proceed."

Brendan leaned forward, frowning. "That implies we'll correct any so-called abuses. We shouldn't commit to that until—"

"For crying out loud, Brendan, we'll be fine even if we have to cut a fish or honey supplier. Don't nickel-and-dime on this tiny shit."

"It's—"

"Enough," Nicholas said. He regulated his voice when he caught the sharp glance his father gave him. "I can handle this."

John harrumphed, but he subsided. "Is there anything more for us to discuss? I need fresh air."

"No, we're done." Nicholas placed his napkin on his barely eaten plate.

"Excellent. Eve, you're still coming over tomorrow? I need some more help going through your grandmother's letters."

"Yes, Grandpa."

John's blue eyes softened. "Good, good. Thank you."

The screen went blank and Nicholas turned the computer off. Brendan shoved his chair back. "Nicholas, I have a meeting in ten minutes. Email me that site survey on the new location in Connecticut."

Eve cleared her throat. "Actually, I have some news."

Nicholas looked at his sister, surprised but ready to encourage his usually quiet sibling. Technically, Eve wasn't employed by the corporation. Since she'd graduated college two years ago, she'd worked for The Maria Chandler Foundation, a nonprofit established by their mother to fund scholarships for underprivileged youth.

Eve had recently joined these meetings at his father's demand. At first, Nicholas had had some hope his dad had softened his rigid, dismissive attitude toward his only daughter and wanted to pull her into the business. But she rarely spoke, and when she did, their father wasn't exactly supportive. Nicholas had decided Brendan only wanted her there because she had a softening effect on John.

Always ready to use any tool in his arsenal. Even if those tools were human. That was his dad.

"Is this about the gala?" Brendan snorted. "Isn't it enough for me to write a big check every year? Do we have to discuss what linens are being used?"

Eve drew back. Nicholas bared his teeth at their

father, ready to bodily defend his sister from the man. "The gala is a huge event and not an easy undertaking."

"Oh yes. Party planning is quite the full-time job."

"It's not about the gala, and it's not about linens. I didn't want to say anything in front of Grandpa because I didn't want to upset him, but . . ." Eve licked her lips. "I heard something, and I thought I ought to bring it to your attention."

Brendan stood, irritation creasing his face. "I don't have time to hear about who's cheating on who at the country club, Evangeline. Gossip with your girlfriends, not us."

Before Nicholas could intervene, Eve lifted her chin and met her father's gaze. "Olivia Kane is home, it seems."

Their father completely stilled. "What did you say?"

Shit, shit, shit, *shit*. Nicholas tensed, his brain clicking into high gear. He'd silenced the cousin who had come running to him but he'd known this was a possibility.

"Livvy." Eve swallowed, but she maintained eye contact with their father. Later, when Nicholas wasn't worried about all of this, he'd be proud of her. "I . . . heard it from a fairly good source, that she's settling in, and even has a job. I thought it may be better you know." Eve's dark gaze slid to Nicholas, and there was concern there. She'd only been thirteen when everything had fallen apart, but she knew how he'd once felt about Livvy. "Instead of discovering about it from gossips."

"People are gossiping about it?" Brendan's words were measured and slow, but it felt like the temperature in the room dropped ten degrees, as it always did when their father heard the Kane name. Their father had done his best to eradicate all mention of Livvy's family.

Cold swept over Nicholas, and he'd never welcomed the iciness more. *Feel nothing. Reveal nothing.* "When do people not gossip about us?" He kept his tone cool and mild. "This is no different."

Eve's hand clenched into a small fist, worry making her lips pucker. "I'm sorry I blurted it out so abruptly, Nicholas. I know you two were once very close—"

"That was a long time ago," he interrupted her. "Don't stress. This doesn't affect me at all." He came to his feet. "It doesn't affect any of us."

"I—"

"This is none of your concern," Brendan barked at Eve. She jumped. Nicholas could see the instant she emotionally withdrew, her face becoming placid and pale. He'd seen that look on his own face in the mirror.

Christ, this fucking dysfunctional family. "Don't speak to her that way," he said, and made sure his voice carried the threat of what would happen if Brendan did.

He and his father had settled into an uneasy balance of power. Brendan needed him—for his brain, his reputation for fair dealing, his ability to get along with people in a way Brendan could not. Nicholas was aware his father resented that need.

It meant Nicholas could flex his muscles now in ways he hadn't been able to when he was a kid.

Nicholas still didn't have ownership interest in the company, though. There was only so far he could push, but he'd push to that point.

Brendan drew back. "Leave me and Nicholas alone. We need to talk."

Eve faltered, but Nicholas gave her a single nod to signal his approval. It was better for Eve to not be in the room if things got ugly. There were things she didn't need to see.

Her footsteps were barely audible, the open and shut of the door a whisper. Nicholas didn't have to wait long.

Brendan picked up his water glass and flung it against the wall. Nicholas didn't flinch at the crash of glass against wood paneling. Someone might have heard it, but he'd clean it up before anyone saw anything more than a damp spot.

Brendan's shoulders heaved and he started to pace the floor. "Goddamn it. One member of that family leaves, and another one crops up."

Feel nothing. Still, his hand curled into a fist by his side. "Paul died, he didn't leave," Nicholas pointed out.

Brendan shrugged. He fucking *shrugged* at the reminder of the death of a young man who had half-lived in his home since he was a baby, who had been his son's best friend.

Nicholas's other hand curled. He wasn't sure if his father had always been an asshole, or if his wife's death and the ensuing speculation had eradicated the portion of him that had given a fuck, but he assumed the former.

Nicholas didn't take his gaze off his father, because you kept your eyes on snakes.

"Did you know?"

A chill ran down Nicholas's spine. "I'm too busy running this company to swing by the water cooler." Nicholas wished he could ask his dad if he was aware Tani had broken her hip. Like Nicholas's generation, Brendan and Tani had grown up together, side by side on neighboring plots of land. They'd seemed like friends.

Until Brendan had invited a grief-stricken, widowed Tani Oka-Kane over to their house after the accident. When she'd left, she walked away from her half of the company, compensated with a dollar amount even the most conservative economist would have said was too low. Bought or stolen, that was the question the world had split on. Nicholas had his own opinion, but he couldn't bear to think about it too much. The bad taste would never wash out of his mouth.

Brendan's lip curled. "Is she back for good?"

"I told you. I didn't know she was back."

"I want her gone."

"That will be difficult, sir."

"How hard would it be to get her fired?"

Nicholas wanted to laugh, even though it wasn't funny. Get her fired? It probably wasn't by design, but Livvy'd picked an employer no Chandler would be able to sway. He had lost touch with Gabe over the years, but the Kanes' former housekeeper's son wasn't going to be in any hurry to take his side. "This isn't a soap opera. Contrary to what you believe, we do not own this town. She has every right to be here, and us interfering in that is only going to cause more talk."

That stymied his dad, as Nicholas knew it would. Brendan stopped pacing. "I don't want any drama."

"I know." Drama was Brendan's mortal enemy.

"You're not to see her."

Nicholas swiftly suppressed the flare of rage. "I hadn't planned on it," he lied. "But I'm not a child anymore. I can make my own decisions."

"Not if those decisions would adversely affect this company." Brendan paused. "Or this family."

Nicholas's lip curled. Yeah, he knew why Brendan didn't want him to see Livvy and it had nothing to do with the company or family, and everything to do with him.

Tongues would wag about the corporate takeover and the fire Livvy's twin had been accused of starting. But most importantly, people would talk about the accident. And how Maria Chandler and Robert Kane had been driving up to the Chandlers' lake house when they'd died, at a time when they were both allegedly out of town, separately, seeing to company and foundation business.

They'd talk about how Maria and Robert had dated in high school, and how strange it had been they hadn't ended up together, because they were fun and normal and relatable, unlike their distant, wealthy spouses.

They'd whisper about an affair.

Suddenly he was twenty-three again, standing in front of his father, the man destroying the softest part of his heart. *Be realistic, Nicholas. If you can't do this for your mother's memory, then do it for the rest of your family. Family first.*

"Think of the family," Brendan said now, and Nicholas knew exactly what he was really saying. *My threat from ten years ago still stands, and you know it.*

Young Nicholas had looked into his father's eyes and fully believed that the man was capable of anything in his blind quest for revenge against the dead man who had wronged him. Including cheating that dead man's widow, a woman he'd grown up with. Including blackmailing his one and only son.

Older Nicholas still believed it.

He tightened his fist so much that pain shot through him. *You are a realist. This should not hurt. Do not let it hurt.*

He slowly released his hand. "I always do."

"Good." Brusque now, mission accomplished, Brendan stalked to the door. "Get me that site survey."

Nicholas listened to the echo of the door as it closed behind his father. Ice cold. The chill had settled in his chest and spread to his arms and legs, the animation Livvy had cranked into him halted.

He had a mountain of work on his desk, dozens of people waiting for him to make some sort of decision on a million different subjects. He'd go and handle all of that. He'd keep busy.

He moved over to the corner and crouched down

next to the broken glass and picked up the pieces, putting the tinier ones inside the bigger base. Then he paused for a second. He reached into his pocket and pulled out his phone, calling up his messages.

Can I help you?
Quit creeping.
If you want a tattoo, you'll have to come inside.

Three texts. One number at the top.
If you want to talk to me, text me.

Only he'd never done that. Texting her would be out of character, out of the pattern.

He watched the cursor in the empty reply box blink. He could send her a message, warning her about his father, but he didn't think Brendan would actually do anything to her. Brendan had railed about Tani and Paul remaining in what he viewed as his town, but as far as Nicholas knew, the old man had never actually confronted them.

He swiped his thumb over the conversation and stared at the Delete box. He should do it. Remove the temptation of even having her number. He accepted the deletion, an odd sense of loss moving through him at erasing his link to her.

It's still in the cloud.

Technology. It ensured no ex was ever truly gone.

He tucked the phone back into his pocket and finished cleaning up the glass. As he was leaving the room, he grabbed the untouched tray of cookies to deliver to his staff.

He picked up a chocolate chip cookie. The dough

was soft, depressing under his fingertips, the chocolate smearing over his thumb. He lifted it to his mouth and took a tiny bite, the bittersweet chocolate exploding on his tongue.

Not healthy.

He licked his thumb and dropped the cookie in the trashcan on the way out. The wind-up man was back in his case, and there he would stay.

There was no other choice, not for him. Or Livvy.

Chapter 4

Every year, after Nicholas left her while she slept—or pretended to sleep—Livvy would roll over in the hotel bed and grab her phone. The first couple of years, she'd read the text that brought him to her and cry, clutching her phone to her chest, aching over the empty space in the bed.

As she grew older, the tears had come less and less, but she'd never been able to stop herself from rereading that single message time and again. She'd also never been able to stop the aching.

Eventually she'd get out of bed, shower, and put her clothes on. Then she'd grab her phone and delete that message. Within a month or so, she'd get a new phone or switch numbers.

Livvy leaned against the granite island and stared at the texts she'd sent Nicholas. For three days, she'd picked up her phone, determined to delete them. Each time, she'd simply reread the one-sided conversation, and put the damn phone down.

She traced her finger over each word she'd sent him, but instead of glass, she imagined she was touching his warm forearm. It had been so long since she'd caressed him like that. They were always greedy and needy, not soft or slow.

Oh God, quit it.

She swiped the conversation to the right. Her thumb hovered over the Delete. Archiving the chat was largely symbolic. She had his number memorized. It hadn't changed in ten years. It wouldn't change anytime soon. God forbid the man had to cope with something like a brand-new number. It would upset his perfect world.

"Livvy?"

Livvy jumped at the booming, deep voice coming from the living room. Feeling oddly like she'd been caught doing something illicit, she shoved her phone into her pocket. "Yes, Aunt Maile. I'll be right there."

Livvy depressed the plunger on the French press and tried to let the scent of Kona calm her.

When she'd left home all those years ago, she'd had a couple years of art school and a tiny bit of experience working at her father's family's little café under her belt. That slight work history had been enough for her to get a job and pay the bills while she apprenticed part-time.

While she prepared two mugs on a tray, she mentally ran through what was in the fridge. She'd lost track of time while she did the laundry and ironing this morning, and she was behind on dinner preparation. She'd tried to use the stack of cookbooks to create nice meals when she wasn't working, but so far, her mother had only picked at every dish she made. Livvy didn't entirely blame her—Jackson had been the twin who had hovered around the kitchen, eager to learn everything he could from their personal chef. Livvy had been much more interested in disappearing somewhere with a sketchbook.

Her hand shook as she poured the coffee and a little spilled on the counter. Son of a bitch. She set down the press and grabbed a towel, cleaning up the granite so it was gleaming again.

Sometimes she managed to go weeks without thinking of Jackson and worrying over where he was and whether he was okay. Curse Nicholas for so many reasons, but especially for bringing up her twin brother yesterday.

You weren't cursing Nicholas in your bed last night. No, she'd been stifling his name on her lips as her fingers brought her body to swift climax. That was hardly new. She had enough Nicholas material in her spank bank that she could probably take care of herself forever.

But she wasn't going to think about him now. That wasn't what she was here for.

Livvy took a second to bundle her hair up on her head and picked up the tray of coffee, balancing it as she left the kitchen, using her elbow to knock open the swinging door. She was met with the sound of a cheering studio audience and the loud clicking of knitting needles, as well as the running patter of her aunt's deep voice.

"Do you think these doctors on these shows have actual medical degrees or—?" Her aunt broke off, a grin creasing her round face. Livvy always got a slight pang in her heart when she looked at the woman. Maile Kane resembled Robert Kane, with the same dark hair and eyes and brown skin. She was large boned and sturdy, her shoulders broad and strong, her hands capable.

Her father's younger sister had been a steady constant in Livvy's life for forever, and never more so than after the accident. It had been Maile who had propped up her and her brothers during her father's funeral; Maile who had tried to talk Tani out of selling her company shares for a pittance; Maile who had helped Livvy find a lawyer for Jackson when he was arrested for arson.

And once the charges against Jackson had been dropped, it had been Maile who had handed Livvy and her brother a few thousand bucks each and told them they could leave if they wished. No guilt necessary.

Livvy couldn't help the guilt, but the money had tided her over through those first lean months. She'd spoken to Maile more over the past decade than her mother, but not by much. Never once had her aunt made her feel bad about that.

"Oh, Livvy, how nice, did you make us some coffee? It's a little late, but you know I read this study that said you should drink a cup of coffee a day in order to maintain a good digestive system and also prevent cancer."

"I did make coffee." Livvy smiled at her aunt. As usual, Maile was dressed fashionably, in black jeans and an exquisite pink cashmere sweater, her shiny dark curls tumbling down her back. Livvy resembled her Japanese-American mother, but in everything else, including her love of dressing up, she could have been Maile's daughter.

Livvy steeled herself to look at her mother, sitting on the couch, prepared for the hit of guilt and anxious need. Tani was patiently winding a ball of yarn for Maile, and didn't glance up at her.

Her mother had been a celebrated beauty in her youth. Save for a streak of white in her hair, she hadn't aged much, maintaining a smooth, unlined complexion and a fit figure. The metal walker next to the sofa seemed out of place.

The surgery they'd done on Tani's hip had been minimally invasive—she'd been out of the hospital in a couple of days, before Livvy could even get to town. The first few days she'd been here, Livvy had matter-of-factly approached Tani to provide assistance in dressing and other basic matters, but she'd been straight-armed away fairly quickly. *I can see to my own personal needs, Olivia.* Since then, Tani had mostly only accepted help from her sister-in-law.

Gregarious, flighty Maile and distant, reserved Tani made an odd pair, but as far as Livvy could tell, they got along well, with Maile chattering and Tani listening. The two women had been living together since her mother had sold everything. This home, a wedding present from Tani's father to Robert's parents, wasn't a mansion, but it was paid for, large enough for the two women and located in a quiet, safe cul-de-sac.

Tani had never talked finances with her daughter, but Livvy'd gleaned enough from their stilted conversations to determine that after she'd sold everything, even at a loss, Tani had amassed enough in savings to support both women. A good thing, since Tani had never worked outside the home. Maile occasionally talked about selling her knitted creations, but Livvy doubted they would cover all their bills.

Livvy skirted the leather couch and placed the tray on the table. She handed a mug to her aunt first. Maile took a sip. "Oh my, is this coconut milk?"

"It is. I thought you'd like it."

Livvy picked up a mug to hand to her mother, but Tani shook her head. "No, thank you. I only drink my coffee black."

"Try it, Tani. It's delicious," Maile urged.

"Too fatty."

"I can make you a cup without milk," Livvy responded.

Tani wrinkled her small nose. "I'll be up all night if I have coffee now."

It was barely three p.m., but there was no point in arguing with her mother. "Sure. I'll drink it, don't worry. What are you watching?"

"This doctor is so smart. It's a show about how to lose fifteen pounds in a week on his new diet. You only eat vegetables that start with the letter *c*." Maile's bright, dark eyes went back to the television.

Livvy'd grown up with little to no television in her home, but her mom had apparently changed her views on T.V. time over the years. The older woman spent most of her day sitting in the arm-chair of her bedroom, switching through various channels like it was her job, pausing only to move to the living room and the T.V. there. "I really hope coffee and chocolate are on that list," Livvy said.

Maile snorted. "And carbs."

"Speaking of carbs, I was thinking of what to make for dinner. Pasta, maybe?" Livvy perched on the arm of the couch where her aunt sat.

"You don't have to cook," Tani said.

"I want to." No, she didn't. But she'd ordered pizza yesterday, and she couldn't do that two days in a row. "I make a really great marinara sauce too." More lies. She could open a jar.

"Hmm, maybe not marinara," her aunt said. "Your mother's allergy."

Livvy looked at her mom. "What allergy?"

Tani shrugged. "I'm allergic to nightshades."

"Since when?"

"A few years back."

She thought of all the meals she'd prepared since she'd gotten home. The omelettes. The pizza she'd ordered.

All made with tomatoes.

Suddenly, Tani's pecking made more sense.

"Why didn't you say something?"

Tani gave another delicate shrug and put the ball of yarn in the basket next to the sofa. "I didn't want to be a bother."

Livvy took a drink of her coffee to hide her an-noyance. This was so like her mother, not to com-municate one simple thing. Livvy had thought

Tani didn't like her cooking, not that she couldn't eat her cooking.

Start a fight. Do it.

No. No. That would be the immature thing to do, and she wasn't immature. At least, not that immature. "Any other allergies I should know about?"

Tani frowned at the coffee table and rubbed a stain there. Cleaning was definitely not one of Livvy's skills, but she'd spent most of the day tidying up in here. The gesture felt like an implicit rebuke. "Dairy."

Livvy thought of the cheese she'd put on most everything. "Got it. Sure."

Aunt Maile nodded at the T.V. "This doctor did a whole episode on adult allergy onset."

Livvy took another sip of coffee. "I'll have to catch that later. Or we could go for a walk around the neighborhood, Mom. Do those exercises the physical therapist gave us. I don't have to work tonight."

Livvy waited, but Tani's only response was silence. She'd talked about her part-time job about a dozen times over the past week, but Maile had been the only one to show any interest. Once upon a time, Tani would have leapt up to tell her exactly what she thought about her only daughter being a tattoo artist.

Olivia, really, I was fine with you not having any interest in the business. I spent a small fortune on art supplies and classes, and this is how you want to use it? To pierce people's skin with ink?

The good old days. She'd never had a close, tender relationship with Tani, but at least her pecking and criticism had been some sort of attention.

When Livvy'd lost her father in that accident, she'd lost her mother too. Tani had effectively withdrawn from all her children, spending her days either sobbing or sleeping. She'd seemed oblivious to Livvy's heartbreak over losing her father and Nicholas back-to-back, Paul's devastation over losing his place as heir apparent to C&O, and—most important—Jackson's run-in with the law and the two weeks he'd spent in jail. At the time, Livvy'd felt blindsided, utterly and totally alone.

As an adult who struggled with maintaining emotional equilibrium, though, Livvy could empathize. In hindsight, she could see a pattern in her mother's behavior that suggested the depressive episode after Robert's death hadn't been entirely situational.

Headaches and fatigue. Growing up, those had been the excuses her mom had given when she'd retreat to her bed for days on end. There hadn't been tears then, only silence. Livvy's father, normally cheerful, would walk around with a worried scowl on his face, shushing Livvy and her brothers. After a few days or a week, her mother would emerge, a little more fragile-looking, but back to her cool and contained self.

Part of Livvy wanted to ask her mother straight out if she'd ever seen a doctor about her depression, but she wasn't sure how to broach the subject. Even when life had been more stable, the Kanes had never discussed mental health. It had taken years for Livvy to seek help and even longer for her to understand there was no cure or magic pill that could fix everything.

In the dark days and weeks following Paul's funeral, Livvy'd finally confronted and acknowledged the scary, lonely emptiness she'd carried inside her for most of her adult life. She'd tried to fuck it and move it and ignore it and run it away, to no avail.

It would never leave her, fine. She was done flailing in the darkness when she could take actionable steps to help herself.

Coming home right now was her chance and she'd take it. Livvy sipped her too-sweet coffee. Even if she had to cook and clean and confront her ex-lover, she'd force her mother to . . . well, maybe not shower Livvy with love, but at least care enough to criticize her a little.

Nobody had ever said her family was functional.

A knock sounded at the front door, but before Livvy could move, the rattle of keys preceded a familiar throaty voice. "Hello?"

Tani straightened. She didn't exactly light up, but her gaze focused on the arched opening of the living room.

"We're in here," Maile called out.

A small, dark-haired whirlwind came barreling through the door. The six-year-old paused only when he caught sight of Livvy and shoved his silky black hair out of his eyes, a shy smile creasing his baby-round face. Kareem had his mother's hair, build, and face, but he had his father's smile.

Livvy wasn't great around kids, but her heart caught, something deep and warm lodging there. She wanted to grab the kid and haul him in for a hug, but he barely knew her and would probably be freaked out. She settled for a smile, dialing up the warmth.

"Hi, Livvy," he said.

"Aunt Livvy," Livvy's sister-in-law said as she rounded the corner of the door and smiled at Livvy. Sadia had been Livvy and Jackson's best friend from the time they were in elementary school, well before she'd fallen in love with and married Paul. She hadn't changed much over the past decade, though motherhood had rounded her already dangerous curves.

"He can call me Livvy," she replied, not for the first time. It felt odd to hear the kid call her "Aunt." She and Sadia had kept in contact more than she had with any other member of her family, but that didn't mean she knew Kareem beyond photos and videos. Before this week, she'd seen him exactly three times in his life. He'd been a newborn the first time, a toddler the second, when Sadia had traveled to meet her in Manhattan for a weekend, and she assumed he'd been too tired and confused at his dad's funeral to remember the third time.

"He'll address you with respect," Sadia said firmly, then came close to pull Livvy in for a hug, which Livvy returned a little awkwardly.

It was odd adjusting to being around someone who didn't hesitate to touch her. She hadn't known how much she craved that kind of casual physical affection. She was a loner by necessity—it was hard to make friends or form lasting attachments when she was constantly on the road.

Livvy held on a beat longer than she needed to, only because she knew she could. At Paul's funeral, her mother had carefully stood on the opposite side of the grave. It had been Sadia who stood next to Livvy, arm wrapped around her shoulders. She didn't know who had been giving who comfort.

"Aunt Livvy," Kareem mumbled, then skirted around her to continue to his grandmothers. He launched himself at Maile, who had thankfully placed her coffee down first. She gave him a fierce hug, squeezing until he wriggled free. With no sign of reticence, he flopped on the couch next to Tani and curled in close to her side. "Hey."

"Kareem," her mother said, and there was a fraction of genuine warmth and happiness in her voice.

"Be careful not to jostle Grandma," Sadia cautioned her son. The boy gingerly readjusted himself next to the older woman, taking exaggerated care not to move her. Sadia hitched the large tote she carried up higher on her shoulder. "Hello, Aunt Maile. Mom."

"Hello. My goodness, Sadia, you look lovely today. Doesn't she look nice, Tani?"

Tani spared Sadia a quick glance. "She looks the same to me."

Sadia smoothed a hand over her round hips and maintained her smile. "Thank you, Auntie."

Livvy gritted her teeth. No, she would not be jealous that her mother had made a passive-aggressive barb at another woman instead of her.

Pathetic, party of one.

"I brought over some sandwiches and those quiches you like from the café." Sadia patted her bag.

"Oh, how nice," Maile said. "We were just wondering what to do about dinner."

And there was probably a nightshade and dairy-free sandwich in there for her mother. *Because Sadia's been here while you've been gallivanting all over the world.*

Funny how the critical voice in her head sounded like Paul.

"I'll go put them away," Sadia said.

Livvy jumped up. "I'll help." Sadia didn't need help, most likely knew this kitchen as well as her own, but she'd take any opportunity to spend some time with her best friend. Sadia was always either working or with her son. Livvy'd barely seen her since she came home.

Sadia placed the tote on the round kitchen table and pulled out a smaller bag. If Livvy peeked, she'd probably see a number of pouches inside the huge tote, along with notebooks and pens. Sadia was ruthlessly organized. "I hope you don't mind me bringing food over. We had some excess from lunch."

Sadia operated Kane's Café now, the place established by Livvy's paternal grandparents. Robert had liked to joke he'd had his eye on Tani his entire life—a reference to the café's location, right across from the original C&O store.

Her father had willed the local landmark to Paul directly, so Tani hadn't been able to sell it when she purged the company and the house from their lives. Running a single café instead of a grocery chain had been a step down for her brother, but it seemed he'd been able to pull a tidy living together for their family.

She hadn't been back to see Kane's yet, though she had fond, warm memories of the place and her grandparents. It was one thing to deal with her mother and family. It was quite another to deal with . . . well, everything else.

Not all painful memories were created equal. And she wasn't convinced confronting each one would be to her benefit.

Like Nicholas.

Or the café. Because if she went to the café, she'd have to see the flagship C&O. Or rather, Chandler's, the building that had replaced the original after the fire.

"Please, how can I mind you bringing us ready-made food?" Livvy accepted the heavy bag and walked it over to the fridge. "I feel like I should be feeding you, though. You're always running around."

"Aw, don't worry about that. I grabbed a sandwich before we left the house and made sure Kareem ate. He's in this phase where he mostly survives on peanut butter and pickles and pizza."

"You raising a kid or a pregnant woman?"

"I'm raising a pit. A bottomless one. Thanks for letting him stay here for the afternoon."

Livvy shut the refrigerator door, then moved back to the sink. "No problem." She was apprehensive about babysitting the kid herself, but Maile and her mother were here, and apparently they took care of Kareem quite a bit. Besides, she figured if she didn't swear, drink, or let him do either of those things, she should be okay.

She poured her coffee into the sink and grabbed a sponge. Doing dishes as she used them felt weird to her—allowing them to pile up was more her speed—but there was no doubt something a little satisfying about having an empty, gleaming, stainless-steel sink.

Sadia pulled a planner and pen out of her bag and dropped into a seat at the table, stretching her long legs out. She flipped the book open. "So my sister will pick Kareem up at 6:30, okay?"

"Which sister? The doctor?"

"Haha. Very funny."

Livvy grinned and scrubbed her mug. All four of Sadia's sisters were either in medical school or physicians. "I try."

"It'll probably be Noor."

"Sounds good. Are you working 'til closing?"

"Yes. We have a barista out sick. But then I have a shift at the bar, so Kareem will probably end up staying at Noor's 'til late."

Livvy shot a glance over her shoulder. Sadia was jotting something down in her planner, giving Livvy a chance to observe her. There were half-circles of exhaustion under her best friend's eyes. Sadia never discussed finances, but Livvy'd assumed things were, if not great, at least manageable. "I didn't realize you were still pulling shifts at the bar."

"Part-time." Sadia closed her planner with a snap. "It keeps my bartending skills sharp. You need something to fall back on."

Sadia's tone was light, and Livvy couldn't detect any hint of a lie. Still, she pressed. "You're doing okay with the café, right?"

"Sure." Sadia raised an eyebrow. "A more important question is, are you doing okay with Mom?"

Sadia calling their mother "Mom" had given Livvy more than some comfort over the years. Paul hadn't wanted to talk to her and Jackson had been mostly unreachable. It had felt like she'd had a real sibling. "Yeah, sure. I mean, we don't talk much, but then, she's never been a talker."

"A person doesn't need to talk much to be difficult."

Livvy grimaced and started cleaning out the French press. "Ugh. Sorry for what she said out there. You look fabulous today, and you always look fabulous."

Sadia huffed out a laugh. "You caught that, huh? Don't worry about it. Your mother is in the minor leagues for backhanded insults. Last time I saw her, my mother asked if I wanted Noor's old clothes. Her *maternity* clothes."

Livvy groaned. "Oh God, Mama Ahmed, why."

"Because she is who she is," Sadia replied prosaically. "Can't change that. Can only accept it."

"Saint Sadia."

"Hardly a saint." Her chair scraped against the tile. Sadia got up and came to stand next to her at the sink. She grabbed a sponge and began efficiently cleaning up the coffee grounds Livvy hadn't even noticed on the counter.

"You don't have to do that."

"I don't mind. Let me help."

Livvy placed the carafe on the drying rack. "You're always helping. You've been here for years taking care of Mom. I haven't."

Sadia stopped cleaning. "Hey. Did you hear that?"

Livvy listened for a moment, but all she could hear was the muted T.V. show, punctuated by Kareem's high-pitched chatter. "What?"

"That shirt you just put on. All that hair is so loud."

Livvy's lips twitched. "Shut up."

"You left for your own reasons, good reasons. I don't blame you a bit."

"Paul did." Livvy winced. "Sorry." Though they'd shared a lot over the years, they'd tacitly agreed the second Sadia had started dating Paul that her role as Livvy's best friend would be separate from her role as Paul's significant other.

"Paul blamed a lot of people for a lot of things," Sadia said, breaking the rule herself. "I know he was hard on you. I tried to convince him to give you a break, but I'm afraid I wasn't successful."

Livvy had barely talked to her brother since the day after Kareem's birth, when she'd driven in to see the baby and he'd confronted her in the hospital hallway. *Mom's getting older, and I'm the one who's been stuck here taking care of everything while you're gallivanting all over the country having fun. Grow up, Livvy.*

Paul hadn't seemed to grasp Livvy wasn't wandering around aimlessly with the family fortune backing her. She'd traveled because . . . well, because she had to, and she'd worked her ass off, more often than not in menial jobs that her childhood of comfortable wealth hadn't exactly prepared her for.

She wasn't sure what her big brother had wanted of her. To stay here and occupy the same role she'd been raised to play from birth, even though their roles had been eliminated?

She supposed it didn't matter. It was too late to ask him. "Thanks for trying to change his mind. It's not your fault he considered me some sort of flighty playgirl."

Sadia made a dismissive noise. "I don't think you were wrong to leave, and I think it's incredibly brave of you to come back right now." Sadia rinsed the sponge in the sink and dried her hands. "And you never need to feel guilty about anything I choose to do. Paul may be gone, but you're still my sister, and Tani's my mother."

"Ah, there it is," Livvy said dryly, in an effort to hide the lump in her throat. "Perfect Asian daughter-in-law sense of responsibility."

Sadia snorted, but she sounded amused. "Lord knows, I've been neither the perfect daughter-in-law or the perfect daughter."

In her worn jeans and soft T-shirt, no one would

guess Sadia had grown up rich. Not as rich as the Kanes or Chandlers, but her parents were both successful cardiologists, which was how they'd been able to afford to send all five of their daughters to the same private schools Livvy had attended.

Sadia's family hadn't had a problem with her dating a man who wasn't Pakistani or Muslim—but they'd had serious opinions about her quitting school and marrying a man who was no longer heir to a fortune. Sadia and Paul's elopement had driven a wedge between her and her family, though they'd softened since Kareem's birth. Livvy dried her hands as well. "You're perfect to me."

"Same." Sadia faced her, leaning against the sink.

She swallowed the lump in her throat. She meant to say thank you, but instead she blurted out, "I saw Nicholas a few days ago."

Sadia's nostrils flared. She crossed her arms over her chest. "Do I need to kill him?"

Livvy gave a half-laugh. Standard. Her friend was forgiving when it came to slights against herself, but hurt a person she loved? She'd pull a knife. And she didn't even know about Livvy's and Nicholas's unconventional arrangement over the years. "I knew there was a reason I loved you."

"There's many reasons you love me. Shall I? Kill him?"

"No."

"Stab him non-fatally? Trip him? Let me trip him."

"We were bound to run into each other sooner or

later." She repeated the words she'd said to herself for the past few nights as she tossed and turned in her bed. *Bound to happen.* Like the inevitability of the situation made it any easier or better.

Bound to have your heart ripped out eventually.

"Probably," Sadia said gently. "But that doesn't make it any less difficult, I'm sure. I always get a little kick in my gut when I see Nicholas, and I didn't have half the investment in him you did."

Livvy shifted. "You see him?"

"Of course. I don't speak to him. Paul would have gone through the roof if I had, and I'm not sure what I'd say anyway. But I'll see Nicholas or Eve at the grocery store occasionally."

Livvy raised an eyebrow. "You shop at Chandler's?" She tried to keep the accusation out of her tone, but she wasn't sure if she entirely succeeded. Nicholas couldn't ever be seen at a competitor store, which meant if Sadia was seeing him at a grocery store, it was *their* grocery store.

No, it wasn't theirs. It was his.

Sadia met her gaze without flinching. "Yes. Paul forbade it, but once—well, I started shopping there. Of course it hurts, every time I step into that place. But at the end of the day, Rockville is my home too. My son's home. They have the best prices and quality and I'm not feeding my son anything but the best simply because of my pride."

"Right, of course. I'm not blaming you."

Sadia regarded her without a shred of anger. "Despite my choice in grocery stores, I'm still more than willing to maim or murder Nicholas for how he dumped you."

Livvy tried to laugh, but it came out more like a sob. "The decision to end our relationship was mutual."

"Honey. I was there."

"Well." Livvy wiped her hands on her jeans, like she could wipe away the past. "It's been forever. I'm over it, and so is he." So many lies. "He seeing someone now."

Her friend pressed her lips tight. Livvy waited for Sadia to tell her it was silly to be upset by that, or ask how the subject of who he was dating had even came about. Instead, she took a step closer and pulled Livvy in for a hug. "I'm sorry, baby. That rat bastard."

Livvy rested her head against Sadia's chest and breathed in deep. She wrapped her arms around her friend and relaxed, marginally. "He is a rat bastard, isn't he?"

"The rattiest bastard." Sadia's hand smoothed over her back.

Livvy didn't care if she was acting childish or needy. She simply absorbed the physical affection like a starved flower absorbed the sun. "I hate him so much."

"I know."

"His girlfriend is probably the worst."

Sadia hummed. "I'm sure she's the most terrible human on the face of the planet. Like, animals can sense how evil she is."

Livvy choked out a chuckle and disentangled herself from her sister-in-law. "Poor Nicholas."

Sadia squeezed Livvy's shoulder. "Let's not go that far."

"I'll be okay."

"You will." Sadia's tone was firm. "You're here. You're trying. You're going to be fine. Promise."

There is nothing wrong with you. You're fine. Livvy smiled mechanically, hiding her disquiet.

Not well enough.

"What's wrong?" Sadia asked.

"Nothing." Jackson hadn't been good at comforting words, but he'd been the only one who'd witnessed her struggles when they were young. He'd always fallen back on a few key phrases.

She'd appreciated the sentiment, but the words hadn't helped. On the contrary, they'd only made her feel more pressure to pretend she was fine. "The way you said that. For a second, you reminded me of Jackson."

Sadia's lashes lowered. "Does he even know Tani was in the hospital?"

"Yeah. I emailed him."

"Maybe he didn't get it."

"I'm sure he got it." He just didn't want to come home. Jackson hadn't even attended Paul's funeral, though she didn't want to remind Sadia about that.

"How do you know?"

"He responds to my emails occasionally."

Sadia frowned. "What email address do you have?"

Livvy rattled it off. She memorized things that

were important. Like Nicholas's number. And her only link to her twin brother.

Sadia blinked. "I've emailed him there. He's never responded. Not once."

Oh. "Emails get lost."

Sadia nodded, but strain had appeared around her eyes. "I sent more than a couple. But that's fine. No big deal."

It didn't sound like no big deal. Livvy knew Jackson hadn't maintained his ties to anyone but her, and then, only in the most cursory ways, but she hadn't realized Sadia had tried to reach out to him. "Do you want me to tell him to contact you?"

"Uh, no. That's fine. I don't know what we'd even talk about, it's been so long." Sadia shrugged and crossed her arms over her chest. "In any case, if he doesn't respond when it comes to his brother's death or his mother's illness, he's certainly not going to pick up the phone because you told him to chat with me."

Livvy winced. She wanted to defend Jackson, but she wasn't sure how. He should have contacted Sadia when Paul died. Especially if the woman had tried to contact him.

"Mom! Can I have chocolate milk?"

"Of course," Sadia called out and strode to the fridge. "Can you go on out there and check on things while I make Kareem some milk?"

Livvy suspected Sadia wasn't really concerned about how her son was faring with his grandmothers, but she respected giving people their alone time when they needed it. "Sure."

In the living room, Aunt Maile was busy at work knitting, and Kareem and Tani's heads were bent over something.

"Draw me another one, Grandma," Kareem demanded.

"What are you doing?" Livvy asked, craning her neck to see what was on her mother's legal pad. She caught a glimpse of a cartoon character before her mom covered the pad with her hand.

A torn-out page rested by Kareem's leg, and Livvy picked it up, recognizing the chubby character instantly. "Hey. This is really good."

"It's nothing. Something to amuse the boy." Her mother tried to snatch the paper, but Livvy neatly sidestepped her, taking in the sketch. This wasn't good, it was excellent, the character's face set in his usual sour lines, his leg raised like he was about to step off the page.

"It's not nothing. I can't tell you how many requests I get for this tattoo."

"People get cartoon tattoos?" Kareem asked.

"Sure," she said, at the same time her mom sternly said, "No."

"You will not be getting any tattoos," Tani told her grandson, ignoring Livvy. "It's not for respectable people."

Her heart jumped at the hint of subtle criticism. It was a happy jump. *You're sick to crave this type of attention.*

Sadia joined them and perched on the arm of the sofa, holding the milk out to her child. Her face was placid again, whatever tension Jackson's name had invoked gone. "Mom's always drawing stuff for Kareem."

"She is? You never drew stuff for us." Her mother had loved and appreciated art, and she'd used a tiny room above their garage to store her supplies. Livvy had started sneaking sketchbooks and materials out of there from the time she was in third grade. It had been one thing they'd had in common.

But that had been a hobby Tani had only occasionally had time for. She certainly had never sat around and drawn pictures for her kids.

"You don't remember the mural on your bedroom wall?" Maile asked.

Tani glanced at Maile, and Livvy didn't miss the frown on her mother's face. It cleared quickly, leaving her brow smooth again.

"The mural?" Livvy tracked the stray memory floating through her brain like a wispy ghost. "Wait. I do." A castle, with a tiny, dark-haired, light-brown-skinned, freckled princess inside, with dark eyes just like hers. She and Jackson had shared a room then, and he'd been featured as a small knight on a steed, his wavy dark hair peeking out from under the helmet. "God, how old was I?"

Tani bowed her head and smoothed the paper out. "Four or five."

"Six, I think she was," Maile said. Her fingers flew, the yarn between them working up rapidly. "But you only had it up for a few months."

After that, her room had been a soft baby blue until she'd hit high school and thrown a tantrum for blood red. "I remember being sad it got painted over so quick. Why did you spend all that time working on it if we were redecorating?"

"Well—" Maile started.

Tani closed her sketchbook with a sense of finality. "A whim."

"I should get going," Sadia said. "Livvy, I texted you all the emergency numbers, though Mom and Auntie have them too. Remember—"

"Noor will be here at 6:30. Got it."

"Are you working at the bar tonight?" Maile asked, then continued before Sadia could answer. "Livvy, why don't you go with Sadia tonight? You've been cooped up here with us since you got back. It's not healthy." Maile's needles moved faster. Livvy had no idea what her aunt was making. She'd once peeked into her aunt's closet to find it filled with plastic containers stuffed with yarn, but she didn't know where the woman stashed her finished goods.

"I haven't been cooped up."

"That sounds like a good idea," Tani said crisply. "You don't need to be here."

Oof.

She hid her flinch. She knew her mother meant she didn't need to be at home tonight, but she couldn't help but interpret it as *you don't need to be here at all.*

Sadia glanced at her. "Sounds fun. It's Friday, so I might get swamped, but we'll surely have chances to talk."

Livvy forced a smile. "Sure. That sounds great."

She didn't know if it would be great or not, but what else did she have going on? Sitting at home and cooking and cleaning and trying to bond with her mom? Or staring and rereading her text messages to Nicholas? Neither of those things sounded particularly healthy.

And damn it. She was going to be healthy, even if it killed her.

Chapter 5

Livvy wasn't sure whether she was so relaxed at O'Killian's because Sadia was here or because she had no memories attached to it. Either way, one drink in and the twisted knot that had turned her stomach into a mess for a week was finally unraveling.

The bar was about one step up from being classified as a dive, with retro booths lining the room, patrons eating greasy pub food and drinking affordable beer and creative cocktails. Livvy tapped her foot on the stool in time to the music coming from the jukebox and snagged a handful of peanuts. Loitering while her BFF worked wasn't exactly the same as a proper girls' night out, but they'd managed to chat between customers.

Sadia drifted over. "There are, like, two men at the other end of the bar who will not stop staring at you."

"Cute?"

"Definite sevens, I would say."

Livvy made a dismissive noise, not bothering to

check them out. "Sevens aren't worth the hassle of a hookup for me in this town."

"They look a little on the young side. They may not know who you are."

"With my luck, they work for Nicholas." A pang hit her when she said his name, but the alcohol had dulled it. Why, she barely felt the urge to pull out her phone and stare at those fucking messages.

Barely.

"Oof." Sadia winced. "That's a definite risk. Never mind, you're right. Can I get you another drink?"

"Sure."

"What are you in the mood for?"

"Hmm. Something classic."

Sadia grabbed a shaker. Her competent hands were a blur as she mixed sugar, lemon juice, water, and gin in a highball glass. She stirred the liquid and garnished it with a couple raspberries before sliding it across the bar. "Gin Fix."

Livvy picked up the glass and took a sip. "Nice. What year?"

"Late 1860s." Sadia wiped the counter down.

The holidays were still months away, but Livvy made a mental note to see what she could find for Sadia in the way of old mixology books. The girl was a history nerd.

"This place has a lot of character," Livvy said.

"Character's a nice way of putting it."

"It's character." She tipped her head down the bar at the man wearing flip-flops and a neon-green suit. "It has characters in it."

"Ha. Well, characters tip well."

"They tip you well, because you're hot."

Sadia gave her a mock glare. She'd changed out of her mom clothes. With her curves poured into tight black jeans and a tank top, she *was* hot. "Excuse me, I'm also really good at pouring drinks."

"Uh-huh. That's what's got that blonde down at the other end of the bar so entranced."

Sadia slid a surreptitious glance down the bar. "The guy or the girl?"

"The girl."

"Huh." Sadia cleared her throat. "It doesn't matter. I'm not looking for a relationship right now."

"Damn." Livvy shook her head sadly. "Now you've done it."

"Done what?"

"Said the words that ensure a relationship smacks you in the face."

"I see you're still a romantic."

Livvy's smile faded, but Sadia was talking, her words rehearsed and practiced. "I have a business and a son. The last thing I have time for is another person."

Livvy shrugged. "An affair might be fun."

Sadia leaned closer. "Actually . . . I've had a few of those this year. Flings."

Livvy opened her eyes wide. "No!"

Sadia's lips twitched. "Okay, okay, Ms. Woman of the World. It was a big deal for me. I'd only really been with Paul."

"Please don't violate our lifelong code of not talking about you and my brother like *that*."

"I'm not giving you details."

Livvy screwed her eyes shut. "Bless you. Anyway, I think you should have as many affairs as you want. I can give you man-slash-woman hunting tips."

Sadia fiddled with the tiny apron wrapped around her waist. "I thought it may be strange for you."

"Since you're Paul's widow? Nah. I want you happy." She took a sip of her drink.

Sadia squared her shoulders. "I'm not going overboard. I realized I'll be hitting thirty soon. It feels like I should do something new and exciting."

Sadia mommed everyone so well, Livvy felt like she could be forgiven for forgetting the other woman was younger than her. "Thirty makes you rethink things, for sure. It's the new twenty, though, or so I hear."

"Will I get back the ass I had at twenty?"

"No, just the financial stress and the sinking feeling that you don't know what to do with your life."

"I'd rather have the ass."

"That blonde doesn't seem to mind your ass."

Sadia leaned forward more, slightly arching her back. "You sure?"

Livvy studied the patron out of the corner of her eye. "Uh-huh."

Sadia gave another surreptitious glance down the bar and her brown skin darkened. "Ahem. I suppose I should go freshen her drink."

"Is that what they're calling it now?"

Sadia's quelling look only made Livvy chuckle, reminding her of their teenage years when they had snuggled in twin beds in her room, giggling over crushes. Then Sadia had fallen for her brother, and giggling over crushes had been a bit more awkward.

Sadia started to walk away, but then froze, looking out at the floor of the bar. Confusion wrinkled her brow. "Huh."

"What?"

Sadia's face went blank. "Nothing. Hey, do you want to go sit on the patio?" A fixed smile appeared. "It's so beautiful out tonight."

Sadia was really shitty at subterfuge. "It's cold and gonna drizzle any minute," Livvy said, and glanced over her shoulder, wondering what had made Sadia's eyes widen.

It was almost midnight, so the crowd had grown over the last hour. Her eye was caught by a small, plump woman sitting alone in a booth, mostly because of the way she was dressed, buttoned up in an expensive black trench coat, pink scarf draped over her head, and oversized sunglasses. "Who's the movie star—" The woman turned her head. Though her eyes were hidden, Livvy could tell the girl was looking at her. She cocked her head, and the gesture, combined with the familiar curve of her cheek, made the breath strangle in Livvy's throat. "Oh."

The last time she'd seen Evangeline Chandler, the night before the accident, she'd been a quiet, shy thirteen-year-old, asking Livvy to read one of her favorite books with her.

Gossip had it that the girl had had to be sedated when she'd been told her mother died.

Livvy jerked around. "Has she come here before?"

Sadia didn't bother to pretend she hadn't also recognized the woman. "I'm not sure. She's not exactly our type of clientele. I've only seen her once or twice over the years. She keeps to herself." Sadia watched Livvy with great concern. "Are you okay?"

"Sure." No, she was not, but there wasn't much she could do about it. "Are you? With her being here?"

Sadia gave a helpless shrug. "I don't subscribe to this family feud, love. As far as I'm concerned, I'm neutral ground."

Livvy didn't subscribe to the feud either. It had been forced upon her. "That's good. I mean, she has as much right to be here as anyone else."

"Now, if she upsets you, I will—"

"Kill her, stab her, trip her. I know."

"Do you want my car keys? You can go home now and come back and get me when my shift's over."

She wanted to say yes, so badly. Her stomach was in knots all over again. Whatever relaxation she'd won in the last couple of hours had disappeared.

A man from down the bar loudly hailed Sadia. "Hey, we gonna get some service here?"

A rare flash of temper lit Sadia's eyes. "Asshole," she muttered.

"No, I'm fine. Go do your work. I'll be okay."

With another concerned glance at Evangeline, Sadia moved away reluctantly. "Call me if you need me."

"Flirt with the blonde," Livvy said, trying to sound like her peaceful evening hadn't just become anything but.

Livvy fidgeted with her glass for a couple of long moments, the back of her neck itching. She'd assumed some people had recognized her, but she hadn't felt exposed until this minute.

She picked up her glass and took another sip. She had a weakness for good, expensive alcohol. She'd tried to shake it, since it was a little too much of a reminder of the extensive stash in her father's office that she'd started sneaking sips out of when she was around seventeen. This top-shelf drink could have been made entirely with water, though, for all the appreciation she could spare it now.

This isn't a big deal. It was entirely possible Eve was simply out on the town and a coincidence they'd both ended up at the same practically-a-dive bar. She was, what, twenty-three now? At that age, Livvy had been hanging out in way more disreputable places than this. But then, Livvy hadn't had much more than a few hundred bucks to her name then. Eve had millions.

Millions that should have been ours, Paul muttered in her ear.

Nope. Adjusting to not having limitless funds had been tough in the beginning, but once she'd grown comfortable, she hadn't missed it too much.

She was moving forward, not looking back.

Livvy swung her leg on the barstool, trying to find the rhythm of the music again. She ate a peanut from the bowl, but it tasted like ashes. She tapped her fingers against the glass and snuck a peek at the sevens down the bar. They were, indeed, still eyeing her, but Livvy couldn't muster up any enthusiasm.

Fuck it.

Pretending to stretch, she glanced over her shoulder. Then looked again, forgetting to be casual.

Eve wasn't alone. Her fingers were clenched tight around her drink while the man who had dropped into an empty seat at the table leaned over the smaller girl. He was big and muscular, every inch of his body screaming predatory animal who had found his prey.

"Hey there."

Livvy cast a single glance at the man standing next to her. One of the sevens. Ginger. Late twenties. Polo shirt. "Hey."

Eve had shrunk back in her seat, her gaze downcast as she picked at the napkin on the table. The man was doing all of the talking.

Not your business. Not your—

". . . Buy you a drink?" Polo Shirt asked.

The man leaned in closer, and Eve flinched back.

Ugh. She wasn't one to cockblock a lady, but Eve's body language was not screaming receptiveness.

Livvy grabbed her glass and her jacket. "Got a drink, thanks. Sorry. I see a friend."

She strode up to the table. "There you are, Karen. I was looking all over for you."

Eve's face turned to her, and Livvy had to control her flinch. Her ridiculous disguise couldn't hide the similarities she shared with Nicholas. Her jaw was the softer, feminine version of his.

"Karen? You said your name was Evangeline," the guy said, disgruntled annoyance on his face. Livvy wasn't sure if it was annoyance at the interruption or at having been given a fake name, but either way, getting annoyed at such a simple thing was a screaming red flag.

"Evangeline? That's a new one." She dropped down in the seat on the other side of Eve and stared coolly at the man. "Girls' night, bro. Scooch along."

"I don't like being called a bro," he sneered.

She glanced over his styled blond hair, spray tan, and V-neck T-shirt. "Okay." She paused. "Bro."

"We were having a good time—"

"You want to talk to this guy here?" she asked Eve. A single shake of her head.

"You heard the lady." Livvy bared her teeth at him. "Off you go."

With a grumble, the man lumbered away from the table. She caught Sadia's attention and ignored the woman's look of surprise. Livvy pointed to her eyes and then the back of the large guy, and Sadia's mouth tightened. She leaned over and whispered something to the man working next to her, who cast an assessing eye at the dude she'd ejected.

Assured that Sadia would keep an eye on things, Livvy turned her attention to Eve. She couldn't exactly get up and leave now, not when the bro was still hovering.

They stared at each other for a long minute. Finally, Evangeline removed her sunglasses and placed them on the table, and unwound the scarf, letting it hang around her neck. Dark eyes met dark and Livvy had to control her flinch. Eve had always favored her mom in looks, but now that she was older, that likeness had gone into doppelganger territory. Eve's hair was stick straight, unlike Maria's curls, and her cheeks were rounder and rosier, but other than that, they could have been twins.

Livvy spoke first. "I'm surprised after you dressed up like a 1920s lady spy, you'd give that guy your real name."

Eve tugged at her scarf. "I was caught off-guard. Dumb."

Livvy shifted, feeling every inch of the years that separated the two of them. "Not dumb. Naive, maybe."

"You're not naive," Eve replied, with no inflection in her voice. She picked up her drink, a pink liquid in a large martini glass, and took a sip. An empty glass sat at her elbow. She'd been here awhile before Livvy had noticed her.

"I'm not. But I'm also much older than you."

"Not that much." Eve straightened and looked her in the eye. "Hello, Olivia."

"Hi, Eve. I still prefer Livvy."

"Most people call me Evangeline now."

Nicholas didn't, Livvy bet. He'd always hauled Eve in close, affectionately squeezing her. *Evangeline is too big of a name for a little squirt like you.* Livvy and the rest of the family had followed suit.

She inhaled. *Rest of the family.* She'd been a part of that family then, yes, but no longer. "I'll remember that."

"I have no preference."

"You should have a preference on your name."

The girl took another sip of her drink. "Whatever's easier."

Livvy bet that was Eve's response to a lot of things. The girl had always been shy, but now, with her downcast eyes and hunched shoulders, she seemed like she was trying to make herself invisible.

"Do you come here often?" Livvy asked, because what else could she ask? Small talk wasn't her forte at the best of times, and that was when she didn't have to navigate the landmine of their past.

"Here? Oh. Oh yes." Eve looked down at her glass. She was lying. "Probably not what you're used to."

"How do you know what I'm used to?"

The hint of a bite in the words surprised Livvy. Okay. Maybe not so timid. "Because I was used to it too. How's the country club?" Her dad had demanded they join the most elite country club in the area after Brendan did. The snobs there had barely tolerated them, but they hadn't been able to turn them away. The green of their money had trumped the melanin in their skin.

The club was a safe topic. Livvy had never cared about the place.

"The same. Nothing changes there."

"I assume you're chairing a committee or two. Some sort of charity work."

Eve stared at her for a long moment. "Why do you say that?"

"Because it's what this social circle expects of those of us with two X chromosomes who have no interest in the family business." Tani had done her stint on a few boards. Maria Chandler had cranked it into high gear by establishing her own foundation.

Though, Livvy could admit, her parents had never tried to shove the gender roles of the rich and mildly famous down their children's throats. They'd figured her desire to be a tattoo artist was a phase, but they'd agreed to art school instead of some fancy degree she wouldn't use and a lifetime of boring social obligations with people she didn't like.

"I do always do what's expected of me," Eve murmured, half under her breath. "I work for the foundation now."

Livvy nodded, unsurprised.

A line formed between Eve's eyebrows. "You don't have to sit with me." Eve took another sip of her drink, this one bigger. "I'm okay being alone."

Good, well, I'll see you later then. And by later, I mean never, because awkward conversations are rarely fun for either party.

Livvy cast a longing glance at the exit, but since the dude who'd been bothering Eve was still in the bar, she stayed put. "I'd like some company. Looks like Sadia's got a bachelorette party in, so she'll be busy for a while, and I don't know anyone else here."

"Sadia?"

Eve wouldn't have hung around Sadia and Paul as much as she had around Livvy and Nicholas. "She was married to my brother. Paul," Livvy specified, feeling guilty at how she rushed to make it clear she wasn't talking about Jackson. She knew Jackson was innocent of arson, but she doubted Eve had been raised to believe that.

"Paul, yes." Her gaze skipped over the table, then away, over to the bar. "I remember her. She looks unhappy to see me."

"Don't mind her. She's protective of me."

Eve blinked and refocused on Livvy. "Does she think *you* need protection from *me*?"

Livvy shrugged. Eve gave a decidedly uncharacteristic snort. "Right. Okay."

"You don't think I need protection from you?"

Eve's smile was grim. She ran her gaze over Livvy. "You don't look scared."

"It's because I'm good at hiding my fear. I'm shaking inside."

She was being utterly honest, but from the way Eve's lips twisted, she knew the younger woman didn't understand that.

Livvy tapped her fingers on the side of her still-full glass. She'd always been shitty at waiting for the other shoe to drop. Livvy ran her hand through her hair, gathering it up in a ponytail before letting it fall back down. "What are you really doing here, Eve?"

"I told you, I come here often."

"We both know that's a lie."

Eve fiddled with the stem of her glass. "Yes," she said softly. "It's a lie. I followed you here."

"Uh. Excuse me?" That, she had not expected.

Eve's throat worked. "I came to your house," she confessed. "I mean, your mom's house. Tonight. I was sitting in my car, working up my nerve to knock."

Oh, yeesh. She couldn't predict what her mother's reaction would have been to opening the door and finding the spitting image of the woman who had died with Robert, but she couldn't imagine it would be pretty. Since Tani had methodically sequestered herself from her old life and only left the house when Paul or Sadia took her somewhere, Livvy figured the odds were low she'd even seen Eve in the past decade. "Why did you do that?"

"I wanted to talk to you. See you. I saw you leave, and at the time . . . it seemed like a good idea to, um . . ."

"Stalk me?" At the very least, Eve was a better lurker than her brother. Not by much, in her weird getup, but it had taken Livvy a while to notice her.

"I wasn't stalking you," she added quickly. "I was . . ."

"You were . . . what?"

Eve shifted in her seat, picked up her glass, and drained it, her throat working. She set it down with a clink. Her words, when she spoke, were precise. Tiny, perfect bombs. "I wanted to see the woman whose father murdered my mother."

Livvy sat back in her seat, the words digging into her flesh and burying in her heart. She almost leaned over to check the floor. Surely blood had formed a puddle under her chair. "Wow," she managed.

You don't want to be seen with the daughter of the man who was responsible for your mother's death.

Similar to what she'd hurled at Nicholas, but not the same.

Eve's face was so serene, almost peaceful, Livvy could almost doubt that the vicious words had come from her mouth. But they had.

Not timid at all.

Since she wasn't sure what else to do, Livvy finished off her own drink, barely tasting the liquid that ran a trail of fire down her throat. "You think my dad—" *Murdered.*

The girl's eyes were cold. "I read the reports. He was driving."

"Yes," Livvy said expressionlessly. She felt oddly numb, and she wasn't sure if it was the alcohol or the conversation.

No, she knew. It wasn't the alcohol.

"Above the speed limit."

Yeah. Her father had always been a careful, cautious driver. Why he'd been speeding when the roads were so icy, she had no idea. "Correct."

Eve's knuckles had turned white on her empty glass. "He was going eighty when he crashed into that tree."

"I've read the reports too, Eve. Evangeline."

"I want you to say it." Her voice rose on the last words, and she pressed her fingers against her lips, like she was trying to silence herself. A hint of moisture gleamed in her eyes.

Compassion bloomed beneath the shock that held Livvy in the seat, but she couldn't give Eve whatever she was looking for. "Say what? That he killed her?"

"Yes."

"I can't." The only people who knew exactly what had happened on that stretch of road were Robert Kane and Maria Chandler. Robert had died on impact. Maria had passed away en route to the hospital, never regaining consciousness. "He wasn't drunk or impaired in any way, and he definitely didn't run his car into that tree deliberately."

Eve paled, her light pink lip gloss garish on her lips "He might have. If my mother threatened to end their affair."

Livvy jerked back from the table. *What?*

Eve's lip curled, and Livvy totally reversed her original impression of the girl. There was a core of steel in Evangeline. If Livvy didn't feel utterly sucker punched right now, she might be proud of her.

"You didn't know," Eve said, each word a little pinprick. "That that's what people said? That the two of them were sleeping together?"

"No." Livvy clenched her jaw. Every second from the moment the police had come to their door had been filled with grief and panic and anger. She hadn't had a second to listen to gossip. Since she'd left, she'd only stayed in contact with friends, and they certainly weren't about to spread lies.

Sure, no one fully knew why Robert and Maria had been together that Friday night. Maria had been in Manhattan on foundation business, and Robert had been scoping out a new site in Pennsylvania. They hadn't been expected home until the following Monday.

But plans changed and the weather had been bad. In the aftermath, Maile had speculated perhaps Robert had picked up Maria as a favor to drive her home. It made sense.

So why had they died on the road to the Chandlers' lake house, thirty miles in the opposite direction?

Livvy shook her head. Sometimes all the pieces in an explanation didn't fit perfectly, but that didn't make the explanation completely wrong.

Her father had loved her mother. They hadn't been an overly demonstrative couple, but Robert had never failed to touch Tani's back or her hand when they passed each other. Livvy had grown up hearing bedtime stories about the first time Robert had seen Tani, when he'd been a kid working at his parents' café. *I thought she was a princess*, Robert had told her and her brothers, a fond smile on his broad face.

Her mother's feelings for Robert had never been in doubt either. Tani's keening screams when she'd learned he was dead were burned into Livvy's heart. It was one of the few times Livvy had seen a display of emotion from her mother.

"This is bullshit. And I don't want you ever, *ever*, approaching my mom with these lies."

"She's heard it." Eve's tone was flat, her gaze hard. "I assure you."

"Not from you. You don't go near her."

Eve's eyes narrowed, calculation glimmering. "I won't. So long as you don't go near my brother."

Livvy ran her hand over her face. She wouldn't ask how Eve knew she'd seen Nicholas. The girl had learned she was in town from someone.

When Livvy didn't agree immediately, Eve squared her shoulders. "I'm prepared to make it worth your while."

Oh, for fuck's sake. This was turning into a soap opera. Or a Shakespearean tragedy. "What?"

"You heard me."

"Like . . . money?"

"Yes, like money," Eve said impatiently.

An odd, completely inappropriate urge to laugh bubbled up inside her. She'd never been bought off before. "Uh, what's the going rate?"

"How much do you want?" Eve countered.

Livvy might not have been groomed to be a CEO, but she had Oka *and* Kane blood running through her veins. Businesspeople, the lot of them. You never wanted to be the one who opened negotiations. "A billion dollars."

"I'm being serious."

"Oh, you're being *serious*. Okay, then. A million dollars."

Eve swallowed. "I don't have a million dollars in liquid assets."

"What have you got? Or I suppose I should ask what's your brother worth to you? Ten thousand? Forty thousand? A hundred thousand?"

"I don't put a value on my brother."

"That's what you're asking me to do. If you can't put a value on the man you love, why should I?"

Eve lowered her voice, though Livvy wasn't sure why. No one could hear them in the rapidly growing crowd. "You don't love him. Don't pretend you do. You don't even know him anymore."

Ouch. "You're right. I don't." She didn't. She'd stopped loving him on a cold afternoon near a small pond in the woods surrounding his grandfather's house, and she'd never looked back.

That was the story, anyway.

"Okay, so why don't we do this, to be fair." Livvy tapped the table. "You can give me the difference between what your father paid for my mother's share in C&O and current market value. Is that too much? Fine. The difference between what he paid and the market value at the time of the sale. You know, when he stole the place from a grieving widow." She paused. "That's still probably more than what you have in liquid assets though."

Eve drew back like she'd been slapped. "He—you—"

"What's that?" Livvy cupped her ear. "Oh. Does it hurt to have your father accused of something shady?"

Eve's lower lip quivered, and she shoved back from the table with a jerky move. "This was a mistake."

"Yeah, it was." Livvy wasn't sure whether she was talking about coming to this bar or coming to this state. It didn't really matter.

"Stay away from my brother." The younger woman stalked toward the door.

"Yikes. That didn't look good," Sadia murmured.

Livvy was only surprised it had taken Sadia this long to rush over. She pressed her lips together, some of her rage melting instantly away at her friend's presence. "Kid's mad."

"She's not a kid, she's a grown-ass woman. What's she mad about?"

"The accident."

Sadia snorted. "Then she should know who to take her mad out on, and it's not you."

Livvy rubbed the spot between her eyes, feeling the tension headache that had been looming earlier turning into a full-blown headache. "She has no one she can take that mad out on. That's the problem." That had been the problem for everyone, right? Even she'd had no one to yell and rail at, with her beloved, bright, laughing daddy dead.

Livvy's eyes narrowed as Eve sidestepped a bunch of frat boys walking into the bar. There was a stumble in the other woman's gait. "How much alcohol is in those pink fruity drinks she was downing?"

Sadia picked up Eve's empty glasses. "A deceptively large amount. Especially for a little thing like her."

Eve stumbled again, catching her balance on the door. They glanced at each other. Sadia sighed. "Go on. Call me if you need help."

"Thanks." Livvy shoved back from the table and draped her jacket around her shoulders.

She found Eve walking rapidly into the parking lot. Livvy zipped up her jacket, the autumn wind biting through her tights. The air smelled like apples and . . . home.

Not home. Old home. Temporary home. "Hey," she called out to Eve's back.

"What do you want?" Eve asked coldly, not turning around.

"Making sure you're okay."

"I'm fine."

Livvy followed the girl. "Do you need me to call a cab or anything?"

"No."

Livvy sighed. "Look, kid—"

Eve spun around. Her cheeks were flushed. Whether it was from the alcohol or her emotions, Livvy wasn't sure. "Stop calling me that. I'm not thirteen anymore."

Livvy stuffed her hands in her pockets. "If you don't want to be treated like a child, you might want to stop lashing out like one."

"I never lash out. I—"

"You hate me for who my father was. If that's not lashing out, I don't know what is."

"I—I don't hate you. I just . . . I was just—"

"Just what?"

Eve straightened. "I don't know."

"Look . . ." Livvy ran her fingers through her hair. "You shouldn't drive home if you're drunk."

Eve gave Livvy an icy, withering look. "I'm not drunk."

"You sure about that?"

Eve opened her mouth, then closed it again. "I might be a bit tipsy."

It would be so easy to wash her hands of this by calling a ride for the girl, but something made Livvy hesitate. Maybe it was how young Eve suddenly appeared, too much like the child she'd once loved. Paul and Jackson had mostly ignored the youngest Chandler—a decade and seven years, respectively, was a large age gap to overcome. But Livvy, starved for girl companionship in her houseful of men, had been entranced with Eve since she'd come home from the hospital.

Plus, at one point, she'd assumed Eve would be her sister-in-law, occupying the same circle of family as Sadia. Another relationship that had been a casualty to the feud.

"I'll drive you home." She'd taken a cab here, and had planned on either driving home with Sadia or getting a ride. It would make no difference if she called for a car at Eve's place or here.

"I don't need you to do that."

"I have no doubt you're over the legal limit. Do you want to risk it?" She made her tone firm, expecting Eve to argue. The girl's chin lifted, and she looked away, her nostrils flaring. Then she held out her keys.

Livvy took them with a fatalistic air. Quietly, deep in her soul, she gave fate the middle finger. She couldn't avoid the Chandlers even when she tried.

Chapter 6

NICHOLAS TRACED the tattoo on her shoulder with his tongue, following the curve of the vine, the prickled point of each leaf, the round delicate flowers. She shivered under his mouth, her biceps contracting as he followed the ink and scraped his teeth over her arm.

His fingers wandered over her soft stomach, dipping into her belly button for a second before drifting lower, into the wet heat between her thighs. Her legs shifted, making room for him without his needing to ask.

One finger, two . . . he pressed them inside her, widening them gently, getting her ready for his cock. His thumb rubbed over the bud of her clitoris, and he was rewarded with a low moan.

The moan grew deeper when he captured her nipple in his mouth, worrying the flesh with his teeth before moving to the other and giving it the same treatment. He wanted to devour her completely, but this wasn't about gorging. This was about savoring, enjoying every second of her. He never got to savor her.

He sucked her for long moments, loving how she squirmed beneath him. It was his turn to groan when her hand found his cock. She gave him the long, slow pulls he loved, milking him from root to tip. He pressed three fingers inside her, filling her up. Her hand faltered on him, but then she caught the rhythm again, rubbing faster and harder. He tried to match her motions, her slick pussy making those wet sounds he loved to hear, but he was far too distracted by her grip on him. He arched his back and let her have her way, her hand speeding up, twisting with every upstroke.

Long hair flicked against his skin and he shouted as her tongue traced the head of his cock and her mouth settled on him, sucking in time with each movement of her fist. A few strokes and he was gone, thighs tensing as he came.

After long moments, Nicholas leaned over the bed and grabbed the towel he'd carelessly dropped on the carpet after his shower. He cleaned his come off his belly, fingers, and cock, hissing as the terrycloth rubbed over the too-sensitive head of his penis.

He balled up the towel and tossed it in the general direction of the hamper. He'd pick it up in the morning. Normally, he made sure everything in his house was perfectly in its place before he fell asleep, but these were abnormal times.

He checked the watch on his wrist. It was past midnight. He was always asleep by 11:30, at the latest. His alarm was set for 4:30 and he functioned best with at least five hours of sleep.

He draped his arm over his eyes and exhaled, the sound loud in his silent, empty bedroom. He would not get anxious about being off his schedule. He would not. He already had too many things on his mind.

Mostly Livvy. Livvy was the biggest thing on his mind. He couldn't escape her, especially not in his fantasies.

He pulled his arm away and studied the skin. He'd scrubbed and scrubbed the damned tattoo when he'd come home. Now he could barely make out the outline of the naked fairy.

Compartmentalize, damn it.

That was his superpower. When he was at work, he thought about work. When he was with his family, it was family. Thinking about Livvy was relegated to one single day out of 365. His cheat day.

But it was far easier to shove Livvy aside when he was hundreds of miles away from her and there was no chance he could run into her. Within driving distance? Impossible.

You need to make it possible. Think of your family. Think of every person who relies on you to be at your peak physical and mental capabilities.

Be realistic.

They could never be together, so thinking of her was silly. He was not a silly man. Done.

He readjusted his boxer briefs and resettled himself into his bed. Closed his eyes. Tried to focus on his breathing.

You can't be with her, but you could fuck. You've been doing that all along, and no one got hurt.

He banged his head back against the pillow. No he could *not*, brain. Because . . . because . . .

With a low growl, he sat up. Because they couldn't.

Back in the case. He had to get back in the case. He could only jerk off so much, so maybe he would go work out again. Run until his feet developed blisters. Abuse his flesh in the hopes that he could excise her.

Before he could move, the ring of his cell phone cut through the silence, and he jumped. He grabbed the device from his nightstand dock. He frowned at the name that popped up on the screen. Why was Eve calling him well past midnight? "Eve? What's wrong?"

There was the static of air. Butt dial, maybe, but it was so late. Evie went to bed far earlier than he did.

Then he heard the murmur of a feminine voice. He reared back and looked at the phone, wondering if his lust-ridden brain was now fueling hallucinations.

Livvy?

No, it couldn't be. Why the hell would Livvy be with Eve?

He pressed the phone tighter to his ear. "Eve? Eve, honey? Eve."

He heard a voice that was unmistakably Eve's, but saying a very un-Eve-like thing. "Shit."

LIVVY FINISHED washing her hands in the bathroom and came out to the bedroom. Eve barely made a bump under her white ruffled coverlet.

She was curled on her side, hands stacked under her flushed cheek. Livvy crept over, feeling foolish until she saw Eve's chest moving up and down under the T-shirt she'd gotten into. She was pale, but there was a bit of color back in her cheeks. Her long lashes fluttered and she looked up at Livvy. "I'm so mortified."

Something eased within Livvy at this miserable confession. "Don't be. We've all thrown up at one time or another."

"After two drinks?"

"Maybe not most people, but my mom and brother have no tolerance with alcohol. The car ride plus the alcohol plus you said you hadn't eaten much today . . ." Livvy shrugged. Eve had just made it out of the car before throwing up in the bushes outside the condo.

She wondered if Eve would tense up at the mention of the other Kanes, but she only closed her eyes. "I've never been good with alcohol either. This is the second time this has happened."

"When was the first time?" Gingerly, Livvy sat on the edge of the bed.

"College. I was trying to impress a boy."

"Ah." College had been expected of all of them. Nicholas and Paul had gone off and gotten business degrees, so the company had been secure. She'd enrolled in a local art program, while Jackson had attended a prestigious culinary school. Neither of them had graduated.

"I promised myself I'd never try that again."

"You only tried to impress a boy once in four

years? Better record than me." She'd only ever tried to impress one boy. Countless times. Nicholas was tough to impress.

"Three years."

Livvy raised an eyebrow, a shot of something that felt strangely like pride rushing through her. "Well, damn. Smart girl."

"Lots of people graduate in three years."

"No, they don't. Be proud of your accomplishments. No one will be proud of them for you." Her tone was probably harder than it needed to be, and she wasn't exactly the best person in the world to play big sister to anyone, but the girl ought to know.

The world was unkind to women. It was devastating to women who didn't believe in themselves.

At Eve's silence, Livvy glanced over her shoulder to find the girl looking at her. Blue shadows ringed her eyes. "You dress differently now," Eve commented out of the blue.

"I'm not a teen living at home with a disapproving mother," she said dryly. "Also, my clothes-buying budget isn't quite what it used to be." The words slipped out of her mouth, and she regretted them instantly. Not because they were false—the hardest part of losing a financial safety net was figuring out the essentials and nonessentials and creating a budget—but because she didn't want to slip into the same barb and parry game with Eve that she played with Nicholas.

Nicholas was her equal. Eve, despite being of legal age, was still a child in her eyes.

Eve nodded. "Yes, I imagine so," was all she said.

The sound of the door opening had Livvy coming to her feet. Eve's apartment was surprisingly small for a Chandler, a two-bedroom place in a quiet, middle-class part of town.

"Don't worry, that's probably my roommate. I texted her." Eve closed her eyes again.

A second later, a pretty black woman wearing jeans and a purple Hello Kitty T-shirt entered the bedroom and gave a sympathetic wince at the sight of Eve in bed. She smiled at Livvy and held out her hand. "Hey, I'm Madison."

Livvy nodded and shook her hand. "Livvy."

Madison bustled closer to the bed and stroked Eve's hair. "Oh, Eve. How many?"

"Two, but in my defense, they were potent."

Madison tsked, dropped her backpack on the floor, and perched next to her friend. "Alcohol and you are not friends. A few sips, max."

Livvy tucked her fingers into her back pocket. "I guess you're in good hands now."

Eve gazed at her somberly. "I am. Thank you." The words were stiff but sounded genuine.

The apartment's front door thudded open, and Livvy jolted. "How many roommates do you have?"

Eve groaned. "Oh God. I accidentally dialed Nicholas after Madison. I hung up, but . . ."

Livvy tensed. *She couldn't avoid the Chandlers even when she tried.* "Nicholas?"

Eve's eyes widened, probably because she'd just realized she'd brought together two people she'd spent the evening trying to keep apart. "Oh, shi—"

"Eve?" came Nicholas's voice from the living room. "Why are your lights on? Where are you?"

"You butt dial him and he charges right over? How did he know you were here?" Madison whispered.

"He tracked my phone," Eve whispered back.

"It's a good thing he's your brother and not your boyfriend, or that would be creepy," Madison grumbled.

"Still creepy," Livvy remarked, trying to tamp down the sinking sense of doom. "Are we going to pretend we're not here, because there's only two rooms for him to check before he finds you."

Eve groaned again, and suddenly Nicholas stood in the doorway, his big body filling the space. He wore dark jeans and a black T-shirt, a sprinkling of rain dusting his shoulders.

Damn it. Livvy was pretty sure the drizzling had left her hair messy and flat. How did he look so good?

His stride arrested as his gaze landed on her, but he didn't look completely shocked. His brows knitted as he took in Eve lying on the bed. "What happened?" he barked out.

Eve draped her arm over her eyes. "Nothing," she mumbled.

"You look terrible," Nicholas said bluntly. "Are you sick?"

"I drank a little too much, okay?"

Nicholas drew back. "You drank? You don't drink."

"Clearly she does," Livvy interjected, something

about Nicholas's overprotective scowl rubbing her the wrong way.

He turned that scowl on her, and a memory pinged in the back of her mind. Paul, hands on his hips, glaring at Nicholas after he'd asked her out on a date. *You better treat my sister right, asshole.*

"Why are you here?"

Her lip curled as his autocratic tone riled up every defensive, contrary cell of her body. "I happened to be at the bar where Eve was," she answered, as pleasantly as possible. "Not that it's any of your business."

"Bar?" Nicholas's gaze cut back to Eve, and he strode to the bed. "You don't go to bars."

"Zero out of two," Livvy said caustically, perfectly fine with having Nicholas's attention on growling at her instead of browbeating his sister. "You're not doing so hot tonight."

Nicholas ran his hand clumsily over Eve's hair until she weakly swatted his hand away. "I'm sorry to have bothered you," Eve mumbled. "But I really am fine."

"That's what brothers are for," Livvy said. "To be bothered. In fact, you should bother him more. I'll go get some vodka."

The siblings ignored her. "You don't look good. You should be at the hospital."

Madison cleared her throat. "I'll keep an eye on her, Nicholas."

His smile was more like an impatient baring of teeth. "I'm sorry, Madison. When did you graduate medical school again?"

Whoa. Livvy raised her eyebrows, insulted on the younger woman's behalf. Snippiness wasn't something that looked good on anyone, but it was especially weird for generally calm Nicholas.

Madison looked amused instead of pissed off. "No med school for me, but I've already taken and passed Drunk Friends 101 with flying colors, so I think I can handle things tonight."

Nicholas bent and peered into Eve's eyes. "You could have alcohol poisoning. We should go to the emergency room."

Livvy straightened, pulling away from the wall. "Let's go, big guy. It's time for us to let Eve get some rest."

"I—"

"Please, Nicholas." Eve turned her face away, the curve of her neck fragile and birdlike. "I'm tired, and my head hurts. I'll talk to you in the morning."

He hesitated, but her plea must have convinced him. "Fine." He bent down and pressed a kiss to Eve's forehead, then walked to the door, his reluctance obvious in every step he took.

Livvy heard Madison whisper something to Eve that sounded like "I like that chick," but she didn't hear Eve's response. The poor girl must be having palpitations at the thought of her and Nicholas being alone together.

They walked out of the condo in tense silence. Nicholas finally spoke. "Thanks for seeing her home." His tone was remote and cold. The display of emotions she'd witnessed inside was gone.

She missed it, even though that concern and caring hadn't been directed at her.

"No problem," she returned.

"What a coincidence you happened to be at the same bar."

It didn't sound like he bought that coincidence at all. She hummed. Let Eve tell her brother about her gentle stalking and bribery attempt.

And her rambling about your parents' affair? Accusing your dad of a murder-suicide?

She pushed that aside, unwilling to deal with it right now. Eve had probably only wanted to upset her, and mission accomplished. She wasn't about to get into that with Nicholas. He either knew about it or he didn't, and the discussion would only mess with her head more than Eve already had.

"You look fresh as a daisy," she said. "Thought this would be way past your bedtime." *Why is that, Nicholas? Why do you look so good? Were you busily servicing your girlfriend?*

"I was about to work out when Eve called."

Oh, thanks a lot. There went an extra bonus image into her spank bank.

Nicholas tapped his keys against his thigh. "You look tired."

Lady boner deflated. "That's a shitty thing to say to a girl," she returned pleasantly. "You might as well say, hey, your face is really looking haggard."

"Sorry."

But he didn't retract his statement that she looked tired. Asshole.

"I don't see your car outside."

"I drove Eve here in her car. I'll get a ride home."

"How?"

Livvy pulled her phone out of her pocket and waggled it at him. "I have like four different apps."

"This neighborhood? You'll have to wait for a while."

She opened an app and tapped her location, then quietly closed it when she saw the wait time. "I'll call Sadia. She can come pick me up once her shift is over."

Nicholas pressed a button on his key fob and the sleek black sedan nearest them blinked its lights. "I'll give you a ride home."

"Uh. That doesn't seem like the best idea."

He rubbed the space between his eyes. "Livvy, it's late. I'm exhausted. Stop being a pain in my ass and get in my car."

"Well, when you're that charming, I don't know how to resist you."

"I leave charming to other men."

Yeah, Nicholas had never been charming in the traditional way. Not in public, at least. In private, he'd charmed the panties right off her.

Ugh. Ughhhhhhh. Could this night get weirder? "Fine. Whatever." She could sit next to Nicholas like a motherfucking adult. It was a short drive to her place.

Since she knew he took pride in opening doors for women, she beat him to the passenger door and got in. As if he was surprised by her acquiescence, he climbed in next to her, shooting her wary looks the whole while.

Pretend this is normal. "You're a lot more overprotective of Eve than I remember."

He shifted, turning toward her, wrist draped over the steering wheel. "Did she say that?"

"No. You rushing over here because she butt dialed you was a dead giveaway."

Annoyance tightened his features, but he dipped his head in acknowledgment. "She was sick for a while."

Livvy raised an eyebrow. Eve didn't look particularly sickly. "When?"

"When she was fifteen or so. She's fine now. She doesn't like to talk about it. But she spent a few months in the hospital. It changed our relationship a little."

Where had she been when Eve was in the hospital? Livvy thought back to all her travels. Los Angeles, maybe? "That makes sense but fifteen was a long time ago. Maybe you should ease off a little. She's only a couple years away from being able to rent a car."

His lips flattened. "Don't worry about Eve and me."

"It's for your own good. I bet your girlfriend doesn't like you flying off like this." There. Totally cool. Addressing his girlfriend, that evil awful bitch.

She's probably nice.

Hmph.

Nicholas froze. "She doesn't mind," he said stiffly. She crossed her arms over her chest and looked out of the window. "What a saint." The *fucking* qualifying the saint was silent.

"She's . . . Goddamn it." Nicholas pinched the bridge of his nose. "I don't have a girlfriend."

She swiveled her head to look at him. "You said you were seeing—"

"It was a lie."

Her first reaction was relief. Then insulted mortification. Her hands curled into fists on her thighs. "Oh. I've played that game before."

"What game?"

"Pretending I have a boyfriend so someone harassing me would leave me alone." She stared blindly at the dashboard. "I read this article once that said the quickest way to get a dude to stop hitting on you was to say that you're with another guy, because men respect other men more than they respect a woman saying no. You didn't have to do that with me. You could have just said you weren't interested."

"Is that what you think? That I said I had a girlfriend so you'd leave me alone?" His laugh was humorless. "My God."

"What am I supposed to think?"

"That I had to come up with some fucking way to stop myself from spinning you around and bending you over the table."

"You—"

His hands tightened on the steering wheel, the knuckles turning white. "I said it to stop me. Not you."

"Oh." *Don't be happy.*

"I know you're not good for me, but I can't seem to stop wanting you."

She barely managed to stop herself from recoiling. There it was, confirmation of how much he hated his attraction to her.

Not good for me.

That was fine. She'd decided he was bad for her too, hadn't she? That was why she hadn't texted him, because she was cutting out things that didn't help her.

So why did hearing him say those words hurt so much?

"It's never been like this before. Every year I'd come back from our . . . meetings, and I'd eventually get back to my life. I'd sleep and eat and socialize and be normal. But you being here, so close . . ."

"I can't leave," she cut in.

"I didn't say you should." His glance at her was savage, his voice dipping to a low whisper she had to sway toward him to hear. "I waited the week of your birthday. The day before. Even the fucking day of your birthday, until the clock struck twelve. Waited for one message that never came."

He was pummeling her with feelings. Giving her bursts of pleasure and a hit of pain.

But didn't that basically sum up their whole relationship?

"You were right. If this was a matter of getting each other out of our systems, we should be done by now. But I don't feel like I've moved on." His tone turned guttural. "Even now, all I can think about is getting you somewhere dark, with a bed. Without a bed. It doesn't matter."

She passed the back of her hand over her mouth, and her brain latched on to his words. *Work him out of her system.* Yes. Yes, that was all she needed.

The tension and desire and need between them could be released like the valve on a rice cooker, and they'd go back to sleeping well and not agonizing over how the other person was so close and so far away. Right?

He cleared his throat and shook his head. "Forget it. What's your mom's address?" he asked gruffly. He cursed before she could respond. "Hang on, I think I left my phone inside."

Livvy ran her thumb over the screen of her own phone while he jogged back to the building.

If you haven't worked him out yet, what makes you think a final screw will?

It wouldn't. She was lying to herself in order to engage in a dumb, self-harming decision. Her body was revved up, the heat between them impossible to ignore.

You said you were going to stop. Move on. Look forward. Take care of yourself. Yeah, she had. But it was far easier to stop when one wasn't in constant proximity to the addiction they were eager to cure. Right now, she was like a recovering smoker who vowed to go cold turkey while a lit cigarette rolled just out of reach.

At worst, she'd wake up with a slightly more bruised heart.

It's so knocked around already, do a few more blows really matter?

She touched her chest with shaking fingers. *Oh, Livvy. Don't do this. This way lies madness.*

But the relief. She'd have relief, even for a few minutes. Respite from her lust and her stress and her problems and worries. Pure pleasure, where she wouldn't have to think about her family or her life or her lost love.

She quickly opened the browser and typed in a search.

Then she texted Nicholas.

Livvy shoved her phone in her pocket like that would make her less complicit in the frankly stupid action she'd just taken, or would make her less ashamed of the shoddy justification she'd given for engaging in said act. Her heart raced, her palms sweating. She wiped them against her bare thighs, her skin almost too sensitive for contact with herself.

Nicholas emerged from the building a few minutes later and walked down the pathway. His face was clean of all expression. He got inside the car.

He could have not seen her message. Or ignored it. She laced her fingers tight together and pressed them against her belly.

Then he placed his phone in the dashboard mount, open to a map with the coordinates she'd texted him.

"The usual rules?"

"Yes. One night," she whispered. "I need . . ."

His hand landed on her thigh, shocking her with

the heavy heat and electrical tingle that ran through her body. His rough fingers stroked higher, moving her short skirt up, clenching on the soft flesh there. They both stared at the way his fingers molded the skin. How many times had his fingers dug into her thighs while he slammed his body into hers?

She needed. Christ, she needed.

Nicholas released her to put the car into drive. "I know exactly what you need."

Chapter 7

THIS WAS a terrible idea. Beyond terrible. Reckless. Dangerous.

All things she made him.

Energy and excitement roared through him. His senses felt like they'd been cranked into hyperdrive.

It was wrong, and his brain knew this was going to end poorly. For the good of everyone who depended on him, the best course of action was to go home and get ahold of these wayward thoughts and irrational emotions.

That is not the best course of action, his boner argued, drowning out the rational part of his brain. He and Livvy would screw tonight, and then they could mosey on with their lives, happy and satisfied the pattern of their behavior had been fulfilled.

Fool. His penis was a fool.

Nicholas drummed his fingers against the steering wheel to the rhythm of the lust beating in his veins.

When they'd been young, they'd come to this motel on the outskirts of town a time or two. The place had been run-down then. Now it was veering sharply into seedy.

She came out of the office, her short skirt fluttering in the breeze, lifting enough that he caught a glimpse of her bottom under the deceptively innocent schoolgirl-plaid skirt, encased in black tights. Her small breasts strained against the white button-down shirt she wore, her red bra visible.

He didn't want to think of her going to a bar in that ridiculously provocative outfit, or about other men salivating over her thighs and breasts and neck.

Neck?

Yes, goddamn it, even her fucking neck was sexy, long and elegant, with that cute little hollow at the base, the perfect spot to suck on while he was fucking her. Surely she wasn't trying to drive him crazy by possessing that neck, but here she was, succeeding nonetheless.

She didn't glance at his car. It had gone against the grain to let Livvy reserve the room, but she'd merely had to make the valid point that he could be recognized, and he'd reluctantly conceded. He could be recognized, depending on how old the clerk was and how long they'd lived in this place. Livvy, though . . .

Despite her ridiculous schoolgirl outfit, she wasn't the girl she'd been when she left town. Her hair, her clothes, even her attitude was subtly different. He'd watched every change happen over the past decade in a time-lapse video. There was nothing he didn't like about the differences in her now.

Dangerous.

Right. Right. This was about sex. Nothing else.

She headed down the walkway, the flickering streetlamp in the parking lot burnishing her hair with red and black. She didn't wobble a bit on her pencil-thin heels, reassuring him that though she'd been in a bar, she wasn't anywhere near intoxicated.

He got out of the car, taking care to pull his collar up and lower his head, feeling ridiculous as he did so. He was a grown man. Who cared if he had sex with another consenting adult?

Lots of people, starting with his father, but he wasn't going to think about them right now.

His strides were longer than hers. Her heels and skirt made it difficult for her to do more than mince. He made it to the door a second after she got it open, and followed her in, kicking the door shut behind him. She stripped off her light fall jacket and tossed it on the floor. "Liv—" was all he had a chance to say before she was in his arms, shoving him back.

It was dark, the only light coming in from the crack between the dingy curtains. Her lips pressed against his, and he inhaled the scent of her, each drugging kiss making his head spin. She crawled up him like he was a pole, her arms and legs clutching for balance.

It took him only a second. One second of having those red lips devouring his hungrily, one second of that hot sinner's body pressing against his own, and all semblance of rational thought flew out of his brain.

Who cared about tomorrow? He was too en-
flamed to wonder about anything but the here and
now. Too excited to even consider this a bad idea.
He kissed her back as if he would die if he didn't
get her mouth, licking and sucking and memoriz-
ing the very taste of her. He slid his hands over her
ass, gripped her luscious cheeks tight, and spun
her around, pushing her up against the door.

He ripped his lips away, holding her from him
when she might have forced her way back. "How
do you want it?" he growled. He had an inkling,
from the signals she was broadcasting, but it had
been a while since he'd had to read those signals.

"Hard . . ." She scraped her nails over the back
of his neck. "Use me. Make me feel it tomorrow."

The wild look in her eyes was sharper than he'd
ever seen it, and it ramped up his own lust. He
dragged his hand over her ass, rubbing the fabric
against her bottom. "This outfit is indecent."

Her lids dropped to half-mast, and she arched her
back. "You don't like my clothes? I'm heartbroken."

"You look like a schoolgirl."

She tightened her legs around his waist, rubbing
up on him. Her heat and wetness was obvious,
even through the twin barriers of her underwear
and his pants. "A naughty one? Who needs to be
punished?"

He should feel ridiculous, but instead his body
hardened more, blood engorging his dick. "So
naughty." His hand slipped up her leg to her hip
and the strip of fabric there. He used his other
hand to arch her back farther, feathering his fin-

gers up her spine. "I could see your ass while you were walking outside." He traced his hand around the waistband at her back and clenched the fabric in his wrist, pulling the bikini and her tights taut, digging into the folds of her pussy. Her eyes widened.

He tightened his grip. "Were you purposefully strutting around in this skirt, your ass hanging out of it?"

"N-no."

"You're lying. Do you know what I do to liars?"

Her nails dug into his skin. "Tell me you spank them."

A red haze swam in front of his eyes, and he pushed her legs down so she was standing. Then he grabbed her by the waist and spun her around to face the door.

He grasped her by the hips and pulled her to stand with her back in an arch, then flipped up that ridiculous plaid skirt. It took him a second to lower her tights to her thighs. Her red panties barely covered the curves of her ass, making him growl. He didn't know what bar she'd been in, but he imagined her seated in some dingy smoke-filled dive, anonymous bastards salivating over her tight body. Fuck, all it would have taken was one shimmy, and everyone could have gotten a free show, these tempting round globes exposed but for the silly scraps of fabric she'd put over them.

You have no right to be jealous.

He palmed her cheeks, rubbing his thumbs over the plump flesh. "Do you know how badly I wanted to pull you onto my lap and flip this skirt up the second I saw you?"

"To fuck me or to spank me?"

"Both."

She arched her back more, her ass wriggling. He didn't think, merely lifted his hand and smacked one full cheek, his rational, caring side standing far apart and watching in horror. He'd never spanked a woman before. As scrappy as Livvy was, he hadn't thought she'd like this.

Her moan suggested otherwise.

He got it. He got the appeal of this, with Livvy bent over in front of him, legs spread, skirt lifted, red panties exposed, and the hot flesh of her ass filling his hand. He slapped her other cheek, and she moaned again, louder. Hell. He could see the appeal of literally doing anything with Livvy, to be honest.

"Was that okay?" he had the semblance of mind to ask her.

Her hands had braced against the door, and her fingers curled in. She nodded, her red-streaked hair rippling over her back.

His next tap was harder. "You've been so bad, Livvy. Tempting all those men tonight. Tempting me." He smacked her again. "You've never stopped tempting me."

She whimpered. "I'll stop."

"We both know that's impossible." He squeezed her left cheek, dropping to his knees behind her. With his teeth, he carefully lowered the panties over her ass to meet the rolled-up waistband of her tights. He stayed there, luxuriating in her body as he pressed soft kisses over each cheek, punctuating each tender touch with a slap of his hand.

When she was rocking back against his mouth, he pulled away. He came to his feet. Unable to take his gaze off her tight body, he walked backward until his knees hit the cheap bed. Nicholas slid down to sit on the floor, his back supported by the bed. The sliver of streetlight illuminating the room highlighted her sweet, reddened buttocks. He tore at his jeans, growling when his hand met his throbbing cock. He needed to jerk off or get in her pussy. Something. Anything. Literally whatever would relieve this ache as soon as possible.

She peeked under her arm and straightened, skirt dropping down to cover her bottom.

A crime, covering that butt.

Livvy stripped off her tights and panties and then turned to face him. "Nicholas?"

He ran his hand down his cock once, then twice when he noted the hunger in her gaze as she watched him fondle himself. He grazed the tip, and his body jerked. "Take off your clothes. Shirt first."

"Do I have to?" Her breathless question was pseudo-innocent.

"Unless you want to be punished." How he'd punish her, he wasn't sure. More spanking? Licking her until she wept with the need to orgasm? Fucking her until she screamed?

These didn't sound like terrible punishments for either of them.

Her fingers fumbled with the buttons of her shirt, and she undid them one by one, so slowly he knew it was a tease. He tightened his hand on his cock, because he knew if he didn't, he'd demand she come over here so he could rip the offending material right off her.

She stripped it off her shoulders, leaving her in her bra, her toned belly inviting his lips.

"Now the bra."

She unsnapped the front snap and drew both cups of red lace away from her breasts. They were perky and lifted on their own, the small handfuls the perfect fit for his palm. Her brown nipples were tight and pointed, giving away her excitement. Her breasts rose and fell, her gaze locked on his hand. He made his pulls slower and more explicit, both to give her a show and to make sure he didn't blow too quickly.

Her hand dropped to the waistband of her skirt, shoving it down, leaving her completely naked. She licked her lips, making the remnants of her lipstick shiny and vibrant. He imagined those lips wrapped tight around his cock, him whispering, *Suck me*, while guiding her head over his lap.

He shook his head, trying to shake the filthy image from his brain, and released his cock. "Come here."

She walked over. Her hand unselfconsciously slid over her belly and pussy. She was wet and hot and plump, nearly hairless, save for a small landing strip. The pot of gold tattooed at her hip was a dark shadow. "Closer."

She planted one foot on either side of his hips. With his position sitting on the floor, her pussy was right at eye level for him.

"Show me how wet you are."

She swallowed, a flush rising up her chest. Her painted fingernails caught the light as she moved over her folds. With her index finger and thumb, she held herself open as she stroked her fingers over her clit and then inside.

He was helpless to watch her pleasure herself. Her head fell back, and her hand moved faster even as he stayed in complete stillness. It was self-preservation that had him gritting out, "Stop."

She halted immediately, her chin lowering, eyes opening. Her hand eased out of her pussy, the cheap lighting casting a glossy glow over them. "Do you want a taste?" she murmured.

"I always do."

Her fingers traced his lips, the scent of her arousal driving his higher. He opened his mouth, waiting for her to slip them inside, but instead she drew her hand away, bringing them to her own lips. Her cheeks hollowed as she sucked each finger, a smug, satisfied look in her eyes.

He tilted his head back against the bed and ran his tongue over his lips, taking in whatever little bit she'd deigned to give him. Nicholas ran his hand up her legs until he could grasp her ass. Quickly, taking her off balance, he yanked her closer so his head was right between her thighs. She cried out and widened her stance, placing her hands on the mattress above his head for support.

Nicholas drew her ever nearer, creating a dark, wet place for him to feast. His tongue slid along the crease of her thigh, tracing the shaking dip, then the other side, before burying against her pubic bone.

He'd seen her au naturel, completely bare, sporting various designs in her hair, and one interesting year, decorated in sparkling accents.

He didn't care how the hell she decorated her private places, so long as he could lick them.

A god. That's what he felt like when he was between her plump thighs, his tongue and lips driving her to madness. If he could, he would eat nothing but Livvy for sustenance.

"Please, Nicholas."

He nuzzled his nose against the strip of hair there. "Please, what?"

"Please lick me."

He gave her a tiny swipe of his tongue, and her thighs went rigid on either side of his head. "Nicholas."

Another swipe.

"Harder."

"Say it." He punctuated his demand with a slap against her ass.

"Fuck me with your mouth."

He growled against her flesh and pressed wet, openmouthed kisses all over her vulva, using two fingers to open her up.

He stiffened his tongue and thrust inside her, spanking her harder than he'd dared before, squeezing and pulling apart her ass cheeks as she gyrated above him. Her cries grew louder and he supported more of her weight as her legs shook.

She'd always been a screamer.

Her pussy contracted around his tongue and he welcomed every tightening and releasing motion, drinking in her pleasure. When she relaxed, he ducked out from her legs and came to his feet. She'd worked most of her body onto the bed and lay sprawled in an undignified heap, face-down, her legs still spread. He quickly stripped out of his clothes, taking a second of sanity to grab a condom from his wallet, before stepping up behind her, selfish desire riding him now. He needed to pound himself so deep inside her she'd feel him for days to come. "Brace yourself."

LIVVY WAS so boneless she could only clutch weakly at the cheap bedding. The hotel hadn't been renovated or touched since she and Nicholas had snuck off here when they were young, and there was an odd nostalgia in grasping the orange-and-green comforter while his hungry hands roved over her.

Except neither of them were young anymore. The tongue that had devastated her was a man's tongue, the big hands arranging her into position, back arched, booty high, were a man's hands. She was his—his woman, his to use and fuck.

Like you'll always be.

There was no way she could excise him from her system. Not with a one-night stand, not with annual meetings. Not ever.

A tiny part of her broke apart as she confronted

her deepest, darkest fear, and she buried her face in the scratchy comforter like an animal sticking its head in the sand. Later. She'd think later. First, she'd pretend she was his, and he was hers, even if only for a few minutes.

His latex-clad cock brushed against her bottom, and lower. She closed her eyes, resting her forehead on her arms.

"Christ, you have no idea how much I love seeing you like this. Laid out and wet and open." His fingers trailed over the crack of her ass, then below, probing her softness, and he made a deep noise of appreciation. "You taste so good. I could lick this all day. You'd let me."

It wasn't a question, but she nodded, stripped of her bluster. Yes, she'd let him. It was the one constant whenever they got together. He dived between her legs like he couldn't get enough, his technique and skill improving every year. She wasn't about to complain. A man who loved to give head and was spectacular at it? He was a goddamn prince.

His fingers slipped away, and his cock replaced them, the pressure promising her untold delight. She pushed her ass toward him so he'd take her. He gave a rough laugh. "You're so hungry. Ask me for it."

"Fuck me." Her voice was high and barely perceptible.

He teased her, the head pushing inside and then pulling out. "I can't hear you."

"Fuck me," she said, louder, crying out when he thrust, seating inside with one push. She gasped, sweat falling into her eyes, her hair sticking to her back.

He didn't give her the steady thrusts that would get both of them off but held completely still, letting her feel every twitch of his cock.

A big hand carefully gathered her hair up, every tug on her scalp sending electrical tingles down her spine and body. She gasped as he wound the strands around his hand the same way he wound his tie to fold it up. When they were secured, he pulled. He lowered over her, plastering his body against hers, resting his lips against her ear. "*You* fuck me."

She shoved her hips back against his hard, immovable body, but he had her almost pinned to the bed, and she could only fuck herself on a couple of inches of his hard dick. It wasn't enough, the thick length barely moving. She sobbed. "I can't. Please."

His mouth descended on her shoulder. She stiffened as his hot tongue traced the tattoo there. This was about as much light as they'd ever had when they screwed. He wouldn't be able to see all of the marks she'd put on herself. That was good, even if it did send a shot of sadness through her. She had to keep him from her soft parts.

Well, not all her soft parts. He bit the flesh right above a prickly flower, and she tried to rock again. "Fuck me. Please, I need your cock so bad. I'll do anything for it." Sex words. True words.

He gave her hair another tug, then reared back, his cock withdrawing from her body, leaving her clenching around nothing. She made a low sound of yearning.

"I shouldn't let you have it," he rumbled above her. "I should punish you for making me want you. For making me need you."

"If you punish me, you're punishing yourself."

There was a moment of silence, their loud breaths syncing together. His big hands settled on her hips, and he flipped her over. His face was strained and covered with sweat. He yanked her legs wide and moved between them, his fat cock shoving in deep enough to make her scream.

She strained underneath him. "Plea—"

"Shh." His cock sank inside her again and he rested his hands on either side of her head. "No more begging now."

She lost herself in the steady roll of his hips, the in and out that was both familiar and altogether new. She had to close her eyes to avoid his intense blue gaze, the way his brow furrowed as he carefully catalogued her face.

"Livvy—"

"Stop talking. Just fuck me. Harder." Hard enough she didn't have to remember this was it, the last time it would happen.

His hips picked up speed, slamming into her. She could always tell when Nicholas was close because he fucked like a train run off course, his hips blurring. She bit her lip to hold back her cries, well aware that these walls were thin, but then his fingers were at her lips, his thumb inserting between her teeth. "You want to abuse a body, abuse mine. I don't want a mark on those lips."

Her body tightened around him, and she moaned, her teeth sinking into his flesh, taking him at his word. She bit harder as she climaxed on his pistoning cock. At the last minute she drew her arms around his neck and brought his face down so his lips were right next to her ear. His breaths soughed in and out, and he groaned, long and low. He shoved in deep and came, his body convulsing in her arms. She pressed her fingertips against his back and stared up at the ceiling, post-orgasmic bliss almost letting her forget this was all she'd ever have of him.

Almost.

He lifted his head, his eyes still closed, forehead creased like he was in pain. He slipped out of her arms before rolling to the side of the bed. He sat there for a long time, both of them breathing hard.

She'd been mistaken. Her heart didn't feel dinged. It felt pummeled.

She stared at his back, the blank canvas of muscles and sinew and bone making her want to roll over and trace her fingers all over it. Tears and sorrow clogged her sinuses. She had no right to that back. Or his cock or his tongue or any part of him. This had been it. A few brief moments of forgetfulness to tide them over.

Say something. Do something.

She opened her mouth, then closed it again, feeling lost.

She jerked when he came to his feet, but he didn't

look at her. The muscles in his butt flexed as he made his way to the bathroom. He shut the door behind him with a thud of finality. A faucet turned on.

The noise was an impetus. She lurched from the bed and gathered her clothes, not bothering to adjust her bra when it gave her a quadri-boob. Once she was dressed, she grabbed her phone and opened an app, muttering a sigh of relief when she saw there was a ride within a minute of her. She called for it and stuffed her feet into her shoes.

The water shut off in the bathroom as she exited the room, and the headlights of the car she'd called cut across the front of the hotel. She hesitated for a second, then typed out, **I'm fine. Got a ride**, and hit send.

She jumped in her ride, her eyes stinging. The car pulled away, and she caught sight of herself in the reflection of the window. Thank God her driver was utterly oblivious. She looked like a girl who had just gotten fucked. Her hair was tumbled, clothes in disarray. She tugged at her jacket to make sure it covered her breasts. *So much for being healthier.*

Her nose twitched, and she placed her finger under it, trying to stave off the flood of emotions. *You're a tough cookie. Hang in there.*

She opened her conversation with Nicholas again, aware she was getting dangerously obsessive. That made five texts she'd sent him now.

A bubble popped up on the bottom of the screen, indicating he was typing, and her breath strangled. He'd never replied. Not once. She waited, hand clutching her phone tight.

The bubble went away and tears stung her eyes. Unable to look at the damn thing a second longer, she typed, **Bye**, hesitated for a second, and sent it. Then she deleted the conversation and sat back, wishing she could delete him from her life just as easily.

She'd lied to herself, but that was nothing new. She was weak. For never being able to stop wanting Nicholas, for using the same dumb rationale every year to see him again, for accepting the crumbs of his physical affection.

She sniffed, hard. She'd said it before, but this time she meant it. She absolutely had to move forward. It was done. They were done. For good.

Chapter 8

NICHOLAS WALKED around the exterior of the house, his polished shoes squelching into the damp ground. His grandfather had left him a voicemail asking him to come as soon as possible. Nicholas had canceled a meeting and gotten in his car.

When John Chandler said jump, no one at Chandler's wasted time asking how high. Except his dad, but then Brendan actively wanted to fuck with John.

He found his grandparent hunched over his beloved late wife's rose garden, carefully pruning the dead heads off the branches. Nicholas came to stand next to his wheelchair. "Grandpa. You called?"

His grandfather didn't stop what he was doing. "There's some weeds over there I can't reach."

Most corporate executives probably weren't ordered to weed in the middle of the workday, but then, most executives weren't employed by a man who had changed their diapers. Nicholas stripped off his jacket, draped it over the banister of the porch, and rolled up his sleeves, tossing his tie over his shoulder so it wouldn't get in the way. He grabbed the soft foam knee rest near John's chair—laid there for him, he assumed—and knelt on the ground, pulling the offending weeds out.

Unlike his grandfather, he didn't count gardening among his hobbies. Nicholas frowned at a stubborn weed. Actually, what were his hobbies? Working out, but that was out of necessity and discipline. When was the last time he'd engaged in an activity for pleasure?

Five nights ago.

He ripped the weed out so hard, dirt sprayed on his white shirt. He glanced down in dismay. He'd have to shower and change when he got back to the office.

"These protests. What's happening?"

Nicholas sat back on his heels and swiped his arm over his forehead. Right. Business. Work. Things that had nothing to do with Livvy and that seedy hotel room where he'd fucked her and left her lying naked on the bed.

Shame and self-disgust wrestled inside him, but he tried to focus past them. "I got the report today. The store the activists are protesting is selling a tomato sauce from a company that uses prison labor to farm tomatoes and a honey from a company that hires inmates to raise bees. There may be a few others. It's hard to source back to every ingredient."

"Have you told your father?"

It was always "Brendan" or "your father." Brendan had stopped being John's son when he'd bought Tani's shares behind John's back. "Yes."

"And what did he say?"

"He said the products are fine sellers and it doesn't make sense to go down the slippery slope of discovering where everything comes from."

"I bet he said, if it became more publicized, we could spin the discovery as corrective rehabilitation, correct? A good deed."

Nicholas reluctantly nodded.

"I looked into this particular program myself. If the prisoners are lucky, they earn a few thousand a year."

"Yes, sir." Nicholas wasn't surprised his grandfather had researched it. John was more than a little technologically adept.

"That's exploitation."

"That's one way to look at it," Nicholas said diplomatically.

"I want no part of it. We will not carry those products, and I want a top-to-bottom review of every supplier we use to ensure none of them are using companies like this. I won't profit off the backs of men and women who have no choice in their employment."

Nicholas pulled off his gloves. "Dad's going to say that's an expensive proposition."

John finished snipping at the thorns and sat back in his chair. His gaze was shrewd when it met Nicholas's. "What do you say?"

"It doesn't matter what I say. I don't own half the company." He didn't mean for his tone to be so testy, and he recalibrated immediately. "I mean, the ultimate decision is up to the two of you."

"Which one of us do you think is right?"

Ha-ha. No. He wasn't falling into that trap. Privately, he agreed with his grandfather, as he often did, but that was an opinion he'd take to his grave. The usual way he handled situations like this was to get both of their visions and then create a perfect compromise neither could wiggle out from. His thoughts were part and parcel of that compromise, but picking sides was a fool's errand. He was Switzerland, a neutral party in this world war. "I'll have to consider it some more."

John harrumphed. "Fine. Consider it fast, though. This could blow up."

In many ways, his grandfather understood public relations far better than his dad. "Yes, sir. I have people drafting a few different statements we can circulate to the media as well."

"Good. Good."

"I think once we come to a decision on this, we should come up with some general guidelines so we can handle these sorts of issues without needing to bother you. Or Dad," Nicholas said.

John smirked. "Are you saying we micromanage you?"

Yes. "Our company has grown dramatically in a short period of time. It makes sense to periodically review all of our job responsibilities."

"I swear, son. You got this diplomacy directly from your grandmother." John removed his gardening gloves. "Very well. Speaking of your grandmother, I've sent Shel to you for a job."

Nicholas racked his brain, but came up empty. "A cousin?"

"Barbara's sister's daughter's niece. She's in a tough spot."

Nicholas didn't bother to try to parse that connection. It didn't matter how anyone was connected to him. If John said they were family, they were family. Besides, he'd probably recognize the girl when he saw her. "Fine. I'll find her a place." He came to his feet and dusted off his pants legs. "Is that all?"

"One more thing."

"Yes?" Nicholas walked to the porch to grab his suit jacket.

"I want to see Livvy."

It was a good thing Nicholas had his back to his grandfather, because it took him a second to control his expression. In the meantime, he pulled his jacket on, his brain racing. When he felt more composed, he turned to face his patiently waiting grandfather.

"I'm sorry—"

"Don't feed me any bullshit," John said bluntly. "I know she's here."

Nicholas didn't bother to ask how John had found out. Though he mostly kept to himself now, in Rockville, John was larger than life. There were few people who he hadn't affected in one way or another. "She's here. I don't know why you think I'd be able to arrange a meeting between you."

"Don't play dumb, Nicholas. I know you've seen her."

"What makes you say that?" He was proud of how cool and controlled his voice sounded when he wanted to grab his grandfather and demand to know who had seen them together and where. They'd been careful. Had he been spotted at that hotel?

His blood ran to ice to think of what his father would think about that.

"Don't worry about it. And relax, your dad doesn't know you've seen her."

Nicholas bit the inside of his cheek. "I don't care whether Dad knows or not." Look at that. He was even able to lie without betraying a hint of his inner disquiet.

John merely nodded. "I need you to do this for me, Nicholas."

He stuck his hands in his pockets, not bothering to pretend any longer. "I don't think I can arrange that. I'm not planning on seeing her again." She wouldn't want to see him. Generally, when a woman booked it after sex with a couple of terse messages, it was a pretty good sign she was done.

Bye.

That bye was haunting him. He hadn't been able to delete it. Ten times he'd tried to work up some sort of response, if only to ask if she was okay or that she'd reached home safely, and he couldn't.

He'd never felt like less of a man.

He couldn't shove the compartment on her closed. His desire for her hadn't eased. On the contrary, he only craved her more than he had before.

Which was why he shouldn't go anywhere near her.

John looked across the yard to the woods, where Livvy's old house sat on the other side.

"Do you know what I promised Sam before he died?"

"That you would take care of his family," Nicholas said quietly. It was a vow he knew his grandfather didn't take lightly, one that had its origins in the history between their two families.

When Sam and John had been little more than children, the Okas had been sentenced to an internment camp for Japanese-Americans. They'd hastily shut down their successful grocery store. Unable to take more than they could carry to the camp, they'd entrusted as many possessions as they could to the Chandlers.

The two families had a lot in common—John's parents had been immigrants too, from England. The Chandlers had simply had the privilege not to be viewed as enemies on sight. They'd carefully guarded the Okas' assets.

When the Okas had been released, Sam and John had headed east, eager for a fresh start. They'd found it. Their tight bond had lasted up until the day Sam died.

"You know, I wasn't a tenth of the businessman Sam was. Everything we have—everything you have, you owe to him."

Nicholas dipped his head, having heard this before. He didn't disbelieve it. His grandfather was shrewd, but he lacked a killer instinct. By all accounts, Sam had been the one to steer the ship during their first tumultuous years.

"I didn't do a good job keeping my promise," John said. "I did the worst fucking job."

"It's not your fault." It was Brendan's fault.

Nicholas tried to beat back that thought. He couldn't survive if he let the seething resentment he felt toward his father surface. And above all, he needed to survive.

"It was my fault." John's trembling, age-spotted hands folded together. "The least I could have done was make sure my own son didn't steal Sam's half of the company."

Nicholas eyed his grandfather with concern. John had been in the hospital when Maria Chandler had died, recovering from cardiac arrest. The news and grief over his daughter-in-law's death had set him back, and so no one had wanted to risk giving him more stress. He hadn't learned of what Brendan had done until it was too late.

Sometimes Nicholas wondered if things would have turned out differently if John had been in commission. He would have tried to block his son on acquiring Tani's shares, without a doubt. Maybe he would have succeeded. Nicholas supposed it didn't matter now.

John's lips pinched together. "I tried to talk to Tani afterward. Even tried to sign my half of the company over to her. She refused to see me."

Nicholas frowned. "I didn't know that."

"I didn't tell you. I didn't know then if you'd take your father's side."

Nicholas's hand tightened into a fist. "Grandpa, you can take my word on it. I'm not my father." Or at least, he didn't want to be like Brendan.

"Ah, I know, son. I know." His grandpa looked away. "You are nothing like your father."

Nicholas shifted, uncomfortable. "Did you ever consider giving Paul your interest?"

John shook his head. "Not when he was so young. He wouldn't have been able to go up against your father, and despite what Brendan would like to think, he doesn't have the qualities that make C&O special. It would have just been another grocery chain then." John gave a helpless shrug. "It had to be me, even though I hated the unfairness of it."

His grandfather often did that, referring to Chandler's as C&O. Nicholas suspected it was deliberate. "The company certainly wouldn't be the same without you." Nicholas knew he needed to prepare for a day when his grandfather wasn't around, and that thought filled him with sorrow and loss. He and his father were the brains, but John was the heart of the corporation.

"I think Sam would be happy I kept our vision alive. Less happy over how his family was treated." John's gaze grew watery. "Livvy's here now, and I . . . I have to see her. I need to make sure she's okay. Please."

It was the *please* that got him. His grandfather rarely asked him for anything that wasn't business related, and he certainly didn't beg.

Nicholas looked off toward the woods. He had grown up a few miles down the road in an ostentatious mansion, but he'd had the run of these houses. His grandfather's house, and the Oka-Kanes' house.

He might owe Sam Oka, though he'd never met the man, but he definitely owed John. "I'll ask her. I can't guarantee anything."

John squeezed his eyes shut. "Thank you."

"Don't thank me yet. She's got a mind of her own."

John's smile was fond. "Didn't she always?"

"She did." He'd always adored that about her. "I'll get back to you soon."

"Don't waste too much time. I'm not getting any younger."

"Yes, sir."

A feminine voice came from behind him. "Nicholas?"

He turned to find his sister walking across the back porch. She looked polished and put together in her sensible pumps and black pants suit. Her white shirt had a frill at the collar. Stiff, formal, elegant. Just like her. "Eve. What are you doing here?"

"Grandpa wanted me to look through some of Grandma's letters."

"Need to get the right ones for our memoir." John's smile held a hit of reminiscing. "She would have killed me for rifling through her stuff, but she'd be okay with Eve doing it."

Nicholas shared a look with Eve. That sounded suspiciously like a task that could have been done at any time, anywhere, not necessarily on a workday, at John's house.

Combined with John's recent trend of not coming into the office, this was worrisome. Nicholas made a mental note to talk to his grandfather's housekeeper. If John was sad or lonely, he needed to know. He and Eve could step up their visits, or perhaps they could look into some activities for the man. "Sounds like a good time."

"You can come over on the weekend and go through the albums, Nicholas," John said eagerly.

Hmm. "I'd like that. But for now, I should get going."

"I'll walk you out," Eve murmured.

He bent down to hug his grandfather, and the older man patted him on the back. Nicholas hid his worry at how weak the hug felt. "We'll talk soon, Grandpa."

His grandfather gave him a conspiratorial look. "Yes, soon."

He walked across the wide expanse of lawn with his sister. She didn't speak until they turned the corner. "That sounded important."

"Everything everyone needs from me is important."

"Must be nice," she said. "Everything I do is paperwork and party planning."

He cast her a sideways look, catching the tinge of discontent in her tone. "Are you unhappy at the foundation?"

"Does it matter? One of us has to carry on Mom's work while the other carries on Dad and Grandpa's. How lucky that it could be split along gender lines."

He'd never seen her smile so sour. "If you don't like your work, we can find something else for you at the company. I thought you wanted to work at the foundation."

Her smile turned fixed, and she shook her head. "Don't worry about it."

He had to worry about it. He had to worry about all of them. He'd assumed Eve was more than content carrying on their mother's legacy.

Despite everything that came with it, he'd never considered doing anything other than what he was doing. He wanted Eve to have that same sense of security.

His car came into view, parked in the circular driveway. Eve rested her fingertips on his sleeve. "Nicholas . . . I wanted to apologize."

He shot her a quick glance. "Apologize for what?"

"For my ridiculous behavior last week. I'm sorry I worried you and you rushed over like that. I'm ashamed you saw me that way."

It took him a second to realize what she was talking about. Jesus, he'd completely forgotten about Eve's intoxication. He'd been so focused on Livvy.

It hadn't been a week since that night. It had been five days. He knew, because he'd counted off each excruciatingly long second and minute and hour, all while burying himself in work.

"You're of legal age," he said gruffly. "It's perfectly fine for you to have some fun."

Evangeline smoothed her unwrinkled jacket. "I didn't go to that bar to have fun."

He nodded and waited. When she'd been a child, Evie had always been slow to confide anything, but she'd spill all in her own time.

"I heard what Grandpa said to you. About wanting to see Livvy."

Nicholas stopped in his tracks. Eve did the same, her head bowed. "How'd you hear that?"

"I'm a very good eavesdropper. The truth is, I wanted to see Livvy too." She twined her fingers together. "I followed her to the bar."

That, he had not been expecting. He stared down at Eve's shiny black hair. "What?"

"I can't explain it. It was like something in my brain snapped after our meeting. I sat there, watching her for a while. I drank, even though I hated it. Then she came over, and I . . ." She lifted her head and swallowed. "I berated her about the accident. Not in so many words, but I was angry and hurt and thinking of Mom. I was harsh and out of line."

"For fuck's sake." He never swore at Eve. Never. But he wasn't quite sure what else to say.

But she absorbed the verbal rebuke like it was her due. She lifted her head. "I'm not proud of what I said or did. I've been agonizing over it for days." She put her hands over her face. "I got angry and it spewed out."

"You shouldn't have done that. No matter what her father or brother did—what her brother was suspected of doing—Livvy wasn't a part of it. She's as innocent as we were."

Maybe you should listen to yourself. He swallowed the sour taste in his mouth. He hadn't treated Livvy well either, in that motel room. And now he discovered that his sister had hurt her before he'd even arrived on the scene.

Just like a Chandler. Selfishly taking whatever you want.

"Eve—"

"You don't have to say anything. I am so mortified and disappointed in myself. Because that isn't all." Eve's round cheeks turned pink. "I offered her money to stay away from you."

Anger was something Nicholas had learned early on how to control. He closed his eyes and counted to ten. Then twenty. Then forty.

Nope. A dull throbbing. "My God. You did *not*."

"I remember how you looked when you came home from ending things with her." Her words tumbled over each other. "I didn't want you to be hurt again."

He didn't remember the direct aftermath of breaking up with Livvy. Had he seen Eve?

Those weeks had taken on a blurry, hazy quality. After the accident, his and Livvy's contact had been limited to rushed phone calls, filled with sobbing on her part and wooden attempts at comfort on his. He'd known she needed him, but so had Eve and his grandfather and the company.

He'd assumed they'd work it all out because they were in love. And love won, right?

Even after his dad had taken over the company, he hadn't considered ending his relationship with Livvy. But then Brendan had called him into his office and pounded the final nail into that coffin. It had been hopeless after that.

She hadn't fought him when he'd told her it wouldn't work. Part of him had hoped she would, even if he'd chosen his words carefully so she wouldn't. It had been as mutual a breakup as it could have been when he'd had to be coerced into it.

"While I appreciate your concern, that was a long, long time ago," he growled.

"That day in the office, when I told you she was back, I saw. You were shaken."

Yes, he had been shaken, but she shouldn't have known that. He was the master at keeping his thoughts and feelings to himself, damn it. "No, I wasn't."

"I know you think no one can read you, but I can. I know you, Nicholas." Eve searched his face. "And what I saw that day in the boardroom, it was the same thing I saw when you came home from breaking up with her."

He shoved his hand through his hair. "I—"

"You don't have to say anything." Eve's voice was gentle.

Unable to stand still, he continued walking, struggling to find the words to express his dismay. "You shouldn't have done what you did."

Eve came abreast of him. "I feel terrible, trust me. I only told you because I figured if you were carrying messages to her, maybe you could ask if she would see me so I can apologize? I don't want to thrust myself on her again."

An unholy urge to laugh came over him. "Why does everyone think I have some sort of direct line to Livvy?"

Eve put her hands in her pockets. "Because we remember how you guys used to be?"

"Key words are *used to be*." They reached his car. She was shivering in the fall air. He reached out and pulled her suit jacket together. "You need a coat."

Her smile was warm, but wobbly. "I'll remember that."

He sighed, the anger seeping out of him. How could he stay mad at Eve? It was impossible. "Don't try to buy any other women away from me, okay?"

"I won't," she said, meek.

He leaned down to kiss her but she surprised him by throwing her arms around his neck and hugging him tight. He returned the hug gingerly. He'd showered her with physical affection when she was young, to make up for their mother's loss, but they'd settled into a pattern of simple pecks on the cheek in the past couple of years. He gradually relaxed into the hug and patted her back.

"When I heard she was back, all I could think about was what life was like before the accident, and the fire. What it was like to have Mom around. How Dad was different," she whispered. "He was, wasn't he? He loved us then."

He tightened his grip on her. That was what he'd led Eve to believe. When he'd sat with her day after day, night after night, in the pediatrics ward of that hospital, he'd told her their father would have absolutely been there if their mother's death hadn't broken him two years prior. What else could he have said to a fifteen-year-old? *Sorry, your father is too busy to care about you.*

No chance in hell.

His father had always had issues. From the time

Nicholas was a small child, he could remember hiding in his room or escaping to the Kanes' when his father grew angry or cold. No physical abuse. His dad was disdainful of men who used their fists. The man preferred to use words and leverage and silences as his weapons of choice. They left no marks. Not obvious ones at least.

Nicholas suspected his mother had shielded him and Eve from the worst of it, especially Eve. He'd taken over after Maria's death. Their grandfather was the only other person who might have an inkling as to Brendan's true nature, but not the full extent. John couldn't know. He'd be devastated to learn what his son was capable of.

Nicholas lowered his head to speak directly into Eve's ear. "Little bit, never doubt it for a moment. You were and always have been loved."

She went so still, he wondered if she'd heard him, but then she dipped her head. "I love you too, Nicholas."

He had things to do. Still, he remained there, content to embrace his sister for however long he could.

He rested his cheek on her head. *Peace.* A different kind of peace than the one he'd experienced briefly with Livvy in her chair, but peace all the same.

"Are you going to see her?"

He didn't need to ask who she was talking about. "Yes." He had to, if only to relay his grandfather's message.

And apologize. For Eve, and also for himself. He'd barely been able to look at himself in the mirror when he shaved this morning.

"Be careful, okay?"

He drew back to peer down at her. "I'm fine."

"I mean, be careful with her." She grimaced. "I'm the last person to say that, after what I said to her, but I saw the way she looked at you when you came to my place . . . she's not invulnerable."

"You were drunk."

"Drunk, not unconscious." She gave him a wry look. "I know we aren't the most sensitive people when it comes to emotions. But I know what I saw."

"We are definitely not sensitive." Their father was an emotional wasteland; their grandfather was sentimental but gruff; their mother had always been cheerful, but that had just been a different kind of mask.

Her small hand stroked over his sleeve. Her fingers were round, the nails blunt. "Maybe we could try expressing our feelings a little more. It might keep us from doing things like stalking people."

Nicholas almost laughed. What would his life have been like if he'd been free to express how he felt? The closest he'd ever come to indulging himself that way was . . .

The time he'd spent with Livvy.

And even then, he'd kept a tight lid on himself, never allowing himself to fully immerse himself, because he knew she'd be gone soon. Except last week. He'd almost lost his control in that motel room. It had scared him so much, he'd had to run away from the bed.

I should punish you for making me want you. For making me need you.

If you punish me, you're punishing yourself.

"We do need to cut down on stalking," Nicholas said wryly. "But I'm not sure if extravagantly indulging our id is the answer."

"It doesn't have to be extravagant. We should make a pact. One feeling, at least one," Eve suggested. "What can it hurt? Try it today. When you experience some emotion, don't run from it or try to stuff it down. Express it."

It could hurt a great deal, when you were sitting on a pressure cooker like he was. Twist the valve, and God only knows if he could stop at one. He would gorge himself, lose himself.

He couldn't explain to her how dangerous and foolish that was. He forced a smile for his sister, because that was what he did for her. Pretended everything was normal, even when it wasn't.

And a part of him recognized the seductive appeal of this exercise. To feel alive and not like an automaton? Even if it was for only one heartbeat. "Okay. One feeling."

Chapter 9

Livvy smiled as her client pirouetted in front of the floor-length mirror, admiring the watercolor lion Livvy had put on her skin. For most of the day, Livvy's entire focus had been concentrated on the expanse of the girl's side, the perfect curves and lines of the design, each pigment, blur, and fade. Her adrenaline was running high now, flush with the rush of a job well done. The girl had been a perfect canvas, quiet and relaxed. "Like it?"

"Love it. It's perfect. Exactly what I had in mind."

"Good."

The bubbly girl grabbed her purse and coat. "I can't wait to show everyone."

"Gabe's in the front and can get you all sorted out. Give a ring if you have any questions or problems."

"Oh, I will. Definitely. Thanks!"

The curtain rustled as the girl bounced out to the reception area, and Livvy began the process of cleaning up her workspace. She'd requested more shifts for the past week. The work was good on a number of fronts: brought in some extra cash and let her avoid the monotony of her mother's home and their depressing inability to speak to each other.

It also keeps you from typing out ten million texts you'll never send to Nicholas.

Well, clearly.

The curtain rustled, and a large man walked into the back room. "Nice job on that lion. Damn, you're good."

She stood and stretched. "Thanks." Her skill at watercolor tattoos gave her a niche not too many artists had. Unlike regular tattoos, with their hard lines and edges, watercolors incorporated blurred lines and gradual spatters, for a vague, airy quality. They were perfect in their imperfections. She'd fallen in love with the designs as soon as she'd seen them and worked under artists all over the country to perfect her skill.

Gabriel Hunter crossed his massive arms over his chest, the flannel of his shirt rolled up to reveal colorful tattoos. With his dark auburn hair and matching beard, the man looked like he should be chopping wood in a cabin somewhere, but Livvy had watched his big fingers maneuver some of the tiniest, most detailed tattoos she'd ever seen.

Gabe was the one who had originally hooked Livvy on the art—his mother had been the Kanes' housekeeper for as long as she could remember. Gabe had been a few years older, friends with Paul and Nicholas.

She wondered if he'd spoken to Nicholas since the accident. She didn't think so, given his close bond with Paul.

Everything leads back to Nicholas, damn it.

"The customer asked how long you'd be here for. I told her I wasn't sure."

Livvy eyed her boss. "Do you need a definite date? Because I'm still not sure when my mom . . ."

"No, no," Gabe rushed. "I only wanted to tell you that if you decided to stay longer, I'm game. That girl came from three hours away and wants to bring her friend up next weekend. It's like I have a guest celebrity artist here."

Livvy blushed but lifted her chin, pride making her want to beam. Celebrity was overselling it, but she did have a small but fierce following. "I'll keep that in mind."

Gabe's green eyes warmed. Despite his outwardly physically intimidating appearance, the tattooed lumberjack was and always had been a pussycat. "You okay closing up?"

"Yup. Got a hot date?"

He winked, the move devastating. Or at least it would be if her body could seem to want anyone other than one particular, terrible-for-her guy. "Only with my remote control. Wanna join me?"

She smiled. His teasing flirtatiousness was second nature to him. She'd never take him seriously, and he'd never crossed the line into sleaziness. "Not tonight, thanks. See you tomorrow?"

"Sure thing."

She finished cleaning up and was about to go lock up when the bell above the door rang. She glanced at her watch and grimaced. Her back was aching. Maybe it was simply a consult? She could hope.

She rose to her feet, but faltered when the curtain split and Nicholas walked in.

Goddamn. All he had to do was appear and her body sat up and panted, lips tingling, nipples hardening, the muscles in her thighs twinging. Like she hadn't had her fill of him a few days ago.

You'll never have your fill of him, you fool.

His gaze was locked on her. "Hi."

"Hi," she returned, too stunned to say anything else. What was going on? She hadn't summoned him in her sleep, had she?

"I, uh . . . I didn't see your car outside. I thought I'd check anyway."

"My car wouldn't start this morning."

"Why not?"

"I don't know. It can be temperamental." She'd considered using her mom and Maile's car, a little Kia that sat mostly dusty in the garage, but it would have required talking to her mom, which would have resulted in Livvy being on the receiving end of that indifferent stare, which would have resulted in her being sad, and she didn't want to be sadder. They lived under three miles away. Walking hadn't been difficult.

"You called a cab?"

"I walked."

"You walked, in this neighborhood?"

She was about to roll her eyes, but then she had to admit she wouldn't have been caught dead in this neighborhood when she was in the same social strata as him. "It's not so bad."

He looked around, like he expected a meth

addict to jump out at him from behind a chair. "Right."

"Did you come here to ask me about Ruthie?"

"Ruthie?"

"My car. Her name is Ruthie."

"No." He shook his head and cleared his throat. "I, uh, came here to give you these." He extended the hand he'd had behind his back and thrust the flowers he held at her.

Yellow roses.

She hadn't touched yellow roses since they'd broken up.

Slowly, like one might approach a predator, she walked over to him, and took the bouquet from his hands. The cellophane crinkled in her fingers. The white tissue was crisp and watermarked with something. She tilted it to the light and made out a simple C shape.

The logo cut her to the core. She'd recognize it anywhere. Chandler's had kept the same font C&O had used.

The pain was so overwhelming she had to remind herself to breathe. In order to cover the hit she'd taken, she spoke in a deliberately light tone. "You came all this way to bring me grocery store flowers?"

"Our floral department is considered pretty high-end now, actually. We do weddings and deliver daily and have top-notch designers—"

She forced a smile. "I don't need the corporate rundown." Though she wanted to appear indifferent and uncaring, she couldn't resist bringing the flowers to her nose and inhaling deeply. She'd considered incorporating yellow flowers into her vine tattoo, but ultimately decided that was too obvious.

When they'd been dating, she'd had a never-ending bouquet of yellow roses. He'd brought them from their store then too. *His store. It's his store now.* In case the lone Cs on the tissue paper weren't enough of a reminder. "What's this for?"

Nicholas rubbed his finger over his nose. "Why does any man bring a woman flowers?"

"Because he wants to get in her pants. Or soften her up. Or impress her. Or because he knows she really likes flowers."

His smile was faint. "I know you really like flowers. I also want to soften you up."

He didn't say anything about wanting to get in her pants or impress her, she noticed. "For what?"

"My sister sends her apologies. She told me what she said to you, and I'm mortified. I apologize as well. She said she'd be happy to tell you this in person, if you ever wanted to meet with her."

Oh. This was about his sister. "No big deal. She needed a target."

"You shouldn't have been her target."

Livvy shrugged. "She's young. She'll learn. Is that all? That's not really rose worthy."

Nicholas frowned and rocked back on his heels. "You don't think—" He stopped, his frown deepening.

"Yes?" she prompted him.

"You don't think I ever used you as a target, right?"

Livvy cocked her head. "Are you asking if I thought you were hate-fucking me all these years?"

He glanced away, his gaze lighting on everything and nothing. "Yes."

"No. Were you?" She was proud of how measured her voice sounded. As much as it ached to only get the physical crumbs of his affection, she'd rather be an object of lust over an object of rage.

"No, never."

The ever-present knot in her stomach unraveled at his immediate rejection. "Oh. Good."

"Was it penance?"

She blinked at his brusque question. "What?"

"When you fucked me." He looked down at her. "Did you sleep with me only because you felt guilty? Like you owed it to me for what your father did?"

She jerked back. "What kind of question is that?"

"A valid one, I think." He swallowed. "I don't want to be a guilt-fuck any more than you want to be a hate-fuck."

"I never slept with you because I felt like I owed you my body. It was always because I wanted it."

"I know I was rough last week." A muscle in his jaw clenched, his eyes dipping over her face and body. A trail of fire followed in their wake.

"Rough . . . physically?" Because she'd felt totally abraded mentally and emotionally too, not that she was about to tell him that.

A dull red flush covered his cheeks. "Correct."

She squinted at him. Did this need to be said? "Uh. I guess I didn't make it clear enough when I moaned every time you spanked me, but I enjoyed myself quite a bit."

"I've never . . ." He tunneled his hands through his hair. "I've never raised a hand to a woman in my life."

"You were pretty good at it." Amusement crept through her disquiet. "Ten out of ten at spanking, I'd say."

"You ran out. I thought maybe I'd traumatized you. I wanted to call or text you, but I didn't want to know if you'd already changed your number like all the other times I've—"

She stiffened. What was he about to say? That he'd reached out to her in the past? When? "I was following our usual script," she said.

"What script?"

What script? The unwritten script they'd been following their entire lives. "We screw. We part ways. That's the script."

"Not like that. That's not our script."

Her eyes narrowed. Now she understood. "Because you always leave. Not me." They'd fall asleep together after multiple orgasms, and he'd sneak out while she slept. Or sometimes, pretended to sleep. She nodded when he looked uncomfortable. "Yeah, I initiate, and you terminate. You're right, *that's* our script." She pivoted and walked to her table, placing the flowers there, trying not to care when the petals smooshed against the hard surface. "Sorry to fuck up the order of things. I adapted the rules to suit our hometown playing field, if you know what I mean."

"There were never any rules."

"Guidelines, then. Patterns. You love those, don't you?" She shrugged, hoping she looked light-hearted. "I can see where you might have misconstrued my bolting, but trust me, I was fine. No trauma. I liked every second of sex we had." She folded her arms together, trying to affect some cool. "Gawd, now you've made this all weird."

He stared at her, and a deep rumble filled the room. It took her a second to realize it was coming from him. He bent over double and grasped his knees, his breath gasping as he laughed. And laughed. Each belly-chuckling laugh made her face turn hot.

She hadn't heard him laugh like that in . . . well, forever. She drifted closer, each peal wrapping around her heart. "I don't see what's so funny—" But that only set him off again.

Finally he subsided, wiping tears of mirth from his eyes. He shook his head, a heartbreaking smile still on his face. It lacked cynicism or icy control. It was young and boyish and happy. "Jesus Christ, Livvy. When has this not been weird?"

Despite herself, a smile tugged at her own lips. "Touché." She tried to sober. "I should close up. You want to reestablish our usual roles? You can leave now."

She turned away to her table, waiting to hear his footsteps, but they didn't come. Instead, she counted each breath he took in the near silent room. "I . . ."

"What?" she snapped, when he trailed off.

"I don't want to leave."

He means now, so quit that little wriggle of happiness in your heart. He'd leave her eventually. "Is that right?"

"I want to stay." He said the words quietly, and then repeated them louder. "I want to stay here with you."

She picked up a pen and put it down again. "What do you want to talk about?"

A long silence stretched out. "Anything. Whatever you want."

She glanced over her shoulder. No clear objective? No agenda? That was unlike him.

She'd vowed not to see him again, ever, not more than five seconds ago. But then he said, "Please," and she wavered.

She couldn't detect any manipulation or ulterior motive in his gaze. Earnestness. Caution. Maybe a touch of confusion, as if he didn't fully understand himself.

As someone who felt perpetually confused, that was enormously endearing. "Anything?"

"Anything."

A blank check to discuss whatever she wanted with him? After years of biting her tongue around him, he couldn't have offered her a more seductive offer. Well, maybe if he'd paired it with his beautiful penis, but it was still pretty damn seductive nonetheless.

The weak-willed part of her that could never

deny him blinked awake, and she nodded to the chair. She hated herself for giving in. She wasn't capable of not giving in.

Argh.

"Take off your shirt."

"Take off my . . . why?"

Because I really, really like how you look without your shirt.

"I told you. You want to talk to me, you have to get a tattoo."

His lips didn't move, but his eyes warmed. His fingers rose to the knot of his tie.

She turned away, because she couldn't stand to watch him undress, and busied herself with rummaging through her markers. When the rustle of clothing stopped, she turned back with a Sharpie. She patted herself on the back for not swallowing her tongue at the expanse of lovely chest that lay before her.

"How are you getting more muscular every time I see you?" she asked, with a touch of annoyance.

"I haven't been able to sleep. I've been working out."

Her shallow first reaction: *Keep doing that.*

She hooked her stool with her ankle and kicked it closer to the chair, then adjusted his seat so he was reclining. "Maybe try some warm milk."

"I'm trying to sleep, not vomit."

She bent her head over his shoulder and ran her palm over the upper muscle of his chest. His pec tightened. Hot. Hairy. Hard.

She swallowed her drool and uncapped the

Sharpie. She started on his left side, drawing a large fin coasting over his chest.

"What are you drawing?"

"Shh. You trust me, remember?" *In this, at least.*

"It took me forever to scrub that naked woman off."

"She was a naked fairy, thank you very much. Didn't you see her pointy ears?" Livvy filled in the detail of the fin, drawing each scale carefully. "Besides, this will be under your shirt. People will only see it when you go swimming or want to bang someone." *That's good. Keep pretending you can think about him banging someone without it bothering you one tiny bit.*

Nicholas craned his neck. "A mermaid?"

"Shh. Wait and see."

She took her time carefully drawing in the scales of the mermaid. On someone else, with her actual needle, she'd do this in iridescent blues and greens so it popped when the person moved. The green marker made her feel a little sad, but this wasn't the right tattoo for Nicholas.

She cleared her throat once she was half done with the fin, unable to keep silent forever. "So, like, what's keeping you awake?"

She looked up at him. His eyes were closed, like they had been last time, furrows deep on his brow.

His lips parted, and for one bright, shining moment, she thought he would say it, that he'd confess it was *her* keeping him awake, but then the words came. "Work stuff."

"Oh." She started to work on the torso of the

mermaid, giving her a slender physique and small breasts. Not covered by a silly seashell bra, of course. She assumed mermaids didn't put stock into absurd human concerns like covering lady nipples at all costs.

Livvy couldn't even stand underwires. Why would a majestic merlady put seashells on her boobs?

A loud vibrating pierced the silence. Nicholas shifted, his chest rippling under her palms, pulled his phone out of his pocket, and silenced it.

"You're not even going to see who it is?"

"It's someone who wants something from me."

She wanted to make a sarcastic *heavy is the head that wears the crown* comment, but couldn't bear to do it. Not when he looked so utterly exhausted. "That's the job of the guy in charge, isn't it? To be in demand?"

His Adam's apple bobbed, and he rested his phone on his leg. "Uh-huh."

The phone lit up again, and she was in the right position to see the caller. *Grandpa.*

Pain blossomed in her chest. "You may want to get that."

He looked at the phone this time, then surprised her by shaking his head. "No."

"You don't pick up calls from your grandfather anymore?"

He pinched the bridge of his nose. "Not when I know he only wants to bitch about my dad."

She raised an eyebrow at the shit-ton of bitterness behind that statement. "Oh. Do they . . . do they not get along anymore?" Brendan and John had always struck her as a mismatched father-and-son duo, but she'd never seen them actively battling.

Nicholas's laugh was short. "You could say that."

"I'm sorry to hear that," she murmured. "Was there a falling-out?"

He didn't answer for a beat. Curious, she prodded. "You said I could ask you anything."

"I did, didn't I?" He cast her an unreadable look. "Yes. Your family."

Her hand jerked and the mermaid's shoulder got messed up. She'd have to give her long hair to cover it. "What?"

"Your family caused the fallout."

"How so?"

Nicholas sighed. "When my dad bought your mom's share of the company—"

"When he stole it, you mean."

He didn't argue. "It left my father and grandfather in equal power. They haven't been able to talk to each other without fighting since that day."

Shocked, she stopped drawing and stared up at him. "What? Why?"

"Because my grandfather can't forgive my dad for cutting your family out."

"John wasn't a part of that?" She hadn't even seen John from the time of the accident to when she'd left. He'd been too sick, and Brendan hadn't permitted any non-family visitors to the hospital.

"No. Of course not. He didn't even know until he was discharged from the hospital. His health was so fragile. It didn't take much for my dad to convince us telling him could kill him."

"Wow." She simply hadn't considered John wasn't in cahoots with his son back then.

"If he'd been there, he would have blocked my dad. I couldn't, but he might have been able to."

Another jerk of her hand. "You tried to stop Brendan?"

He went silent.

The day they'd broken up, she'd met him in the woods and tried to make sense of her upside-down world. *What's Paul talking about? He's stomping around and yelling at Mom and saying your dad stole the company from us. That's not true, right? You wouldn't have let him do that. Nothing's changed.*

Nicholas had moved away. *What's done is done, Livvy.*

"Why didn't you tell me then?" She'd had another tiny piece of her heart shattered, thinking Nicholas had betrayed her whole family.

His chest rose and fell, the unfinished mermaid looking utterly silly. "I assumed it wouldn't matter. Would it have made a difference to you?"

It's impossible for us to be together now. They won't let us.

"Are you asking if we would have stayed together?"

"Yeah. Could we have survived my father taking your family's company? Even if you knew I'd opposed it?"

Livvy had seen the finality in Nicholas's eyes when they'd ended things, had felt the creeping foreboding when she'd met him that day in the woods.

She'd never met her grandpa Sam, but she'd heard stories about the man and the odds he'd overcome to become a wealthy businessman. One of Sam's favorite sayings had been *Nothing's over 'til you quit.*

Nicholas had quit. It was over.

"Probably not." Which wasn't a total lie. She sniffed, hoping that the tickling at the back of her throat didn't actually become tears. God, would that be embarrassing. "I'm real glad John doesn't hate us. That's . . . that's cool to know."

"He wants to see you. He asked me to arrange a meeting."

Yearning made her heart clench. John had been a surrogate grandfather to her, showering her with as much love and kindness as he had his own grandchildren. "He knows I'm here?"

"Yes."

"Did you tell him?"

"No."

No, he wouldn't have. She was Nicholas's dirty little secret.

Don't get snarky; he's your dirty secret as well. "I don't know if that's such a good idea."

"He would be kind to you. I promise."

She took pride in her steady hands, but they were shaking now. "If he's not?"

"We would leave."

"You'd come with me?"

"Of course."

The immediate agreement shouldn't have soothed her, though she knew his main goal in chaperoning was to protect his grandfather, not her. "I have to think about it."

He tilted her chin up and her breath caught. His eyes were soft. Warm. She couldn't remember the last time he'd looked at her like this, without his guard up and a layer of frost in place. She wanted to savor every second of it as much as it terrified her. "He missed you."

It was sad how much she wanted him to replace that *he* with an *I*. Pathetic. "If . . ." She trailed off, the words clogging up inside her throat.

"If what?"

Fuck it all. No ifs. Ifs opened a land of possibility, led to a universe where anything was doable. Where the children of feuding families could unite and overcome the odds and ugly history between them. *If* was a word for fairy tales, not reality.

If was to be avoided at all costs.

You said you were done for good.

But that *look* he was giving her, exacerbating her need for ifs. It was short-circuiting her brain.

She did what she always did when she stopped being able to think around this man. She kissed him.

FOR THE second time in a week, Nicholas found himself swept into the hurricane force that was Livvy. She took his lips—forcefully, perfectly—leaving him without a need to think. With a jerk, he pulled her off balance and dragged her up and over him so she was straddling his lap.

She tore her lips away. "The door. Let me lock . . ."

"I already did it when I came in." He'd flicked off the neon Open sign too.

Someone might call him presumptuous, but he hadn't anticipated their lip-locking. He simply hadn't wanted anyone to interrupt them.

She didn't seem to mind his foresight. She went back to kissing him, her tongue slicking over his.

You shouldn't be doing this. Don't do this. Why are you doing this?

Because he really couldn't help himself, and neither could she. Their conversation had been raw and real and without snark or animosity, something neither of them had engaged in since . . . well, since well before they'd broken up.

And all because he'd indulged one feeling—the desire not to leave her.

Each honest word he'd spoken had made him feel better, calmer, stronger. It had always grated on him, the betrayal in her gaze when they'd ended things, the knowledge he hadn't corrected her when she said he wanted the takeover. He'd kept the truth in his heart, unable to utter it. *My dad's blackmailing me to stay away from you, and I can't stomach the thought of you fighting in vain for us when I know I can't be with you.*

He'd made the rational choice, acting as cold as he could, convinced he was ultimately making the right, least painful decision for everyone involved.

Who's being rational now?

Not him, and he didn't particularly know if he cared.

Her fingers tunneled through his hair and tightened on his scalp, and he bit her lower lip, trying not to leave a mark but hoping he did anyway. His hands slid down her back, under her skirt. The thong she wore gave him complete access to her round flesh, and it overflowed his palms. Her touch ghosted over his chest, his stomach, to the fastening of his pants. A butterfly caress trailed over the thickness of his cock, and he sucked in a breath. She pulled her mouth away and pressed a hot kiss on his neck.

There was a spot—yes, *there*. He groaned and arched up, his cock pushing against her palm when she licked the hollow of his throat, then nipped the same spot. She rubbed the bulge in his pants, rasping the cotton of his boxers over his hard, ready flesh.

He tilted his head back to give her better access, closing his eyes to block out the harsh fluorescent overhead lights. He could pretend they were somewhere else. A soft bed in a nice hotel. His place. Her place. Places where lovers went to have sex. "What do you want?"

She sucked his neck, and he bit the inside of his cheek. "I want your dick in my mouth."

His dick was in perfect agreement, hardening to a painful degree. That would feel so good, her slick, wet tongue slipping over him, cheeks hollowing with suction. Too good.

He gripped the back of her neck and pulled her away from him. "How about you come on my tongue first?"

Her brow furrowed, and she sat back on his legs. "Why do you always do that?"

He struggled to concentrate, which was hard when he had Livvy perched on his lap. "What?"

"Every year, you would go down on me. Always. But the instant I tried to get my mouth on you, you'd haul me up. Distract me. Why is that?"

Discomfort gripped him. He shrugged. "I got older. I'm not some twenty-year-old who can get it up multiple times."

She snorted. "I don't think getting it up has ever been your issue."

"Do you *not* like my tongue between your legs?"

"See? Distracting me with silly questions." She fiddled with the button of his pants. "When we were dating, you used to break speed limits to get to me if I ever so much as teased you about a blowjob."

Truth. "Let me," she'd whispered in his ear one night in his car, her hand rubbing his cock through his jeans.

How could he have denied her then? "I did love it. I'm just . . . not accustomed to it anymore."

She blinked. "Are you saying you don't let anyone go down on you?"

He cleared his throat, embarrassed. "Not in a long time."

"How long?"

Since you. But he couldn't admit her mouth had been the only one on his cock. That was far too uncomfortably revealing. "A long time."

She searched his gaze. "Do you not like it?"

"No. It makes me feel . . . I don't know. Vulnerable." He'd always felt powerless during their encounters. He couldn't stop himself from coming to see her or leaving the next day. He couldn't stop himself from having to go back to his passionless, unexciting life.

He hadn't wanted to give up any more power. Even if that meant cutting out something he'd once adored.

He didn't know how to explain all of that. It wouldn't make sense to most people, maybe not even her. He opened his mouth to stutter out some sort of explanation, but she spoke first.

"I get it."

He blinked.

She slipped her thumb over his lips. Up and down, side to side. Unable to look away, he bit her thumb, laving the spot with his tongue.

"Can I . . . ? Can we try? If you hate it, I'll stop."

Nicholas swallowed. The silence stretched between them. She didn't push or prod, merely sat on his legs and waited.

That patient, calm waiting was what convinced him. Livvy wouldn't get mad or sad or make him feel like less of a man if he demanded they stop. "Yes."

Her hand left him, and she gathered her hair up high on her head, securing it with a ponytail holder on her wrist. His body went taut with expectation beneath her, and her lips curved in a knowing smile. "You couldn't not get hard when I was putting my hair up, could you?"

Going down on him had been the only time,

save when she was working out, that Livvy had ever put her hair in a ponytail. It had gotten to the point that he damn well couldn't see her jaunty little hairstyle without wanting to see her on her knees. "You always had one of those elastics on your wrist."

"I always will. Sometimes tying my hair up is the only task I can accomplish in a day," she joked. Or at least, he thought it was a joke.

She shifted, flipping her ponytail over her shoulder, and slid down until she was between his thighs. He wanted to close his eyes from the potent picture she made, her body tight and toned, dressed in black leather pants—where did one even find black leather pants?—and a long-sleeved, low-cut gauzy top. Her fingers danced over his fly, unbuttoning the placket, letting his cock jut out. Her cool hand wrapped around it, stroking the hot flesh. He groaned and tipped his head back.

Her fingers ghosted over his hipbones. "Do you know my favorite part of your body?" she mused, with a dreamy air.

"Are you holding it?"

"No, baby." Before he could recover from the casual endearment, she traced her free hand over the indentations at his groin. "I never know what to call these dips right here. One of my friends said they were come gutters."

He huffed out a laugh, as always amused and mildly scandalized by her ribaldry.

She stroked over the second dip, her expression absorbed. "I think the proper name is Apollo's girdle. I like hip-dip sexy things. What do you think?"

Think? How could he think when her mouth was level with his cock? "I don't care."

"You have good ones, whatever they are," she breathed, and ran her tongue over the dips in question. "I approve."

He tightened his hands on the seat's armrests. "Fuck."

"Ask me."

There was a steely command in her voice. He stood poised on some precipice, one where he handed her all the power, where she turned his ordered world into chaos, and he couldn't stop.

"Suck my dick," he said, his voice guttural.

Those red-slicked lips grinned, and she rubbed her cheek affectionately over the bulge of his cock. "Whatever you want, sir."

She licked the underside, tracing the vein. "I like doing this too," she whispered, her breath a puff of air on his cock head. "I'd always get so wet when I sucked your cock, remember?"

God, he did remember. Nothing had felt better than sinking his fingers inside her after she'd gotten off her knees. Knowing his pleasure had gotten her excited had been its own form of arousal. "Livvy."

She traced the tip of his cock over her lips, leaving them shiny. *Shiny with him.* "Do you feel out of control yet? Helpless?"

"Yes."

"Is it so terrible?"

"It's . . . unusual."

"I'll let you have some power." She pressed dainty, tiny kisses down the shaft. "Pull my hair."

He exhaled. "Are you sure?"

"You know I like it rough."

"I don't want to feel like I'm using you again."

"Maybe I want to be used." Her dark eyes flicked up at him. "Maybe I get off on that."

He raised both hands and slid them over Livvy's scalp. Her head felt small in his hands, the hair like coarse silk against his fingertips. He used one hand to gather up the strands and wrap them around his fist. All the while, he was cataloguing her reactions, so apparent in her expressive face: the way she bit her lip, the way her eyes narrowed in pleasure, how her short lashes fluttered. He used his grip to pull her away from where she was teasing his dick, leaving his cock just out of reach of her lips.

"Suck my dick."

Her lips curved. "Whatever you'd like. Sir."

It was the *sir* that broke him, that made every dark fantasy he'd ever had about being serviced flare to the surface of his mind. Livvy on her knees in his office, his car, her bed. Her lips surrounded the head of his cock, and he arched his hips higher, letting her take him deeper. He used his grip on her hair to move her how he wanted, when he wanted.

It had been so long since he'd had this, he felt awkward at first, but they found their rhythm.

"Remember when I would sneak into your room?" he rasped. "You'd be waiting for me with your hair tied up."

She moaned around his cock, and he groaned in return, his hips picking up speed, working in tandem with his hands on her head. He was full-on fucking her face now, possibly too savagely, but just when he grew worried that he should slow down, he noticed her arm shifting.

"Are you fucking yourself?" he said, the question more of a statement, because yeah. Her fingers were busy and hard at work, her leather pants unzipped just enough to let herself play. The knowledge that this was turning her on as much as it turned him on had him fucking her mouth harder and faster, the wet tightness and suction making his head spin. Her moans grew, the vibration of the sound sending tingles of pleasure straight to his balls. For a second he wondered if he should withdraw, but she shook her head, taking him deeper, her throat closing around the tip of his cock, and he exploded, spurting on her tongue. It took him long moments to recover, and he tilted his head back, gasping. "God. Thank you." A thank you wasn't enough. Not only for the orgasm, but for the heady, brief moments of freedom he'd found with her mouth.

He'd been powerless and, yet . . . powerful.

He hadn't felt both those things at once in years. It was thrilling and scary and exciting.

Clothes rustled, and he opened his eyes to catch her shimmying out of her pants, her strong muscles flexing, the ink covering them dancing. A dragon wound itself around her right leg, the scales blue green and vibrant, eyes blood red. A flame licked her upper thigh, a blur of crimson and orange and yellow.

That dragon had appeared on her body four or five years ago, but it had always been too dark for him to see it properly. He wanted to inspect every scale, but she was moving, climbing on top of him. She faced away, her legs draping over his thighs, his sensitized cock brushing the small of her back. "You want to thank me properly?" she asked, glancing over her shoulder.

He nodded dumbly. She grabbed his hand and brought it between her legs. He took over, and slid his fingers under the lace waistband, lifting her panties away from her skin, to catch a glimpse of her mound.

She let him play, her hands reaching over her head to grip his neck, nails digging into his skin. He looked down her body as it moved and writhed on top of his, loving every inch of her pleasure. Her moans grew louder and faster, her breathing deepening, and he followed her cues, his cock perking up at the way she was massaging it with her back.

Recognizing the signs of her impending release, he pressed his lips against her ear. "You're so close, aren't you?"

"Yes."

"Come on me. Let me feel that pussy squeeze."

She inhaled deeply, her body bearing down on him. "Give me more."

"More what?"

"More fingers. I need you to fill me up."

He thrust three fingers inside her, widening them. "There. Better?"

"Yes."

"Better than my cock?"

She whimpered, her hips moving faster. "No."

He pressed his thumb tight against her clit and sent his fingers deeper, curling them to hit the spot that always made her body rock. She cried out as he massaged that flesh, not giving her a second of reprieve. He bit her neck, harder than he'd ever previously dared, and her body bowed, her inner muscles tightening and releasing on him.

When she was finally done, he stroked her flesh softly, loath to leave this wet, warm place. He wanted to do everything to her.

Every little thing. Every sexual act he'd missed and hadn't had in so long with this woman.

His phone rang, puncturing their bubble of sexual bliss. He cursed it mentally, because she immediately slid off his legs, grabbing her pants. Whatever this interlude had been, it was at an end. He sighed and buttoned up his trousers, grimacing at his renewed erection.

His phone stopped ringing, then started again.

"You should get that," she muttered. "Sounds urgent."

Annoyed, he pulled his phone out from where it had fallen in the crack of the chair and glanced at the display. His father this time. His grandfather, he could ignore. Brendan, not so much. The man wouldn't quit calling until he picked up, even if it was for the tiniest of details.

With a rough sigh, he stood and turned his back on Livvy. Though he wanted nothing more than to watch her ass jiggle as she wrestled her pants on, he couldn't do that and speak to his father.

"Yes?" he answered the phone shortly.

"Nicholas, what the fuck is this?"

"What?"

"These protestors. We have ten stores now with picketers. An anonymous source leaked that we're selling countless products made by prisoners. Who the fuck did that?"

Nicholas straightened, eyes narrowing. "Countless? No one knows that we've confirmed the two products except for you, me, and Grandpa."

"Well, those two have been blown up to hundreds and thousands. There's a fucking *hashtag* calling for a boycott. Why the fuck is there always a hashtag?"

Because hashtags got people to listen, but he wasn't about to sit here and explain social media to his dad. "Listen, I'll handle it. We'll issue a statement tonight. Say we're committed to our mission statement, as always, and while we have identified a couple of products, we have no evidence of any others."

"Say we're discontinuing those products, effective immediately."

"That's a good idea. I could also say we're going to do a comprehensive review of all suppliers to ensure no others are engaging in practices that run counter to our policies." He held his breath, ready to launch ten million arguments to achieve the outcome his grandfather—and he—wanted.

"Yes, fine, whatever. Just make this go away, for crying out loud. I'm getting harassed on every end here."

"Yes, sir." Without bothering to say goodbye, he hung up, and only then saw the string of texts he'd received in the last half hour. Had he checked his messages first, he would have seen a rundown of the situation from their public relations vice-president. He responded with instructions.

When he heard footsteps behind him, he pivoted, having temporarily forgotten where he was or who he was with. Livvy was fully dressed, shifting her weight from one foot to the other, her face wary. "Sounds important."

He lifted his phone. "I'm sorry. Small emergency at work."

"Hmm. Well, uh. I gotta get home. This has been real fun and all." She scooped up his shirt and tossed it to him.

It hit him in the chest, and he grabbed it automatically. "Listen—"

"You're gonna want to cover up that tail."

He looked down at his chest, having forgotten the mermaid. Even in permanent marker, the drawing was cute. Not something he'd want on his skin permanently, but Livvy's talent was evident in the mischievous look in the sea creature's eyes, the fluid lines of her body. "I'll drive you home."

"You're busy. I can walk."

Making certain to imbue his voice with every ounce of command he possessed, he repeated himself. "Not that busy. I'll drive you home."

It was the tone that got people to jump and scrape the second he spoke to them, but she looked unimpressed. "There's no need—"

"If you don't let me drive you, I'll creep along beside you while you walk home," he said flatly. "It'll take ten times longer, and we've established how terrible I am at lurking."

Her lips twitched. That was one of the things he'd always appreciated about Livvy. No matter how stubborn or angry she got, she never lost her sense of humor. That hadn't changed. "I guess you wouldn't look so handsome in an orange jumpsuit."

"It's not my color." He caught her wrist before she could move away. "You asked if it was so terrible to feel helpless." It should have been. For a man obsessed with control, who used coldness to keep himself from falling apart, he should have been terrified.

One feeling.

Yes, the Pandora's box was open, and he could sense all those emotions he'd carefully kept locked away struggling to get out, but he'd ignore them for now. He'd focus on that one feeling, that desire to be with her.

Her lips quivered, but then they firmed. So tough, she was. Tougher than him.

He stared into her dark eyes. "It wasn't. It wasn't terrible at all."

Chapter 10

"Drop me off here."

Nicholas didn't appear thrilled, but he complied with Livvy's order, stopping at the end of the cul-de-sac. It was dark out, but the lights from the dashboard illuminated his face in a greenish glow as he turned to her. "Will you think about meeting up with my grandfather and sister?"

She bit her lip. In all the other stuff they'd discussed, she'd almost forgotten about John and Eve. "Not your sister. Tell her we're cool." She believed Eve was remorseful. There was no need to have another stressful discussion, especially if it was going to drag up totally false stories about their parents.

He accepted that response with a single nod. "My grandfather, though?" When she hesitated, he pressed. "He's getting old, Livvy. I don't want to lay that on you, but I don't know how much longer he has."

Her stomach sank. "Is he sick?"

"No, nothing urgent." Nicholas grimaced. "Still. You never know. I'll beg you to do it, if that's what it takes."

She opened and closed her hands in her lap. For Nicholas to beg? That was indeed serious. "I came here to make peace with my family. That's it. I didn't ask for all this."

"I know." He traced his fingers over the steering wheel. The fingers he'd had inside her. "I'm sorry. I don't like bothering you, believe me."

"It's not a bother to see John. It's painful."

"I get that." He didn't say anything more.

She sighed. "I'll think about it."

"Thank you. Let me know either way."

She opened her door, the interior light coming on. "I guess, I'll, um, talk to you soon then?" The words felt weird in her mouth. It had been so long since they'd parted ways with actual goodbyes and the expectation of seeing each other again.

He rested his palm on her arm and she stopped. "Can I—"

She waited for him to finish but then he only shook his head and removed his hand. Her skin felt a little colder. "Never mind. Yes, we'll talk soon."

Were they supposed to kiss? Hug? She gave him an awkward wave and what she imagined was a pretty close human imitation of the gritted teeth emoji and exited the car.

She was supremely conscious of his vehicle idling behind her as she walked into the cul-de-sac. He wouldn't leave until she got to her mother's house. She tried to view the neighborhood through his eyes—it was solidly middle- to upper-class, but the four-bedroom brick home she was walking toward was a far cry from the estate where she had grown up.

She tucked her fingers into her jacket pocket, brushing velvet softness. While Nicholas had been distracted on the phone, she'd stuck the roses he'd brought her into an empty glass of water. She couldn't have brought them home without serious questions.

That hadn't stopped her from foolishly tucking a few petals in her pocket, though. She removed her hand and tugged her jacket tighter around her body. All her nerve endings felt tingly and too sensitive, as they always did after an encounter with Nicholas. Something was off, though, and it took her a second to realize what it was.

She didn't feel terrible.

That repetitive cycle of pleasure and pain. Where was the pain? Where was the aching inside of her, threatening to swallow her whole?

There was worry, yes, but she was calm. Why was that? Could it have been the talking when usually they were silent? The sense of making some sort of non-physical connection with him? The range of emotions he'd displayed? His vulnerability when he confessed he was nervous about a woman going down on him?

She mulled over the idea of oral sex therapy as an as-yet-undiscovered area of psychology as she skirted the motorcycle parked at the curb. Her aunt had complained the neighbors were letting their guests park willy-nilly in front of their home. She'd tell Maile about the hog in the morning.

She mounted the steps of the porch and waved at Nicholas. His headlights flashed and he drove away.

Livvy almost had her key in the door when a creak had her straightening, body going alert. A large shadow separated from the rickety chair on the porch, and she took a step back.

The shadow spoke. "It's me, Livs."

"Me, who—?" Realization struck, and she took another step back, this time out of shock. No one called her Livs except . . . "Jackson?" she whispered.

The hulking man stepped into the thin circle of light cast by the porch lamp. She and Jackson shared the same eyes and lips, but otherwise, no one would know they were siblings, let alone twins. Both her brothers had always been large-framed, taking after their father's side of the family.

In the ten years since she'd seen him, Jackson's face had grown leaner, more sculpted, his cheekbones high and slashing, his thick brows lowering over piercing eyes. He'd turned his solid frame into muscles packed on top of muscles, his large forearms and biceps revealed by the white T-shirt he wore in defiance of the fall chill.

"Jackson," she said again. Then she burst into tears.

She and Jackson had been like two peas in a pod, sharing a room until they were eleven, though the house they'd grown up in had had plenty of space. She liked chatter and noise; he'd been a silent, shy kid. Her father used to joke they made up for each other's weaknesses. Together, they were one perfect individual.

The first time they'd been apart had been when Jackson was arrested for the fire. That had kicked off a decade of separation.

She and Jackson had never been physically affectionate—like her mother, Jackson shied away from overt displays of fondness. But nothing could have stopped her from throwing herself at her brother. She tried to wrap her arms around his neck, but even in heels, on her tiptoes, he was far too tall.

She spoke against his chest, "Pick me up," but it came out more like "Schmoop rump."

"Uh, what?"

"Pick me up!"

A resigned sigh came from deep in his belly, but he did as she asked, lifting her so she could properly cling to him.

A big hand awkwardly patted her back. "Please stop."

She ignored the pleading in that rough voice. "Don't tear-shame me. I can cry if I want. I haven't seen you in forever." Not since the charges had been dropped. He'd left town sometime that night, with only a terse note for her, a duffel of clothes, and the money Maile had given him.

She'd left a couple days later, unable to find a reason to stick around in a place that no longer seemed like hers.

The patting turned more frenzied. "How long is this gonna last?"

"As long as I want, asshole," she snarled between sobs. "Deal with it."

Another sigh. "Livs, you know I'm not good at this."

He never had been, bless him. She inhaled, struggling to stop. A few ragged breaths later, her tears eased enough for her to speak. "No, I don't know that. I don't know anything." She twisted her head. A flash of black peeked out from under his T-shirt sleeve. Her tears turned to indignation, and she shoved herself away from him. "Except I see you got some tattoos. From someone who obviously wasn't me." Like a wife discovering lipstick on her husband's collar, she jerked his shirt up and studied the half-sleeve there with a sneer. Her outrage melted into sharp nostalgia. Jackson had incorporated Hawaiian designs, reminiscent of the single tattoo their father had had on his arm. Whenever she'd asked her dad about it, he'd laughed and rolled his eyes, telling her it was a remnant of his wild youth.

She sniffed and lifted Jackson's other sleeve to find something written on his inner bicep. Damn it, too bad she couldn't read Japanese. "This is ridiculous. You went to some strangers somewhere for our people's heritage?"

"Since when are you an expert on our people?"

She wasn't. Her father had been estranged from and never met his extended family in Hawaii, and her mother had only ever made half-hearted efforts to teach her kids about their Japanese side.

But *still.* "I know how to do research."

"I got this one in Tokyo and the other one in Maui. I think that was better than you hitting up Wikipedia."

She nudged him into the moonlight and peered closer at the lettering. "Some nice line work," she admitted grudgingly. "I could do better, of course, but it's not terrible. What does it say?"

"Google it."

She glared up at him. She and Jackson might have been close, but he was still a brother, with all the annoying traits that came along with that. She smacked his arm. "You want to permanently alter your body? You come to me from now on. No one else."

He rubbed his arm where she had hit him, though she imagined her hand stung more than his hard flesh. "Yeah, yeah."

She took another step back, and silence fell between them as they studied each other, cataloguing the differences ten years could make. His hair was shorter now, his face roughly hewn and matured from his baby roundness. There was an odd sense of deep familiarity that came with seeing someone you'd spent twenty years with, but the strangeness of meeting someone after a decade who had lived a life that was so remote, she had no idea what it had even consisted of.

They'd emailed occasionally and talked on the phone at least once a year, either around their birthday or the holidays, so they'd had a vague idea of where the other one was, but that was it. While she'd stuck to the States, Jackson had back-packed the world, doing God knows what. When she would ask if he had a job or enough money, he'd only tell her vaguely he was doing fine, and then change the subject.

He was the first to speak. "Still a pipsqueak, I see."

Her inhalation was shaky. "Still big and mean, I see."

His full lips curled. "Hey, Livs."

"Jackson." She shoved her hands in her pockets, unsure of what to do with them now that she was done grabbing him. She fingered the rose petals, their smoothness calming her. "I'm surprised to see you."

"I know."

"What . . ." She trailed off, uncertain what to say. There were a million questions she wanted to ask, and a million ways for him to dodge her.

A trickle of anger undercut her joy at seeing him. It surprised her, that anger, but she supposed she'd been carrying it around for a while. "Fuck you, Jackson. How could you not come home for Paul's funeral?" Oh, she tried to keep the tinge of bitterness and judgment out of her tone, but she feared she failed.

Yeah, that anger and resentment was real. It didn't matter what Paul and Jackson's relationship had been at the time of their brother's death. Hell, Paul had been estranged from her like whoa. She'd still wept when she learned he'd died alone and cold on a hiking trail, had rushed home to put her arm around Sadia.

Jackson nodded, not a trace of surprise on his broad face. "So, we're leading with that, huh?"

"Yeah. We're leading with that."

"I couldn't come then."

"Was someone stopping you?"

He ran his hand over the back of his neck. "A few guards. I might have been in a jail cell in Paris."

The anger vanished. She stared at him in shock, every fear she'd had about her brother rushing back. He'd always been so good. A little surly and quiet, yes, but he'd walked the straight and narrow far more than she ever had.

Being accused of arson had pushed him over the edge, it seemed. Dear Lord, had he spent the past few years bumming the world and getting tossed into jail cells? "For what?"

"It was nothing."

"It was something, if you were in a foreign jail."

"I had to pay a fine. No big deal. But, yeah, I missed the funeral." He walked away and sat down on the porch steps, linking his hands between his legs. "How was it?"

She wanted to grab his arm and snuggle close to him, force him to love and hold her, but she'd already pushed her luck. She didn't want to shove him right off the porch onto an international flight.

Tentatively, she sat on the step, with a good amount of distance between them. "It was a funeral. Pretty small." Most of the friends Paul had were ones he'd made after she'd left town. He'd cut ties with most everyone they'd grown up with. Not surprising, since most of them were also either friends or employees of Nicholas. Sometimes both.

"I'm sorry I couldn't come."

She deflated, all of her resentment gone. "I guess you had a good reason. I wasn't any closer to Paul than you were, at the end there. But he was still our brother." It was easy when you were estranged from someone to always focus on their weaknesses, but Paul had been a pretty decent big brother before life had come between them. Stubborn and sometimes annoying, but protective and loving too.

"Yeah. I know." Jackson cleared his throat. "I should have contacted you after, at least."

"And Sadia."

He looked out over the yard. Livvy wondered if he was comparing it to their old home, where they'd been surrounded by woods. Here, the houses were close enough she could see Carol's television on in the living room next door. "Did her family come to the service?"

"Yes." Sadia's parents had left early, but her sisters had hovered around her.

"Good. That's good." He rubbed his nose. "I got your e-mail about Mom."

"I assumed." She'd worded the e-mail carefully, laying out the facts only. She figured Jackson had the right to know about their mom, but as angry as she'd been over him not coming home for Paul, she hadn't been ready to guilt him into rushing home for their mom.

It had been her decision to come here. Jackson could make his own decisions.

He rolled his big shoulders, like he was trying to get rid of an annoyance. "I was in the state anyway.

Thought I could at least check on you." His eyes cut to hers. "How's Mom?"

"Not bad. She's getting around with the walker now. A physical therapist comes a few times a week. She'll be walking with a cane soon, probably."

"Thought only fragile old people broke their hips."

"She's not young anymore, Jackson. And it can happen to anyone who takes a nasty fall and has a touch of osteoporosis. Luckily, Aunt Maile was able to get help for her immediately."

Jackson's smile was faint. "Aunt Maile. She still a chatterbox?"

"Who isn't a chatterbox to you?" Livvy grinned, though. "Yeah. Still hoarding yarn. She helps Mom a lot, especially when I'm at work."

"You're working here too?"

"Part-time. At Gabe's shop."

Like her, Jackson had been friends with their housekeeper's son, but he showed little reaction to hearing his name. "You've really settled back home nicely."

Though there was no inflection in his voice, Livvy bristled. "What's that supposed to mean?"

"Nothing."

"If it was nothing, you would have said nothing. The fact that you said something means something."

Jackson tapped his fingers on his knee. "You still think you know me so well, pipsqueak?"

"I will always know you," she said quietly. *I'll always love you. No matter how far we run from each other and this place.*

Jackson's Adam's apple bobbed. "Why'd you come back here?"

"To look after Mom."

"Bullshit."

Her eyes narrowed. "Watch your language. There's a lady here."

He snorted. "You always swore worse than me."

"That's because I talked more than you. Clams talked more than you."

He ignored the dig. "Why did you come here?"

"To look after—"

"Bull. Shit."

"What do you want me to say?"

"The truth."

"It's the truth."

"Fine. I'll hire a nurse for her tomorrow. Full-time, twenty-four hours. You can leave."

She eyed him. If Jackson was kicking around prison cells, she imagined most of his money had probably gone to bail and lawyers. If he had money. Lord knew what he did. "How do you have that kind of cash?"

He ignored the question. "So you're going to leave, right?"

"No."

"Then why are you here?"

"Because I want my family back!"

They both froze at her almost-shout. She covered her mouth with a shaking hand. Shit, she hoped she hadn't woken up her mom or her aunt.

Jackson had stilled. "Ah," he breathed.

After long, tense minutes, she lowered her hand. "I got depressed after Paul died."

His lashes lowered, hiding his eyes. "How bad?"

She swallowed, aware of what he was really asking. *Were you suicidal?*

She couldn't say yes, though it would be the truth. She'd spent a solid week in bed, unable to function, the darkness growing so large it incapacitated her. Thoughts of self-harm had slithered through her brain, finally scaring her enough to pick up the phone. "Not as bad as . . . you know," she said carefully. That wasn't a lie. The time after the accident had been the worst episode she'd ever had. Which was not unusual, her therapist had assured her, given all the traumatic upheaval that had preceded it.

"But bad." Jackson's lips tightened. "I should have called you."

She hesitated. Jackson had appointed himself her sole comfort when they were young, but they'd been away from each other for so long. She craved the security of familial support, yes, but that support had to be rooted in something. "Don't beat yourself up over that. I got help. I've been in therapy for a while now." The first time she'd gone to a psychiatrist, she'd felt vaguely guilty, like she was doing something self-indulgent and silly. But it had helped. It hadn't cured, but it had helped.

Jackson nodded, but tension had carved lines in his forehead. "That's good. I'm glad."

"Yeah. Anyway, I did a lot of thinking and talking and I acknowledged my depression is exacerbated by a lot of things, and one of those things is being so alone." She ran her hands over her thighs. "We lost one member of our family and it was like we lost everyone. Paul's gone now, for good. I'll never fix things with him. But it's not too late for Mom and Sadia and Maile and Kareem. They're mine. I want that connection. I need it. Even if I don't live near them, to know I have that base . . . it would help me." She could especially use a re-connection with her mom, but she didn't want to remind Jackson of his own troubled relationship with Tani.

His sigh was long and low. "Oh, Livvy."

"I know. I'm a marshmallow."

His shoulder bumped hers, an unexpected show of comfort. "Being a marshmallow isn't a bad thing."

"Marshmallows melt." Weak, soft, blobs of sugar. That was her.

He squinted. "On the inside, but their outsides get all crisp when you stick them in a fire."

"This is a strange metaphor. I think we should drop it." She paused. "And, uh, maybe don't say the word *fire* around here."

She was gratified when he smiled faintly. "Probably smart. Have you been by the store?"

She hid her surprise that he could speak about the building he'd been arrested for burning down. She couldn't drive past it. "Not yet."

He nodded, like he'd expected that answer. "Have you seen Nicholas?"

It was a lot harder to hide her reaction to that question. She cast a glance at Jackson, noting the direction he was looking. Down the road, at the point where Nicholas had dropped her off. It was clearly visible from the porch. "I—"

"You don't have to answer. I know." He gestured at the house. "You don't get to pick and choose. You face one part of your past, Livvy, you have no choice but to face it all. Around here, everything's bound up together. And if we're talking about things that exacerbate your depression . . ."

Hadn't she thought something similar? *Not all painful memories were created equal.* Her annual encounters with Nicholas weren't great for her mental health, no lie.

Livvy bit her lip and nodded. "I know. But I want my family."

His lips went taut, and he nodded. "I understand, believe me. But you're better off getting out of here and starting over. Find a nice group of people who love you. Have a house like this in some other suburb."

"Is that what you did? Start over?"

"Basically."

"Are you happy?"

Jackson's eyes gleamed. "I'm alive."

"Is that good enough for you?"

He didn't answer that. "You're going to get hurt."

Probably. She already had been hurt.

Yet there was today, and her strange lack of hurt with Nicholas.

Pleasure and pain. It's a circle. You're just still stuck in the pleasure part of the cycle.

But it felt so good. Dangerously good. The kind

of good that could persuade a woman to reach out annually to a man who could only give her his body and nothing else.

"You're saying I shouldn't deal with any of it, because I can't deal with all of it. What if I can? Leave some of my baggage behind when I go?"

"Some things are unresolvable. You're living in a fantasy land if you think you can have it all."

Not a fantasy. A fairy tale.

As much as every cynical part of her believed him, she couldn't stop the tiny kernel of desperate optimism unfurling inside her. "I can't leave."

Jackson's lips curved up, but it wasn't an amused smile. "I didn't honestly think you would. You're so damn stubborn, Livs."

"A stubborn marshmallow?"

"All marshmallows are stubborn. Nothing that soft could hold its shape if it wasn't stubborn as hell." He got to his feet. "I gotta go."

"Where? Do you have a place to stay tonight?"

"Yeah. I'm expected in New York City tomorrow."

"For what? For work?"

He only shrugged.

"You didn't see Aunt Maile or Mom." Now that she thought about it, she wondered why he'd been lurking in the dark. Had he known Livvy was out? Or had he not been able to risk Maile or Tani answering the door?

He ran his hand over his head. The faint moonlight danced over his black hair. "I didn't come home to see them."

She wanted to argue with him, but she wasn't

going to project her own desperate desire for family on her brother. "When will you be back?"

"I don't know."

"Will you . . . will you come back?"

He thudded down the stairs. The last time she'd watched him stride away from their house, led away in handcuffs, she hadn't seen him for a decade. She had to bite back a cry for him to stay.

"Yeah."

It wasn't a hug or a kiss, but she held that yeah close to her chest. "I'm going to expect to see you then. Soon."

Jackson walked to the motorcycle and then turned around. "Be realistic and do whatever you gotta do quickly, Livs. It's not healthy to be here." His gaze lifted over her head and darkened.

She turned to look over her shoulder and scrambled to her feet. Her mother stood in the doorway, one hand on the door, the other resting heavily on her walker, dressed in a pink nightgown, her hair neatly combed.

How much had Tani overheard?

The woman was motionless, staring after her son, even as the sound of the motorcycle revving and driving off filled the air. Livvy approached slowly. "Mom? I thought you'd be asleep."

Her mother didn't respond, and Livvy's heart clenched. Was that a sheen of wetness in the older woman's eyes? "Mom?"

Tani blinked and looked at Livvy, and that wetness was gone. "The noise woke me up. I thought it was a neighbor. Then I heard you talking."

"What's going on?" Aunt Maile's voice piped up behind Tani, and then the other woman was there, crowding around her sister-in-law. She tightened the belt around her silk purple robe.

"Jackson was here," Tani said. There was no inflection in her voice.

"Jackson!" Aunt Maile clasped her hands together. "Where is he? Why didn't you bring him inside?"

"He didn't want to come inside," Tani replied.

There was a snap in her mother's voice that made Livvy flinch. "He had to go. He's expected in New York. For work, I think?"

"What kind of work does he do?" Maile asked.

Jesus, no one knew anything about Jackson, did they? "I don't know."

"Is he coming back?"

She didn't want to say yes. What if he didn't? "I'm not sure," she hedged. "Come on, let's go inside. Mom, I can help you get back to your room."

"I can get to bed on my own," Tani said stiffly. Ignoring Livvy's hand, she turned away and made her way slowly down the hallway, to the first-floor bedroom she'd taken for her own while she recovered.

Maile lingered behind, her wistful gaze on the street. "Did he ask about me?"

"He did." Livvy closed the door.

"How did he look?"

Livvy spoke without thinking. "Like Dad."

Maile closed her eyes briefly. They were teary when she opened them. Unlike Tani, she didn't bother to hide it. "If he comes back, you tell him I miss him terribly."

"*If* he comes back," Livvy emphasized. "He's gone years without seeing me either."

Maile nodded, her face troubled. "Do you want to talk about it?"

Livvy's heart squeezed. If she'd reached out at any time over the past ten years, Maile would have been available as a resource and comfort. She hadn't needed to feel so alone.

It was good to know that. "Not right now, thanks. Why don't you go back to bed?"

"I was awake, watching television. I didn't know if you'd need a ride home. You didn't walk in the dark, did you?"

In all the drama, she'd almost forgotten Nicholas and what they'd done together before he'd given her a ride home. She fought to keep the blush off her face. "No. I got a ride."

"Good." Maile turned and walked to the stairs. Her thick hair was caught up in a braid that almost reached her waist. It swished when she walked. "I'll go watch some more T.V. Or I'll start that new knitting project. I want to make a sweater for the Kims' new baby."

Livvy did her usual circuit, making sure the windows and doors were all locked, before making her way to her room, unable to get her mom's face out of her mind.

Marshmallow.

Calling herself a fool, certain the gesture would be rebuffed, she went to her dresser and pulled out the sketchpad she kept there. She always kept a few pads on hand, in case of inspiration. Her hand hovered over her box of pastels, but she chose the charcoals.

She went back downstairs to her mother's room. A light was visible beneath the door, a late-night talk show blaring on the television. She knocked lightly, peeking in at her mother's response.

The room was decorated rather barrenly, like most of the house, with only a bed and furniture. Nothing on the walls. Her mother's regular room upstairs was pretty much the same. It was a far cry from her childhood home's master bedroom, which had been graced with priceless artwork.

"Hey. I, uh, just wanted to drop these off. The physical therapist said it would be good to keep your hands busy," she made up on the spot. "I don't have any puzzles or Rubik's Cubes or whatever, but figured you could sketch. Or write letters. Whatever." She walked into the room and placed the sketchbook and charcoals on the table.

After a quick glance, Tani returned her attention to the television. "Thank you." The dismissal in her tone was unmistakable.

Livvy hesitated at the door. "Do you want to talk about—?"

"Good night, Olivia."

She bit her lip, aching inside. *Marshmallow.* "Good night."

Upstairs, Livvy removed the bruised petals from her pocket and placed them carefully on the bureau. She shed her clothes and tossed them on the floor while the tub filled. She'd been pretty good at keeping her guest room here incredibly tidy, each article of clothing hung up neatly. She was simply so tired. She'd pick up tomorrow.

She sank into the hot bath, letting the water ease the muscles that had locked up during the day. From hunching over her clients and from the load of tension she carried.

What would it feel like to shed some of the baggage she carried?

She'd be happier, wouldn't she? That dark emptiness would always be there, but if she could grasp more ways to keep it from swallowing her whole, that was a good thing, wasn't it?

Do whatever you gotta do quickly, Livs.

Livvy grabbed her phone from the ledge of the tub. She opened a new message and typed out, **I'll see John.**

A bubble popped up at the bottom of the screen and she held her breath. Part of her didn't believe he would actually reply. He never had, after that first time laying out their arrangement.

And then her phone vibrated as the three little dots became three little words.

Is tomorrow okay?

She ran her finger over those words before she caught herself. Nope, no. She was going to be cool about this. This was not a big deal, even if it was the first message she'd gotten from him in a decade.

You can try to work out your issues with him, but that's it.

She typed with purpose. **Yes. I have to work during the day. Say, 5:30?**

Perfect. I can pick you up?

No. Then he'd drive her home again and that seemed far too date-like. **I'll drive. I can meet you . . .** She hesitated, then finished the thought quickly. **I can meet you behind Kane's.** If she could stand to see John, she could stand to see her grandparents' café as well as the flagship C&O—Chandler's— across the street, damn it.

She nibbled on her nail, watching the dots pop up on the bottom of the screen. They hovered there for a solid minute, and then came his reply. **Okay**.

Like a mature, healthy individual, she placed the phone on the ledge of the tub instead of fondling those messages. Livvy tipped her head back, trying to clear her mind.

Some things are unresolvable.

Maybe they were. At this point, though, she wasn't sure what other option she had but to try.

Chapter 11

NICHOLAS STUMBLED downstairs, exhaustion weighing at his eyelids, his phone glued to his ear. Between his staff, father, and his grandfather calling him about this prison-labor scandal, the damn thing had been ringing since the crack of dawn. He'd missed his usual workout, which, combined with his preoccupation over meeting Livvy later today, meant his already stretched-thin patience was in perilous danger of snapping.

He waited until the P.R. guy finished speaking. "Call a press conference for today at noon. In the meantime, we're at no comment. We'll talk more once I'm in the office."

He hung up with a terse goodbye and stalked into the kitchen. He tossed his phone on the counter and reached up to grab a mug from the cupboard. He was so preoccupied, it took him a solid minute to process the loud, out-of-place crunching noise coming from behind him. Instinctively, he grabbed a knife from the rarely used set on the counter and pivoted.

Holy shit.

Past and present overlapped as he stared at the big man sitting at his kitchen table. His heart stuttered, his lips forming a soundless word. *Paul.*

Except Paul was dead, and Nicholas didn't believe in ghosts, especially ones who hung around their ex-best friend's homes to eat cereal.

The Kane siblings had all occupied specific roles. Paul had been the dutiful and charming heir apparent, Livvy the dramatic rebel, and Jackson . . .

Well, whatever role Jackson had occupied, he'd lost it when he'd been arrested on suspicion of arson.

A witness had identified him fleeing from the burning C&O. He'd had motive and opportunity, and a gas can with his fingerprints had been found behind some bushes in the Kanes' backyard. Though the evidence had been flimsy, it had been enough to arrest Jackson and have him held without bail.

Before he could go to trial, though, the witness recanted his account. Despite the dropped charges, no one had been terribly convinced as to Jackson's innocence.

Especially Nicholas.

He and Jackson had never been particularly close, but whatever relationship had existed between them had vanished when the man had thrown a Molotov cocktail through the window of the store their grandfathers had built.

Nicholas didn't care about the physical damage. Someone could have been seriously hurt, and that he couldn't forgive.

Jackson's dark, oddly flat gaze moved between Nicholas's face and knife with the easy skill of someone who had been in more than one brawl. "You gonna stab me?"

"No one would blame me."

"Because I'm so scary, huh."

"No. Because you broke into my home." How had he broken in, anyway? Nicholas had a state-of-the-art security system.

Well, he used to have one. He was fucking calling the company right after he figured out what was going on here.

He wasn't able to gauge any weapons in the other man's big hands, other than the spoon he was holding. Gingerly, Nicholas placed his knife on the counter. "If you were hungry, you could have knocked on the door."

"You would have invited me in for cornflakes?"

"Sure."

Jackson took a bite of cereal, crunching louder than necessary. "Liar."

Nicholas's gaze narrowed. "I didn't realize you were in town."

"Got in last night. Comfy couch you have, by the way."

"You slept on my couch?" Who the hell *was* this guy?

"Wanted to make sure I caught you this morning. I gotta head out soon."

"Most people call and make an appointment."

"You wouldn't have agreed to see me."

"Then you knock."

"You wouldn't have answered."

"Then you would have gotten the hint," Nicholas bit off. "That's how society works."

"Never been very good at all that social stuff." Jackson bared his teeth. "Not like you."

Nicholas gave up. "What are you doing here?"

Another grunt. Nicholas's eyes narrowed. "So you came over here to what? Sleep on my couch, silently eat my breakfast foods, and brood? Wild take on Goldilocks, Jackson."

Jackson took another bite, seemingly unfazed.

"Have you seen Livvy or your mother yet?"

Jackson picked up the bowl, and loudly slurped the milk. Nicholas gritted his teeth, well aware this was a deliberate rudeness. The man had been raised in the same social circle as Nicholas. Tani would have swatted him for such impoliteness, just like Maria.

Jackson finally put the bowl down and stared at him. Christ, he looked like his brother, only a leaner, rougher version of the man. Not even the milk mustache on his face detracted from his generally vicious appearance. "The more important question is, have *you* seen my sister?"

"None of your fucking business."

The chair screeched as Jackson shoved it back across the expensive tile floor. "I think it is."

Nicholas tensed, rocking up on the balls of his feet. Jackson had the air of someone who had never heard of fighting fair, but they had enough bad blood between them that Nicholas couldn't say throwing a punch or two would be entirely unwelcome. "You're mistaken."

"You haven't seen her?"

"No. You're mistaken as to anything I do being your business."

A muscle in Jackson's cheek twitched. "It's my business when you fuck with my sister. I'm here to tell you to stay away from her."

The anger warmed Nicholas, loosening his tongue. "Aw, did you fly all the way here to play overprotective brother? How's that role feel for you? New?"

A flash of something hot and angry moved behind those dark eyes. "The fuck does that mean?"

"It means I know you haven't seen her since you left town."

"And you have?"

He faltered. Yeah, actually, he had seen her consistently in the past decade. But no one was supposed to know about that.

"Don't try to lie. I know you've been with her." Nicholas stiffened, but then Jackson continued. "I saw you dropping her off last night."

Last night. So he didn't know about their unconventional arrangement.

Still, Nicholas's hand clenched into a fist. There was no need for him to feel guilty. *Imagine if her mother had seen you. Imagine if your father had seen you.*

Would it matter? Would you have changed what you did with her yesterday?

The answer to that was frighteningly clear. He

couldn't regret a second of what had come after he'd indulged that one feeling. Not when it had made him feel so good. He met Jackson's eyes. "Don't tell her you came to see me. Or that you saw us together last night."

"So you can keep on fucking with her?"

"No. Because it would stress her out."

Jackson blinked. "Your concern for her is heartwarming."

"Don't presume to know anything about me or my concern for your sister," Nicholas said coldly. "You don't know shit about us."

Jackson crossed massive arms over his chest. Jesus, what had the guy been doing over the past decade, bench-pressing cars? The Kane men had all been big, but this was excessive.

"I know that you think there's an *us*. I'm not too keen on there being an *us* when it comes to you and Livvy."

"And again—it's none of your business."

Jackson rubbed his hand over his face, and Nicholas suddenly noticed the bags under the other man's eyes. Livvy's twin may have broken in and slept on his couch, but it clearly hadn't been a restful nap. "I don't like you, Nicky. I never really have."

"The feeling's mutual." Actually, he'd never given Jackson much thought. He and Paul had been fast friends from the moment they could walk. Before he and Livvy had been lovers, he'd adored her platonically. Jackson . . . Jackson had been way too distant for anyone to really be close to. Except Livvy. And maybe Sadia.

"After you broke my sister's heart when you dumped her ass ten years ago, my dislike turned to hate."

"I didn't dump her ass, as you so disgustingly put it. It was a mutual breakup."

Jackson laughed, but the sound was without mirth. "Yeah right. Our father died, our mother checked out, your dad maneuvered a takeover, and you cut her loose." He sneered. "It was a perfect storm of assholery."

It *had* been mutual, not that Jackson would necessarily know that. Nicholas didn't much recall the aftermath, but the breakup, that was engraved in his mind. Livvy's hair had been purple then, fading to lavender because she hadn't bothered to color it in the two weeks since the accident. Her eyes had been puffy, face scrubbed clean of makeup.

Telling her about his father's threats was impossible, not when he'd been groomed his whole life to keep their family business private. Besides, if she'd known about the blackmail, she would have tried to tell him they could still be together, because their relationship was so fairy tale perfect, and wasn't that how fairy tales worked? The prince and princess stood up to the evil wizard and life worked out?

Be realistic, Nicholas.

The truth would have only made things more difficult for both of them. So he'd convinced himself their ending things was the rational, realistic thing to do. He'd rehearsed a speech, suppressed every desire he had to fight for them both.

They couldn't have survived everything that had gone down. To believe they could would have been the height of fantasy. "Is that why you burned down the store that week? Because you thought I hurt her?"

Anger twisted Jackson's face, and he took a few giant steps toward him. Nicholas held his ground. He might not have the younger man's brawn, but he wasn't about to be pushed around by some . . . some . . . *criminal.*

Alleged criminal.

Whatever.

"There it is," Jackson sneered. "You're nothing but a fucking robot in a suit. You never cared about Livvy more than you cared about the fucking business. I was the one who had to hold her after you broke her heart. I was the one who had to tell her she would be okay when she sobbed so much she threw up. I was the one who had to hide every pill in the goddamn house because she kept saying she wanted to die because you didn't love her anymore. Don't you *dare* tell me it was mutual."

Nicholas jerked. "What?" he rasped.

He'd misheard Jackson. Surely that couldn't be right.

Jackson's mouth tightened until it disappeared, and he took another step. This time Nicholas backed up against the counter and let the other man shove him in the center of his chest, accepting the pain of his index finger. "Stay away from my sister," Jackson enunciated. "Or I swear to God, you'll wish I was only an alleged arsonist."

She'd wanted to die? His vibrant, sweet, rebellious Livvy? Because they'd broken up? No, Jackson was lying.

Except Nicholas was good at separating lies from truth, and that had sounded pretty damn true.

His vision blurred. He wasn't in his kitchen anymore, but back in that clearing in the woods, standing a foot away from her. He'd refused to touch her as he spoke the final words in his carefully rehearsed speech. *It's impossible for us to be together now.*

And then, because he was human, he'd slipped, speaking the truth for a few seconds. *They won't let us.*

To cover, he'd blurted out the rest. *I think we should end this.*

She'd nodded, pale and composed. They hadn't hugged or touched, merely retreated to their respective homes. She had surely hurt, just like he hurt, but she'd agreed with him. She hadn't even put up a token resistance.

You made sure she couldn't.

Jackson grabbed his shirt in his fist and hauled him close, until they were nose-to-nose, bringing Nicholas back to the present. "Are you listening to me? Fuck with her and—" Jackson looked down and frowned.

Nicholas glanced down as well. He hadn't buttoned his shirt all the way. Jackson's grip had revealed a smidgen of the mermaid Livvy had drawn on him yesterday, the green marker vivid against his skin.

That was his, a souvenir of his time with Livvy,

not to be shared. He shoved Jackson away, stepping back. This was all too much. One feeling. He'd been right to be wary of indulging that one feeling, because now he was being flooded with every emotion under the sun.

There was no way he could bury them all and get back in the box.

He needed time and space. And Livvy, but that wasn't new. What was new was that he'd actually get to see her soon. Before they got together, he had to think, and he couldn't do that with her brother lurking in his home. "Get out."

Jackson watched him for a second, then stalked to the back door. The alarm beeped, but didn't go off. Disarmed. "Fuck with her, and I'll fuck you up."

Nicholas's jaw clenched, but he couldn't speak, his mind still in a tailspin.

"By the way, your security is shit, but it might help if you changed the code." Jackson smiled. It wasn't a comforting smile. "I guessed it on the first try."

Chapter 12

Livvy was early for her meeting with Nicholas, which was a pretty good indication of how nervous she was for it. Tardiness was more her speed.

She came to a stop in the parking lot of Kane's Café. She had vague memories of her dad's parents, who had owned this small but popular establishment. Her grandfather had been as big as her dad with a similarly booming voice, her grandmother as sturdy as Maile with a soft lap.

Once Livvy had asked her dad why he'd kept the café after they were gone. It hadn't made sense, especially since their family didn't need any income from the place. He'd ruffled her hair. *Sometimes it's okay to make irrational decisions because of sentiment. The café reminds me of your grandparents.* He'd winked. *Plus, it was the first place I saw your mother.*

It was here that her brother and Nicholas had taught her how to shoot milk out of her nose when she was nine, where she'd consoled Sadia when she'd broken up with that asshole Tim in ninth grade, where she'd had her first tea, her first coffee, and her first job.

Livvy was in no hurry to get out of the car and face those memories, even if they were, generally, good. She rubbed her hands together to warm them. Winter would be here before she could blink and Ruthie's heating system wasn't the best anymore. One day, she'd have to lay her precious car to rest, and the thought had her preemptively choked up. She had a lot of good memories attached to this baby. Bad ones too, but the good outweighed the bad.

Livvy took a deep breath and forced herself to look at the grocery store across the street. When she'd lived in any of the four states where Chandler's had stores, she'd carefully avoided them, averting her eyes when she caught sight of that telltale font. Oh, but this store. This one was the most painful. The original, or at least, the store that had taken the place of the original.

It looked the same, though they'd rebuilt it bigger. The Chandler name looked too large for the building, in the space where C&O had once perched.

A flash of empathy for Paul ran through her. How hard must it have been for him to stay here and see this sign every day? She hadn't expected to run C&O, and it still hurt to see the reminder that it wasn't hers.

She got out of her car and slammed the door shut, ignoring the way the thing rattled a bit. Livvy wondered whether it similarly hurt Nicholas to see the Kane name every time he came to Chandler's. As CEO, he spent most of his time in the office, no doubt, but he was expected to frequent the first store.

Like now.

A tall, familiar figure was striding toward the furthest reaches of the parking lot. It appeared as though he'd decided to come early to their meeting as well.

Of course he parked far away from the entrance, lest the boss take up a customer's spot. Her heart leapt, then sank when she noticed the leggy blonde walking next to him, dressed sharply in a tailored business suit.

Livvy tugged on her crop top, wishing she'd opted for something with a bit more coverage. It was fine. So her former love was walking next to a woman who looked perfect for him, like the living embodiment of the fake girlfriend he'd pretended he had. Big deal.

What even was her life.

As she tortured herself by watching, the couple stopped next to a car and Nicholas bent his head.

No, no, no.

He kissed her.

Her breath strangled in her throat. Those lips that had captured her mouth last night were on someone else's skin.

None of your business. It's none of your business.

As if he felt her eyes on him, his gaze lifted over the woman's head. Surprise flashed, and then something else, something determined and needy. His lips moved.

Livvy spun, breaking whatever ridiculous hold

he always exerted over her. She knew they were supposed to meet shortly, but she needed a second. She could either get in her car and drive away or head into the café.

She chose the café, because damn it, it was closer, and it made slightly more sense.

Besides, Nicholas wouldn't come in here, surely. It was Kane territory. She'd have her second.

Had she wondered where the pain portion of that pleasure-and-pain cycle was? Oh. It was right here.

She stepped inside the café, the scent of baked goods and coffee not reviving her spirits. She wanted to go home and burrow under the covers, hiding from the world. Now that she'd watched Nicholas kiss another woman could she be done with him?

It hadn't been passionate. A peck on the cheek. He'd used to give her those as an afterthought, when he wasn't going to see her for a couple hours.

He hadn't kissed her cheek in a decade. He'd kissed her on her lips—hot, openmouthed, passionate kisses. He'd sucked her nipples, bitten the inside of her thighs, licked her between her legs. He'd given her hickeys all over her throat and breasts.

So why the hell was she envious of a peck on the cheek? Why did that feel like the height of intimacy?

Her fingers itched to touch her cheek, but she kept her hand at her side and walked woodenly to the line, standing behind a teenager blasting music through his headphones. Sadia wasn't in sight.

Maybe she was in the back? Livvy could use a dose of her best friend's steady, pragmatic wisdom right now. Or the other woman's threats to shank someone for Livvy, preferably the perfect, svelte recipient of Nicholas's kisses.

She sucked in her stomach. Her arms, her pride and joy, were still sculpted as fuck, but she was starting to get a bit soft around the middle. That woman hadn't been soft anywhere. She'd been tall. Elegant. Dressed perfectly.

Livvy wrapped a strand of her hair around her finger. That strawberry-blond shade would look terrible on her, but she coveted it anyway.

Stoppppp.

She didn't hear any footsteps behind her, but she stiffened, prickles of awareness causing goosebumps to rise on her arms. She didn't turn around. *Please go away. You can't see me like this.*

Naked. Vulnerable.

"Livvy," he breathed, and she almost crumbled.

It took her a beat too long to shore up her defenses. She stared determinedly at the teenager in front of her. The line was about six deep. "What are you doing in here?"

"I don't know."

Hell, at least he was honest. "Someone will recognize you. There'll be gossip. Scram."

"I can't."

"Nicho—"

"You look tired."

"Remember when we talked about how that's a

shitty thing to say to a girl?" she returned pleasantly.

"I—I'm tired too."

She frowned and finally glanced over her shoulder. She took in his bloodshot eyes, the slight circles under them, and swiveled back around. Yes, he was neat and tidy otherwise, but he was telling the truth. He did look tired.

"That was my cousin."

Her heart stopped, then started again. "What?"

"That woman is my cousin. Shel?"

"I can't keep track of your cousins."

"Neither can I. She's taking a position at the company. A tour of the flagship is standard."

She bit her lip. Her anxiety and upset edged away. "Oh." She recovered her aplomb. "I didn't ask who she was," she said defensively.

"If I'd seen you with someone, I'd want to know who it was."

"It's not my business."

"Yes it is."

She cast him a sharp look. "What is with you?"

He met her gaze steadily. "Damned if I know."

"You don't want to be in here."

As if suddenly reminded of where they were, Nicholas looked around, taking in the café with the air of a man waking up from a dream. She did another quick survey. She didn't spot anyone she knew, but that didn't mean anything. It was quite possible someone in here knew her even if she didn't know them.

Nicholas cleared his throat. "I didn't think before I walked in."

Not thinking? That was totally un-Nicholas-like behavior.

The line inched forward. "Please leave before someone recognizes you."

He moved closer instead, so close she could feel the brush of his breath on her nape. A featherlight touch landed on her spine, and she almost jumped. His fingertip traced the hollow of her back, under her jacket, revealed by the crop top. It barely lasted a second, no longer, and then a coolness where there had been heat.

She glanced behind her in time to catch the door closing behind Nicholas.

Shaken, she made it to the counter and placed her order with the teenage barista. He gave her the total, then grinned. "Sadia's at Kareem's school. Some kind of parent-teacher thing, if you were looking for her."

Livvy forced a smile. See? Entirely possible someone knew her. She'd never met this kid before. "Thanks." She checked his nametag. "Darrell."

"No problem."

She grabbed her latte from the counter when it was ready and walked to the door, part of her certain Nicholas would be gone, the rest of her hoping he'd still be there, waiting for her.

He was, standing next to her beat-up old car, leaning against the driver's side. His muscles were tensed, his hands curled into fists. She didn't know who he was looking to fight, but then she realized where he was looking.

The sign. *Kane's Café.* "Have you been inside since . . . ?"

"No." He cleared his throat. "I have not. Not since that double date we had with Sadia and Paul."

She had to think for a second, mine through her memories. She remembered that. A week or so before the accident. They'd had coffee and cookies.

"You were wearing a polka dot sweater," he murmured.

"I can't believe you remember that."

"I remember putting my arm around you, and Paul rolling his eyes and telling us to quit getting physical around him."

She huffed out a laugh. "I think I told him to stop hassling us."

"You did. Then you kissed me. He flicked water at us." His smile subsided. "How was that us?"

She understood what he was asking. Her life prior to the accident sometimes didn't feel like hers.

A spasm of pain crossed his face and she drifted closer to him. Understanding and echoing hurt coursed through her. "Yo. Stop leaning on Ruthie. She's delicate, you know."

He blinked and focused on her, some of that pain subsiding. It took him a second, and then he moved away from her car. "Paul didn't change much in there."

"No. I think he liked it the way it was." Paul had kept the same menu from her grandparents' days too. "Sadia's trying to upgrade things, but it's kind of expensive."

His face softened. "How is Sadia?"

"She wasn't there." Livvy took a sip of her latte, barely tasting it. She glanced around, but it wasn't quite five, and the parking lot was fairly empty. She'd parked closer to the edge, and they were hidden from the main road by a large tree.

It wasn't as good as meeting behind the place like a pair of clandestine lovers or drug dealers, but it would have to do.

"No. I mean how is she? In general?"

"She's good. She says she sees you around town sometimes."

"Yes. We don't talk to each other, because, well . . ."

"For what it's worth, she wouldn't react like Paul, if you did talk to her. I mean, she doesn't love you, but she'd be civil."

"It would be hard to top Paul's hatred of me." His eyes glinted. "We didn't cross paths much, but when we did, he was really good at looking right through me."

Her lips twisted. "If it makes you feel any better, he and I couldn't really see eye to eye either."

Nicholas shook his head. "No, that doesn't make me feel better. You should have had your brother."

She shifted her weight, surprised at the criticism on her behalf. "I couldn't be who he wanted. It's okay. I've kind of made peace with it." Much of her mourning after Paul's death had been over the loss of a possibility of a relationship with the man.

"Maybe someday I can too." Nicholas shoved his hands in his pockets. "Three days after Paul died, my father told me to buy this café from Sadia. I told him I approached Sadia and she refused to sell."

Livvy lifted an eyebrow. "You never approached her," she guessed.

"No." Nicholas smiled, but it was grim. "Paul would have haunted me forever for trying to rip his place from his widow. But if she needs money, I'm happy to pay over market value for it. I'm also happy to just give her money."

Despite any financial troubles Sadia might be having, Livvy doubted the other woman would be eager to sell the café or take charity. "I'll tell her, but I don't think she wants to sell. And she definitely wouldn't take your money."

"I figured." His smile was forced. "All you Kane women are on the proud side."

"Pride can keep you warm sometimes." Especially when you lost all of the people who kept the cold out.

"Tell me about it." He rolled his shoulders. "You're early."

There was something different in his tone, something hesitant. "Yeah, unlike me, I guess." She nodded in the general direction of Chandler's, unable to bring herself to look at it. "I thought maybe I could go inside there, face my past, blah blah, but couldn't manage it. Silly. It's just a store."

He glanced at the small café again. "Not silly at all."

"Someday," she allowed.

"Someday." He cocked his head. "We can head up to see my grandfather. We're a little early, but he won't mind. He was excited when I told him you agreed to see him."

"Okay, then. Do you want to take Ruthie or . . . ?"

"You never told me why you decided your car is a woman."

"Because no man could ever handle my ass for this long."

Nicholas smiled, his eyes softening. She had to look away. "I'll drive. Ruthie might be able to handle your ass, but she probably can't handle driving up a mountain."

Chapter 13

Nicholas had been exaggerating by saying his grandfather's house was up a mountain, but not by much. The trees were older, the growth of lawn heavier, but she knew this hilly road like the back of her hand. When Sam Oka and John Chandler had moved to this then-rural place in the middle of nowhere, they'd purchased neighboring tracts of land. After they'd established their empire and each gotten married—in a joint ceremony, no less—they'd built their homes.

Livvy gazed in the direction of her old house, her late grandpa Sam's home. She and Nicholas had run wild through these woods as children. As young adults, they'd made love in these woods.

And then later, Nicholas had broken her heart in these woods.

"Stop the car."

Nicholas didn't even hesitate, coming to an immediate halt. She stared out her window.

"Do you want to leave?" He didn't sound surprised.

She ran her hand over the pristine leather seat. "How's he doing?"

"Grandpa? Well, for his age. He has some pretty bad arthritis, so he uses a wheelchair now."

"Are you sure he doesn't hate me?" She wasn't proud of how plaintive she sounded.

She also wasn't proud of the rush of soothing comfort she experienced when his thumb brushed the back of her hand. "He doesn't hate you."

She rolled her shoulders. Shedding some of her baggage. "Okay. Let's go then."

"Are you sure?"

No. "Yes."

Livvy braced herself for the first sight of the house, but even then she felt like she'd been punched in the belly when the large stone estate came into view. Someone was maintaining it well, the garden John's late wife had so adored still thriving.

Nicholas parked in the circular driveway. She didn't wait for him to come around the side of the car, fumbling her way out of the passenger side.

Sweat broke out on her brow as they climbed the porch and he stopped in front of the door. "Are you sure, Livvy?" he asked again, this time with more than a touch of urgency.

Yearning and longing and terror whirled inside her, but she nodded. Fearful she would take him up on the next out he gave her, Livvy rang the doorbell.

It opened after a brief pause. The man standing behind the door was young and handsome and a stranger to her. His polite smile turned to familiarity when he caught sight of Nicholas. "Hey there."

"Hi, Chad. My grandfather's expecting us."

The younger man's gaze moved curiously between the two of them. "Sure. I can let him know you're here." He stepped aside.

The knot in her belly got worse as Livvy entered the home. Little had changed here, though the paint on the wall looked fresh, and the carpet had been swapped for hardwood. The air still held the familiar scent of vanilla and cookies.

Nicholas's fingers brushed the small of her back. "Still okay?"

"Yup." She firmed her spine. Without waiting for his urging, she walked into the living room, her feet retracing steps she'd taken for years.

Nicholas was behind her, but she forgot all about him when she saw the framed photo. She forgot about everything.

What was it doing here?

It wasn't a particularly large piece. It didn't have to be. She could close her eyes and recall every detail of the black-and-white photograph. Two young men, barely out of childhood, dressed in simple jeans and shirts, their arms around each other's shoulders, in front of a storefront. The white boy was solemn, the Asian boy's lips slightly curved, a devilish gleam in his eyes.

It had been taken a couple of weeks before Sam and his family had been sentenced to an internment camp for Japanese-Americans.

Another picture of her grandfather hung in a

museum in D.C., but that one had been taken by a photojournalist in the Central Utah camp where the Okas had been imprisoned. Sam's smile had been missing then, his eyes somber, his body leaner, having had to endure things no child should have.

This photo had graced the first C&O from the minute it opened to the day it burned down.

"How does he have this? This was destroyed in the fire."

Nicholas came to stand next to her. "I'm not sure. He tracked down the photographer, I think, and managed to get a copy."

"What took its place?"

"Nothing. My father wanted to put up our family portrait, but Grandpa blocked him on that. There's a blank spot in the front of the store."

She nodded, her body numb. That was good. Bad enough to be erased, but maybe worse to be replaced.

The whir of a power chair came from behind them. Livvy turned, that numbness protecting her from her anxiety. She dropped her hand from the frame.

John was older, of course, but he sat straight and tall in his wheelchair. Thick, bushy eyebrows lowered over eyes remarkably similar to Nicholas's. His mouth worked. "Livvy."

She took a hesitant step forward, part of her still caught in fear, though he'd been the one to ask her to come here. The fear he would tell her to get out, or that her family had ruined his.

But still, she couldn't stop that hopeful, needy step.

His jaw trembled, and then he did the best thing she could have imagined he'd do. He opened his arms.

Her pulse sped up at the gesture, at the pure, unadulterated eagerness to love her.

Without thinking, she crossed the room and crouched down, allowing him to pull her into his arms. He wasn't as strong as he used to be, his arms weak, but that didn't matter. He smelled faintly of cigars and dirt, of home and family and roots.

John smoothed her hair away, his calloused hand rough. He leaned back and beamed into her face, unashamed or unaware of the tears running down his cheeks. "Livvy?" he asked again, and another fresh wave of happiness ran through her at her name uttered in that gravelly voice. "Look at you. All grown up." He shook his head. "You're the spitting image of your grandma and mother."

She sniffed, long and loud, and wiped the back of her hand over her nose. "It's so good to see you."

"You're back. I can't believe you're back."

"No. I mean, yes, I'm back, but temporarily."

"How long will you be here?" John asked eagerly. "I don't know."

Displeasure crossed his face, followed by resignation, but he rallied. "Are you hungry? Nicholas, go tell that jailer you've hired that we could use some food and drinks. He's probably in the kitchen getting dinner ready."

"Stop calling Chad your jailer. He's your housekeeper."

"I know an old-people caretaker when I see one."

"He's here to help you with anything you need. A housekeeper," Nicholas said firmly.

John snorted as Nicholas left. "The boy thinks I'm an idiot." He squeezed her hands. "You have no idea how wonderful it is to see you. I've dreamed of this, you know."

"Me too." She hesitated. "I was scared to come here. I thought . . ."

"I'd shun you." He nodded, unsurprised. "After what my son did, that's a reasonable assumption for you to make."

"After what my father did, you mean," she corrected him. Her father and her brother, if John believed Jackson had set the fire.

"What your father did was an accident. What my son did was deliberate." John's nostrils flared.

She looked away, at the photograph of Sam and John. "It was a shock to see that here. A shock, but a nice one."

"It's yours."

"What?" She turned back to John.

"It's yours. I have another copy. I kept this for you and Jackson. That's part of your heritage. You should have it."

Her first instinct was to take it, but then reason prevailed. "I travel a lot. I—I have no home or anything to put it in."

John frowned. "Why do you travel?"

Because I keep trying to find what I lost. "I love seeing the country," she said brightly.

"Hmph." John didn't look convinced by that explanation. "Is Jackson here?"

She glanced at the doorway, which remained empty. If she could keep Nicholas from discovering Jackson was back, that would be good. No need to rile him up. "He was here briefly."

"I'd like to see him," John said, surprising her. "If you would tell him that."

"I can't guarantee he'll come."

Sadness came and went in the older man's gaze. "Tell him . . . the past is dead and buried for me. In case he fears anything."

"I will."

John stroked her hair again, as if he couldn't stop himself from touching her, and she leaned into the paternal gesture, so hungry for familial affection. It was all she could do not to demand more hugs.

"Now, tell me everything about you. You travel. Where have you been? What have you been doing?"

"I'm a tattoo artist."

"I know that much. I may be old as dirt, but I can google."

She smiled. "You're not old at all."

His lips quirked. "Keep lying to me, sweetheart. I knew you'd be an artist. Always doodling and coloring. Like your mama, when she was young."

Livvy wondered anew if her distant mother had ached after losing John in her life. "Mom never considered me an artist. I just—"

"Just permanently put your art on people's skin? Don't let your clients hear how little confidence you have in your work."

She wrinkled her nose. "Right. Reflex."

"Your mother is a good woman. If she puts pressure on you over your chosen profession, don't hold it against her—she probably sees too much of herself in you. I was always saddened that your father discouraged her from having a career as an artist."

"No, you're mistaken," Livvy said slowly. "My father didn't have a problem with my being an artist. He even convinced my mom to let me go to art school."

"Sometimes men have different goals for their wives and daughters. I say this with no animosity toward your father, Livvy, over what happened, but it was pretty obvious when Robert married your mother that part of her appeal was her wealth and social status. Her working as an artist didn't quite mesh with that."

The mural.

She remembered suddenly, her father's deep voice, sweet as always, as her mother put the finishing touches on the fairy tale mural in her and Jackson's bedroom. *Really, Tani, does this match the rest of the house? It seems a bit tacky to have this in our children's bedroom, no?* They'd painted over it not long after.

"I'm sorry. Forget I said anything. I didn't mean to speak ill of the dead."

"No, no. I'm an adult. I understand my parents weren't perfect." Except . . . as a child, it was natural to make one parent right and the other wrong. Her father, so loving and boisterous and generous and indulgent of her. Her mother, closed off and distant. Right. Wrong.

Livvy pushed the thoughts away, disquieted by even a hint that maybe there had been complexities in her parents' relationship she'd been unaware of. "My mom doesn't hassle me about my career anymore." *Because we don't talk about anything anymore.*

"How is Tani doing? Recovering from her injury?" John said her mother's name like a verbal caress. Tani and John's relationship had always been like parent and child.

"Yes, nicely."

"Getting old is fucking awful."

She smiled. "Yes, it is."

"I'm sorry about Paul. I wanted to come to the funeral so badly. But I feared upsetting you and Tani further."

She dipped her head, acknowledging his condolences. Would she have been less miserable that day, standing by the grave of her brother, if she'd known John and Nicholas had wanted to be there? Undoubtedly. It warmed her now, to know that support had been out there, even if she'd been unaware. "Thanks."

"A tragedy, that's what it was."

"Yes. A tragedy."

Nicholas reentered the room, his gaze softening as it rested on her and his grandfather. The old-fashioned tea cart he pushed didn't distract a bit from his rugged masculinity.

Nostalgia shot through her. The delicate porcelain tea set was white with pink roses on it. "Grandma Barb's tea set."

John's wife had been a kind, matronly sort who

had adored having all the grandchildren over for tea. She'd passed away when Liv was a child, but she'd had a few years to get to know the woman.

John's age-spotted hands curled in his lap. "I barely use it now. I don't have many visitors."

Nicholas snorted and set the cart in front of them. "You could, if you weren't so grumpy every time one of your old friends came to see you."

"I barely liked most of those bastards," John grumbled. "Can I be blamed for preferring the company of my garden?"

"Then don't complain you don't have any visitors," Nicholas said calmly.

"Asshole," John said affectionately.

Livvy grinned, glad to see age hadn't taken any of John's sharp tongue. The words this man had taught her.

John accepted the teacup and turned to her, a gleam in his eyes. "Now, tell me some sordid stories about life as a tattoo artist."

LIVVY HADN'T come home looking for a grandfather's love, but she'd found it. And she'd never be able to express how grateful she was.

She could easily have stayed on this couch for hours. Nicholas and his grandfather's relationship was as easy as it had always been, half joking, half loving. Nicholas barely swore, but he had no problem matching the elder man's salty tongue.

There was only one spot of tension, when John brought up some sort of media hubbub. "We're handling it," Nicholas said.

"I want to make sure we aren't slipping, Nicholas. People. Quality—"

"I know, Grandpa."

"Your father will want to pursue the bottom dollar. Well, that's not what Sam and I . . ." He paused and shot a guilty look at Livvy, who pretended not to have noticed the slip. "We didn't start this company with an eye toward only making a profit."

"Dad would say we're in a position to make the world a better place if we can make a profit."

"I—"

"Grandpa." Nicholas gave a single, firm shake of his head. "Not now."

His grandfather sighed, long and heavy, but subsided. "Very well. Keep me informed."

Livvy tried to pretend she wasn't absorbing this unusual new dynamic between grandfather and grandson, but that would be a lie. She guessed this was what Nicholas had been talking about when he said he was often in the middle of the two older Chandlers.

Nicholas took a bite of his cucumber sandwich, his big hand practically dwarfing the tiny, crustless sandwich. "I always do."

John grunted and nudged the plate of lemon squares toward Nicholas. "Here. I made your favorite dessert."

"Lemon squares aren't his favorite dessert."

Both men looked at her, and she ran her tongue over her teeth. "Or at least, they weren't."

Nicholas shook his head, taking the attention off her. "No, thanks, Grandpa. I'm good."

"You remember the sweet tooth he had, Livvy?" John mused. "He barely eats the good stuff now."

"You don't like sweets anymore?" He'd used to gorge himself on anything remotely sugar filled. He'd been lucky to have an equally fast metabolism.

"They aren't good for you," he said briskly, and picked up a cucumber sandwich.

She met his gaze. "Do you only like things that are good for you?"

"I try."

"Boring," John muttered, and passed the plate to Livvy. She picked up the lemon square and ate it slowly, catching the surreptitious glance Nicholas cast at her mouth as she nibbled on the tart sweet.

They talked more, Livvy relating a couple of the lighter, funny stories about her travels. She finally noticed the sun slipping away and checked her phone, wincing. "I have to get going."

"Is Tani by herself?" John asked.

"No, my aunt's with her, but I didn't tell them I'd be out so late." Tani probably wouldn't notice, but Maile would worry.

John looked disappointed, but nodded. "Of course."

"I can come back," she said tentatively, heartened when John beamed.

"Yes. Please."

Nicholas pushed his chair back. "Let me make sure Chad knows we're leaving, Grandfather."

He left the room, and Livvy watched him go.

"Do you know what Sam and I used to joke about?"

Livvy turned back to John and shook her head.

"That Tani and Brendan would grow up and fall in love. I even told Sam we should have betrothed them when they were young." His smile faded. "That wasn't to be. But then, you and Nicholas . . . ah, I had such dreams for you two. Uniting the two families would have been magnificent."

She licked her suddenly dry lips. "John, you understand, we're not back together."

"Nicholas grew up into a fine man," John replied, with enough hopeful eagerness that Livvy grimaced.

"He did."

"Of course, you already know that."

There were a million benign ways to read John's words, but a shiver ran down her spine. "What do you mean?"

John regarded her sympathetically, but there was a certain shrewd quality that reminded her of a fact she bet a lot of people overlooked. Yes, Brendan and Nicholas had been the ones to expand their empire, but John had been the one to lay the first brick. "I know your birthday, Livvy."

That shiver turned into a tremble. "So?"

"In the beginning I thought . . ." John stroked his finger over his late wife's teapot. "Well. Chandlers fall hard when they fall in love, after all. I assumed Nicholas was going off to mope somewhere. Then, one year, I happened to look at our flight records. He was flying somewhere, a different destination each time. All over the country." He inhaled. "I assume that was to see you?"

Her body ran hot, then cold. Mortification and panic mingled. "It meant nothing. Don't tell him you know about this. Don't tell anyone, please."

"I've kept it a secret, haven't I? Even covered for the boy when he got sloppy. I'm not telling you to embarrass you now, my dear."

"Then why?"

"I'm telling you if something were to develop between the two of you, I would approve. In fact, I would assist, in any way I could." He patted her hand.

"Nothing's going to happen." She thought of her and Eve's tussle at the bar. Of Brendan, and how he had coldly taken the company from her mother without a shred of remorse. "And I don't think the rest of your family would echo that sentiment."

Pain flashed in John's eyes. "If Nicholas didn't make it clear, my son and I don't speak to each other much anymore. I don't care what he thinks. I would protect you both from his foolishness for as long as I have breath in my body."

His generosity made her want to weep. "He mentioned you were estranged. I'm sorry. I know how that feels."

"I'm sure you do." John's shoulders hunched forward. "We've had a rough time of it, haven't we? Sometimes I wonder what Sam would say about all of this." John looked out the window, toward her old house. Sam's old house.

"He'd ask why we quit, maybe."

John turned to her. "You remember, huh?"

"Nothing's over until you quit," Livvy intoned.

John's smile was nostalgic. "Sam really was a rebel in certain ways. Like you. But no, I think he'd say something more along the lines of, how the fuck did you all get here?"

"Is that what he'd say, or what you would say?"

"One and the same, love." John sighed. "We were one and the same."

Chapter 14

NICHOLAS SHOT Livvy a glance as they walked out of the house, trying to read her expression. He wanted to ask her how she felt, if she was over-whelmed at seeing his grandfather, what the man had said to her. He wanted to gather her close and smooth her tangled hair. He wanted to do every damn boyfriendly thing under the sun he didn't have the right to do.

They reached his car, and he beat her to the pas-senger door. He opened it for her and waited, but she'd turned away to look west. The sun was setting over where Sam's house was hidden by the forest.

"Do you know who lives in our old home?"

"No," he answered honestly. "It was a family di-rectly after it was sold. Then an elderly couple, but they left. I think it's been vacant for a while." He hadn't checked the property records, though that would be easy to do. He hadn't particularly wanted to know.

She only nodded, but didn't move.

Nicholas had used to sneak into Livvy's room in

that house. The walls had been painted blood red, her comforter and furnishings all shades of black and white.

She wanted to die because you didn't love her anymore.

Jackson's words had been looping in Nicholas's head all day. He hadn't been able to concentrate on work, or his father's latest demands. All he could think about was a younger Livvy sobbing on the bed he'd lain in countless times.

She shifted, cocking her hip, a power pose she often adopted. Like him, she'd been raised to be assertive, powerful, certain of her place. She'd also been raised to keep a part of herself away from the outside world, visible only to the inhabitants of their privileged sphere.

No wonder she didn't betray the depth of her pain when you helped yank that place away from her.

He'd tried ignoring his own past and history, burying his emotions so deep he could go long stretches without feeling anything. He'd tried binging on her in secret, stolen, isolated bites, telling himself that the small hit of excitement was enough.

It wasn't now. He couldn't roll away and walk out the hotel door, shove her in a compartment and move on with his life. He'd been taken out of that box and wound up so tight he wasn't sure if he'd ever be able to go dormant again.

That didn't scare him, oddly enough. For all his worries over the cauldron of emotions inside him, for the first time in a long time, he felt as though he was on the right path. Not the perfect path. But the right path.

He pulled his phone from his pocket.

Her cell beeped, and she took her time getting it out of the back pocket of her low-slung jeans. Her fingers hovered over the message and she glanced at him.

The silence grew heavy and weighted, but then she gave a single nod and started walking toward the woods. He knew she wouldn't need to look up the coordinates he'd texted her. The numbers were burned into his mind as well as hers. She'd whisper them to him when they were kids, from the time they were fifteen and eighteen and wanted to go for a swim or hang out or meet up to chat. It had been innocent then. After they'd started dating, it had stopped being innocent.

He shut the car door and caught up to her, keeping his strides short. Funny how some things came back to him so easily, like how to match his walk to hers.

She looked up at the sky. "It'll be dark soon."

He gauged the remaining time they had. "Will your mother need you?"

"No. Aunt Maile's always home, and Mom's actually pretty self-sufficient." She shrugged, but the action looked heavy, like her shoulders weren't well equipped to carry the weight they did. "I'm not needed."

He curled his fingers into his palms, the sadness in those words making him ache. Did her family know? Livvy thrived on feeling needed. He used to murmur the words in her ear, simply to watch her blossom. *I need you. I want you.*

She grew stiffer as they drew closer to their special place, but she didn't demand they turn around. When they walked into the clearing, he caught the nostalgia and pain on her face. It was gone quickly, replaced by a blank stare.

She'd worn the same look when he'd told her they were finished.

Told her. It had been a speech, in the truest sense of the word, hadn't it?

She strolled around the small pond in the center of the clearing and knelt to run her fingers through the water. They'd played here, loved here. And in the end, they'd broken up here.

He hadn't sent her the coordinates that last time. He'd merely told her to meet him in the woods.

"Have you ever brought anyone else here?" she asked, staring at the water trickling through her fingers like they held the secrets to the universe.

He wasn't fooled by her nonchalance. "Of course not."

Another handful of water, seeping through her closed fingers. "Why not?"

"I would have felt like I was cheating on you."

Her throat worked as she swallowed. "That's dumb."

"It's probably why I haven't been able to maintain any long-term relationships," he said conversationally, pacing to the tree opposite the pond. "You either, right? You bristled when you saw me kissing Shel today."

"We have no claim on each other."

He chuckled, but he didn't feel any humor. The words he spoke were naked and revealing, and he couldn't stop them. "Livvy, for God's sakes. How can I be with anyone else when I spend three hundred and sixty-four days waiting for you to draw me a map?"

She went statue-still. "Is that what you do?"

"Yes. It's exactly what I do."

Her light brown skin paled. "I—"

"It's what you do too, isn't it?"

"It might be what I did." She shifted. "I stopped. Like I said, ten years is long enough to get it out of our systems."

"Yeah." He traced the letters carved into the tree. "You'd think so."

The soft pad of her footsteps behind him made him ache. Her smaller hand came to rest just above the inscription. "I can't believe it's still here."

"Where would it go?"

"Thought you might have chopped the damn thing down." There was a quiver to her tone, belying her cockiness.

The words were carved in deep, made in the first flush of their love affair, not long after the first time they'd had sex.

NICO + LIVVY = 4EVER

A childish sentiment. A promise they'd made when they hadn't understood what forever was or how it could be destroyed. "Remember when I carved this?"

"Yes."

"You said the only bad part of our relationship was that it was so easy. We slipped from friendship to lovers so quickly. We never had to woo each other."

Her lips trembled into a smile. He doubted she was aware of how wistful it appeared. "Could you blame a girl for wanting a grand declaration of love every now and again?"

"No. I could never blame you for anything." His hand dropped away from the tree. "Why'd you agree with me, that night?"

"What night?"

"The night we broke up."

Her guffaw was loud. "I don't want to talk about this."

"Why not?"

"It wouldn't change anything."

"The past can never be changed."

"Right. So why bother tearing it apart now?"

One feeling. "Someone smart told me talking about stuff can help."

She crossed her arms over her chest. "Has a pod person taken over your body? I'd like to speak to Nicholas, please."

"Livvy, I'm not going to move until you tell me why you agreed with me back then."

"Then I'll walk home," she snapped and pivoted.

"Why don't you want to talk about this?"

She stopped, her shoulders hunched. He kept forgetting how small she was. Her personality was so big. "It's not something I like to think about."

"I need to know."

She looked at him. Annoyance, fear, and, finally, resignation flitted across her expressive face. "What you said made sense. Being together would have been too hard after everything."

No, he hadn't said being together would be too hard. He'd said it would be impossible. *It's impossible for us to be together now. They won't let us.* "Did you want to end things?"

"No!"

He couldn't breathe. "No."

"No, okay? I wanted to fight. I wanted to fight for you, and I wanted you to fight for me, and that didn't happen, because that shit only happens in fairy tales."

He was choking under the weight of their history. "You lied. You told me I was right. You agreed it would be impossible." Every time he'd doubted himself, he'd tell himself she'd wanted their breakup too. That it had made rational sense, even without his father's meddling.

"Fighting for someone only works when the other person wants to be saved. I couldn't fight for you knowing that you'd already given up." Her smile was bittersweet. "Nothing's impossible until you quit, remember?"

Chandlers aren't quitters.

She took a deep breath as if to brace herself. "You did quit, didn't you?"

"I had to."

"No, you—"

"I *had* to." His raised voice startled the birds in the trees, sending them flying away in a great flock.

A line formed between her brows. "Because of the accident? It colored your feelings for me."

"No." He licked his lips. His heart was beating fast, his blood rushing in his veins. It felt . . . it felt so right. *Tell her.* "I didn't end things with you because my feelings changed for you. The last time we stood here, I loved you. I honestly did." *I never stopped loving you.*

No, too soon.

She didn't look impressed. "You loved me but—"

"My father made me."

Livvy drew back. "What?"

Nicholas ran his hand over his mouth, the words tasting like betrayal.

Family came first.

He knew that shouldn't apply when that family was abusive. His brain was at war with the reflexive instincts that had been honed in him since he was a child.

He had to overcome those instincts. The questions in Livvy's dark eyes demanded honesty. "My father made me do it. He made me break up with you."

"You mean he disapproved of us being together."

"It wasn't only disapproval." How could he explain a lifetime of dysfunction and resentment and emotional manipulation? "Brendan hated your dad. Despised him."

"For driving that night."

"Partially."

Livvy's gaze was hooded. "Eve said there were rumors my dad and your mom were having an affair."

He jerked back. "Eve said that?" He hadn't known Eve was aware of those rumors, though of course she wouldn't have discussed them with him.

"I assumed she was trying to hurt me . . . but that's what people believe?"

"Some people," he admitted reluctantly.

"That's foolish. My father would never have cheated."

Nicholas wasn't as certain about his mother. His parents had displayed a near-perfect image of marital bliss for the world, but he could remember the fights. He couldn't blame Maria if she had gone elsewhere to find affection. "I don't think my mom would've betrayed Tani like that. There were a million innocent reasons for them to be on that road, in that car together." He'd believe them too, even if it did mean a lot of questions went unanswered.

Sometimes all the questions couldn't be answered.

"Is that the other reason Brendan hated my dad? Was it the rumors?"

Nicholas raised one shoulder. "He does hate any kind of negative gossip, but honestly, I think he despised Robert even before the accident. Your dad got promoted to co-CEO with John. My dad had to technically report to both of them." Robert had been an outsider, neither Chandler nor Oka, yet he'd leapfrogged over Brendan, who had occupied Nicholas's current subordinate position at the time. Nicholas had always sensed a barely hidden resentment in his father's attitude toward Robert. "After Robert died, Brendan transferred that anger and resentment over to your whole family. He wanted you all gone. He got rid of Tani by taking the shares, but then there was us."

"When you said your father made you break up with me, what do you mean? Specifically?"

"He put financial pressure on me."

"He threatened to disinherit you?"

His jaw clenched. "Not me."

Her eyes went wide. "Eve?"

He closed his eyes, only opening them when a small hand ghosted over his arm. "Livvy, she was thirteen. I felt like I had no choice." On a practical level, even if Brendan cut Eve out, Nicholas would have taken care of her. But the damage would have been done. Young Nicholas hadn't been able to bear the thought of Eve knowing Brendan viewed her as nothing more than a disposable pawn.

Hell, he still couldn't bear to see his sister's pain every time Brendan ignored or dismissed her. But their father's negligence toward her was a step up from outright disowning, or so he told himself.

"Why didn't you tell me then?"

"I couldn't." A pleading tone had entered his voice, one he didn't recognize. The Kanes had been as close to family as one could get, but Brendan had always been very careful about making sure no one but his wife and son saw the true extent of his coldness. "I didn't know if you'd believe me and I didn't want to make things harder than they had to be."

She slowly moved her head from side to side. "I would have wanted you to tell me. I was so hurt after."

She wanted to die. His heart thudded.

"I would have loved having a villain. Someone I could fight." Livvy's smile was tremulous. "I would have made you fight."

"I don't know if I could have fought," he admitted, unable to hide the trace of shame in his words.

"I know," she said, surprising him. "I get why you kept it from me. In hindsight, you probably made the right call. Either way, your family would have been destroyed like mine was. Present me finds that thought really terrible."

"My family was destroyed anyway." His voice was so guttural he could barely recognize it.

A tear leaked out. "It would have been worse."

Her concern humbled him. Yes, this was the woman he'd fallen in love with all those years ago. Soft and sweet and considerate, hiding under multicolored hair and a layer of pure steel. Nicholas took another step closer, until they were standing toe-to-toe. He dipped his head and breathed in her sweet, delicate scent. Vanilla cream.

He lowered his mouth to hers. The kiss was soft and sweet at first, only their lips brushing against each other. He ran his palm over her cheek and angled her so he could deepen the kiss. His tongue sank into her mouth and she stood on her tip-toes, rubbing up against him.

Her mouth was criminally addictive. It always had been. He tilted her head back and kissed his way along the curve of her neck, finding the spot that revved her up. She writhed against him and he gripped her hips and backed her up against the tree, her hands falling to the rough bark. "Livvy," he breathed.

"Yes," she whispered, both consent and appreciation. She shrugged off her jacket. He licked her lips and brushed his tongue against hers, pulling it into his mouth to suck and lick at it. His hands slid over her back and bottom, pulling her close so his cock nestled into the cleft between her legs.

"I want to . . . right here."

"Yes," she whispered again. With a jump he had her hoisted between him and the tree, her legs wrapped around him and interlocking at the base of his spine. His hand rested against the bark, the scrape a harsh reminder that her delicate skin would get messed up if they actually fucked here.

He whirled around and fell to his knees with her still wrapped around him like a koala, and tumbled her down to the ground.

He couldn't begin to count the number of times they'd made love right here, their bodies straining together under the sky, back in the days when they'd been so hungry they could barely keep their hands away from each other. Each time they'd come together in some generic hotel room, part of his brain had been fantasizing that they were both right here.

Where they belonged.

He ripped at the buttons of his shirt, and she helped him before unbuckling his belt and unzipping his trousers. Her crop top—why wear half a top, he wasn't sure—left her belly bared, but he shoved it up so he could get to her breasts, pulling her bra down so he could fondle her flesh.

He kissed his way down her neck, biting and sucking at the flesh at the hollow of her throat, knowing he was skirting the edge of pain, that he'd leave a mark.

Not caring.

He paused to strip her jeans down her legs, then her panties. "Sorry," he panted, when the fragile silk came apart in his hands. "Is this—?"

"It's fine. Just—yes. Yes, fuck me."

He stopped when he was poised on the edge of penetration. He didn't push his way inside her, but waited, teasing her lips with the tip of his cock. "I love this. This moment, right before I get inside you," he said in a gravelly voice.

She ran her hands up his biceps and pulled at him, but he wasn't budging. He dipped his cock inside, letting her wetness coat his flesh.

"Stop teasing me."

Didn't she get it? He wasn't teasing her. Something momentous had shifted in his brain, some understanding that had taken ten years to get through his thick skull.

He'd made a terrible mistake. Clouded by grief and fear and yes, anger. He'd quit and thrown away someone he should have fought for.

Her legs tightened around his waist like a vise and she yanked him forward. Unable to resist the call of her body, he sank inside her with a deep groan, the shocking heat of her pussy making him shake. He raised himself on stiffened arms the second she froze beneath him.

"No condom," he rasped. It had been so long since he'd fucked her bare. Whenever they'd met, she'd flung a strip of rubbers at him, or he'd produced his own.

Her nails stroked along his spine. "I'm on birth control. And I'm . . . I'm clean."

He shuddered. "I am too."

Those nails dragged down to his ass. "Just do it."

Oh, God. "Do what? Fill you up with my come?"

"Yes."

"Say it."

"Fill me with—" He hit a particularly deep spot, and she shook. "Fill me with your come."

He fucked into her with slow strokes. He gazed down at her, mesmerized, as her head tipped back, and she moaned. The sun was almost gone, the hazy blue-gray sky turning her body into a dreamy portrait. Past and present and future melded together, forcing his body to move faster. He needed her to feel him inside her, in every inch.

She communicated in breathy gasps, her hands coming up to encircle his neck. She arched below him, her thighs falling wide. He wanted to be tender. He wanted to be kind. But his lust took over, until he had nothing in his brain but the elemental, desperate need to fuck her until she couldn't walk, until he couldn't move.

His hips snapped back and forth. Faster, and faster, until her body clenched all around his. Each contraction squeezed his throbbing cock like a vise.

His balls drew up tight, and he thrust deep, spurting inside her. Each pulse simultaneously weakened him and filled him with strength. He locked his arms to keep from collapsing on top of her and hung his head, panting.

They were both covered in sweat, but the cool air was working through his lust-induced warmth. Nicholas sat back, attention riveted on his still-hard cock withdrawing from her. He grasped his dick, his hand feeling too rough and unwelcome after the paradise of her pussy, and rubbed the wet tip against her slit.

"Look at that," he rumbled. "What a mess we made."

He stroked up to her clitoris. His heart stuttered when she breathed, "Nico . . ."

He went still. No one had called him Nico since her.

He batted the head of his cock against her pussy, then braced himself on one arm above her and pressed his lips to her neck. "You want more?" He rubbed her clit with his cock in a slow circle. "I can give you more. I can give you everything."

She stiffened beneath him then pressed her

hands against his chest, straight-arming him away. Shit. Had he said the wrong thing?

Nicholas moved back immediately, though with great reluctance. He didn't want to separate their bodies. That meant they'd have to go back to thinking.

She sat up and scrambled to her feet way faster than he would like. It took him a second to get his legs under him and stand without wobbling. "Hey."

She ignored him and scooped up her jeans, shoving them up over her legs.

He adjusted his own clothes absently. "Hey," he said again.

"What?" she snapped.

Uh-oh. He *had* said something wrong. "Listen, what if—?"

"I don't like that word."

"What word?"

She readjusted her bra. "If."

"Then I won't use it. But can we talk?"

"I need to go. Take me back to my car."

He needed time to figure out what was happening between them, or, hell, what was happening in his own head. "Livvy—"

She turned away and started walking, jerking her jacket over her breasts. Leaves clung to her hair. "Either take me back to my car, or I'm walking."

"Don't be like this."

"Like what?"

Poking and prodding. Overwhelmed from all the confessions he'd shared with her, her snotty tone rubbed him exactly the wrong way. "Dramatic," he snapped, and then grimaced, a chill running through him at the way she spun around and glared at him.

Maria, for God's sake, stop acting so dramatic.

Drama was cold Brendan's sworn enemy. *Like father, like son.*

Oh, fuck. Never.

"That's what I am." Her shoulders were set and rigid. "A moody drama queen. Now take me back to my car."

Chapter 15

Livvy flopped on her bed, face-down, like a proper drama queen.

Dramatic.

Well, fuck you too, Nicholas.

She'd refused to speak with Nicholas in the car ride back to town. She'd held her emotions in admirable check on the drive home. She'd showered quickly and then smiled throughout the delicious steak and potatoes dinner her aunt had saved for her and ate every bite, though she wasn't hungry. She'd gamely tried to engage her mom in conversation about the sitcom they watched after dinner, only to be rebuffed. She'd cleaned up the kitchen, thrown a load of laundry in the washing machine, and whistled while she did it, every ounce of energy being poured into appearing calm.

Dramatic. Moody. Emotional. Temperamental. Artistic. There were so many adjectives she'd been tagged with from people who couldn't and wouldn't understand her.

I can give you everything.

She pressed her hand over her heart, the spike of

hope and excitement coursing through her again. She hated him so much for giving her that high, because the truth was simple and stark.

He couldn't.

She wasn't a fool. She believed Nicholas when he said his father had made him end things with her. Brendan was totally capable of something so ruthless—hadn't he cheated her mother out of her half of the company?

Livvy believed he'd been reluctant to leave her and loved her then, and that did bring a measure of peace to her heart. But the second he'd started to talk about *ifs*, she'd reached her limit.

He might still have feelings for her, but that didn't mean he'd ever want or be able to give her more. She deserved more. She did.

Keep saying that, squeaked the tiny defenseless part of herself that sometimes wondered if she deserved anything.

Lethargy tugged at her body, the desire to crawl under the covers and not get up. Resolutely, she rolled to her feet instead. A few more things. She could manage a few simple tasks first. Opposite action.

Livvy placed her phone on the nightstand. After she got under those covers, she knew she'd stare obsessively at the coordinates he'd sent her for the first time in forever, tracing every familiar number, but she'd put that off as long as humanly possible.

She took off her clothes and popped them in the hamper in the corner. She grabbed a button-down flannel sleep shirt from a drawer and drew it on, pressing the fabric to her nose to inhale the comforting scent of laundry detergent and softener. It only marginally calmed the emotions twisting her insides into a knot.

As she buttoned it up, she glanced around, wishing she'd left the place a mess so she could tidy it up and feel accomplished about something. She opened the closet door, but all her clothes had been neatly unpacked from her duffel and hung on hangers. Cursing past-her for her diligence, she started to pace, stopping when she realized how frenetic her motions were getting.

She wrapped her arms around her waist and inhaled and exhaled deeply. Okay. Okay. She needed a breather. Boxes. Her feelings were too big and overwhelming, and they were leaking right out of her. Time to contain them.

Livvy skirted the bed and plopped down on the floor, resting against the wall.

She ran her hand against her leg and slowly, using her index finger, traced a box around the head of the dragon inked into her flesh.

Look at you. You're a disaster.

Put the negative thoughts into the box. Find a counter thought. "I deserve compassion," she whispered and moved to the pot of gold at her hip. A tiny box around that, her very first tattoo.

You shouldn't have come home. You're not tough enough for this.

"I've been through a lot of shit, and I survived. Life is worth living, even with the shit in it." The vine now.

He doesn't love you.

"I can love myself." Another flower. "I'm a good person." Her finger pressed deeper into her flesh. "I can keep figuring it out. I'm doing the best I can."

She arched her back and reached behind her, though the twist was awkward. She bled her feelings into every design but the compass was her favorite tattoo, with its watercolor splash and blurred pigment, like a drawing left out in the rain.

She couldn't quite contort enough to draw a box here, so she stroked it. "I deserve compassion," she repeated, and then kept repeating it until she could feel the knot inside her unravel.

It was a tiny easing, but it was enough to stave off her panic spiral. She closed her eyes and rested her head against the wall, not releasing contact with her compass.

She wasn't sure if she fully believed the words her therapist had given her to keep in her arsenal, but they helped. And one day, if she said them enough times, maybe she could absolutely believe them.

Her phone beeped, shattering the silence of the room. She wanted to ignore it, but it was late enough that it could be an emergency. Her movements were sluggish as she got her feet.

Nicholas. A new message, right below those damn coordinates.

I was going to throw a rock against your window, but I'm not sure if it's yours.

Her *window*?

She texted back. **???**

His reply was immediate. **Look outside.**

No. He couldn't possibly be . . .

She walked over to the window, brushed the curtain aside, and peered into the darkness. She was situated on the side of the house, a large lawn right below.

And on that lawn stood Nicholas, looking up at her. The moon was full, gilding his dark hair and the sharp angles of his face. He'd changed out of his suit into a pair of worn jeans and a light-colored, long-sleeved sweater.

What the hell?

She tried to yank open the window. The damn thing was stuck, dried paint sealing the jambs.

"What are you—?" she started to say loudly, but then realized she might wake up her mom and aunt by screaming through the glass. She typed into her phone instead. **What are you doing??**

He glanced down at the phone in his hands and responded. **I wanted to see you.**

> **So you're lurking? I thought we established you're shitty at that.**

His half-smile made her want to smile back. Instead, she scowled.

> **I think I'm doing a pretty good job.**
>> **No lurker wears white. You wear black. You want to meld into the shadows.**

He ran his hand over his chest. Ugh, why did he have such a hot chest? **The moon is full tonight. I wouldn't be able to meld even if I wore black.**

Her fingers flew. **Then you should leave lurking to the professionals. There's no value in it for amateurs.**

I don't know. It gets your attention.

The phone rang, and she hesitated for a beat. He raised his device to his ear and mimed picking up.

She pressed her lips tight, unable to resist him. "What?" she snapped. "I'm busy."

"You don't look busy." His voice was low, designed not to carry. His gaze dropped over her body. The flannel shirt covered her arms and up to the tops of her thighs. It wasn't sexy.

He looked at her like she was wearing the tiniest of negligees.

"You look beautiful," he finished.

Call her vain, but she absorbed his compliment like a sponge soaking up tiny droplets of water. Livvy was suddenly glad she'd left the top button undone, the upper curves of her breasts visible. "Thanks."

"Unbutton that shirt a little more."

She regularly wore corsets and miniskirts, but she clutched the lapels of her shirt together like an outraged aunt and glared down at him. "I will not."

"Come on. If I'm such a creeper, give me something to creep on."

She was tempted to smile, but she controlled her face. "Creepers don't get rewarded."

"Probably a good policy." Nicholas moved closer, into a brighter patch of moonlight. His lips moved, his husky voice caressing her ear. "I'm sorry I called you dramatic. I want to see you again."

She swallowed, hating that leap of happiness. *I can give you everything.*

He couldn't. "You're seeing me."

"I mean see you properly. Not because I'm escorting you to my grandfather or because you're driving my sister home, but because we want to be in each other's company."

She twisted the button on her shirt. "I don't see the point in that."

"I thought I showed you the point of it in the woods." He screwed up his face. "Ah, that was not supposed to be a euphemism."

Her lips trembled, but she controlled her smile at the unexpectedly silly joke. "Like you said, I'm not good for you." She wouldn't be able to forget his words anytime soon. *I know you're not good for me, but I can't seem to stop wanting you.*

"I *did* think you were bad for me."

She managed to stop herself from showing pain. "Yeah, well, I'm trying to be healthy too, Nicholas."

He ran his hand over his face. When he finally spoke, his voice was hoarse. "I said I *did* think you were bad for me. Now, though . . . Didn't you feel better today? After we talked?"

"Yes." *Until I felt myself latching on to the crumb*

of a possibility for a future for us. She couldn't allow herself to do that.

"I think I need that."

"You've never liked chatting before."

"When we were young, I did. Remember how we'd lay on the ground and talk for hours?"

"I talked."

"You talked more than me. But I talked."

She conceded that with a reluctant nod. He'd always been reserved, from the time he was a young boy, but he'd shared a lot with her, even before they started dating.

He pressed his fist over his heart. "We've tried staying away from each other. We tried just fucking each other. It hasn't gotten me anywhere, and I don't think it's helped you either. Maybe we could . . . I don't know. Try spending time with each other. Talking."

She could feel herself weakening, responding to the pleading in his voice. She should hang up, right now. She knew she was too weak where he was concerned.

She worried that button. "We can't talk without boning. I think that's pretty apparent."

"So we'll bone." He put his hand up when she would have talked. "The sex isn't the problem. Yeah, what we were doing, our arrangement all those years, that was bad for both of us. We could make things healthier between us. No binging. Guilt-free, rules-free, two consenting adults who respect each other."

She pressed her fingertips against the window, so tempted it hurt. Livvy could see the sense in what he was saying. That burden on her shoulders had eased a tiny bit every time they'd honestly engaged with each other.

"No one will know. This won't hurt anyone," he said quietly. "But it might help us."

The second part of their long-standing agreement. *One night. No one will know.*

You can't ever think anything will come of this. No dreaming of weddings or walking hand-in-hand next to a duck pond. He didn't know everything about her, all the dark and messy things. She'd kept those from him even when they were young. A not-so-tiny, insecure part of her had always feared he wouldn't want her if he saw it all.

Plus, if she took her heart out of the equation totally, she could say she didn't want a relationship with him, not when it meant he'd have to fight his family. She also didn't want to fight hers, not when she was here to rebuild those ties.

She was so tired of fighting. "Okay," she murmured, tracing a circle on the window.

"Okay?"

"Okay."

A smile split across his face, and her finger jerked. She'd forgotten how breathtakingly handsome Nicholas was when he smiled. "Now will you take off your shirt?"

Her lips twitched, and she acknowledged the dare in his eyes. He thought she wouldn't? She wasn't sure what she'd ever done to give him the idea she was inhibited when it came to her body.

She tucked the phone between her shoulder and her ear so she could flick open the buttons, appreciating both the flare of heat in his eyes and his increased breathing. When the shirt was open, she ran her hand down the center of her chest, over her belly, and cupped her naked pussy.

"Come downstairs," he murmured.

"I shouldn't."

"You should. What we did in the woods wasn't enough for you. Come out here and let me take care of that wetness between your thighs." He hung up before she could reply or agree.

Because he knew she wouldn't not come, the bastard. She tossed her phone on the bed and buttoned her shirt as she left the room, creeping through the dark house.

She went out through the back door and padded barefoot over the grass, barely conscious of the chilly air or the goosebumps it left on her exposed skin. She didn't see Nicholas at first, jumping when he spoke from the shadows closest to the house. "Come here."

She drifted closer to him, the sense of danger making her wetter. "I take it back. Not bad at skulking."

"I've graduated from lurking to skulking?"

"It's a definite upgrade."

He hooked his arm around her waist, and in two seconds had her pressed against the vinyl siding of the house. Nicholas's booted feet came between her bare ones as he crowded her. "Are you cold?"

"Yes." She wrapped her arms around his neck and stood on her tiptoes to whisper in his ear. "Warm me up."

He hummed. "You smell so good."

"That's the flowers." A trellis was right next to her, a few blooms of a fragrant flower from the last remnant of summer still clinging stubbornly to the vine.

He dipped his head and buried his face against her neck. "No, it's you. Vanilla and sweetness." His big fingers quickly manipulated the shirt, opening her to his touch. His hand went to her breasts, fondling the flesh, coaxing the nipples to tight, rigid points. When she reached for his belt buckle, he leaned back, grabbed her wrists, and brought both hands above her head. "Let me," he whispered, and waited for her nod.

He kept her wrists up and away, and stroked his fingers down over her stomach, smiling when her muscles tensed. That teasing touch slipped between her legs. He hissed a curse when he found her slippery and wet.

He pressed his forehead against hers, his eyes trained on her face as she shivered and shook under his leisurely caresses. When she strained closer, he gave her a kiss, but his kisses were as shallow and teasing as the play of his fingers on her clit.

"Please," she gasped into his mouth. She twisted her caught hands until they could grasp his, their fingers twining together.

He drew away, enough so he could speak, his breath puffing against her lips. "Please what?"

"Harder."

He circled her clit and released her hands. "Hold yourself open for me."

Trembling, she slid her hand down her body, until her fingers could slide over her pussy. She made a vee of her fingers and spread her lips.

His hand left her for a second, and then three fingers landed on her clit in a gentle slap. She tilted her head back, crying out, but his big palm was there to capture the sound.

Her breath came in shallow gasps, and she stared into his dark, merciless eyes. "Do you like this kind of spanking too?"

She nodded.

His lip curled up, and he delivered tap after tap, alternating with lazy fingering, speeding his motions up when she grew grasping and greedy.

He captured her cries with his lips when she came, making sure no one could hear them. When she was finished, he drew away and carefully buttoned her shirt. Then he dropped a chaste kiss on her cheek. "Come to my place tomorrow."

He'd just spanked and finger-fucked her, but that innocent, careless kiss was what made her blush.

Intimate.

No. Talking was fine. Putting their past to rest was fine. Dreaming of more was not. She shook her head. "Not your place. Someone might see."

His lips compressed, but he only said, "Right. I'll text you a location then."

His thumb stroked over her cheek, the caress making her feel temporarily cared for and protected.

She shivered. That was the key word. She couldn't lose sight of that qualifier. Temporary.

Chapter 16

Livvy blew on the surface of the hot coffee she held, the silence of the café calming her. She'd only stopped by Kane's after hours to pick up some of the day's excess sandwiches for dinner—she'd officially given up on navigating the kitchen at home—but she was glad she'd accepted Sadia's offer of a cup while her sister-in-law got the food together.

Livvy took a sip, a frightening level of contentment filling her. For most of her adult life, Livvy hadn't been able to experience happiness without pain. Guilt and sadness and darkness were like a fine overlay on her entire life, a veil with the power to tarnish anything good that came her way.

For the past week, though, every night she'd spent with Nicholas had been simply . . . happy.

There had been a little twinge when she'd snuck out to see him. A prick when she had to creep back into her mother's house or lie about having a shift at work. A wince when she drove up to another hotel room. A trickle when she grew relieved that her mother was rapidly improving in stability and mobility so she didn't feel so bad about not being home when she wasn't working.

Other than that, though, she was wallowing in this extended-pleasure portion of her Nicholas Pleasure/Pain Cycle.

They didn't just fuck, though—Livvy shifted in her seat, wincing a bit—yes, there was definitely fucking happening. When they were finished, she snuggled into his arms, her head on his chest, and they would talk.

They spent most of their time discussing the things they'd done separate from their shared history, tip-toeing around their families and the company. The places she'd been, the things she'd seen, how she'd grown her skills and business while moving constantly. He'd traveled internationally quite a bit, while she'd never gone farther than Canada. They'd had the money for it when she was a kid, but her mother had been terrified of long flights.

She listened quietly as he told her about Paris, and then badgered him about his visit to the Louvre, forcing him to recount in excruciating detail every exhibit he could remember.

She'd ached when he'd drowsily pressed a kiss to the top of her head and murmured, "You should go there sometime."

She'd go, maybe. But not with him, and she wanted his perspective on every painting and sculpture.

The first night, she'd woken up after they'd fallen asleep, certain he'd left the hotel room. But, no, there he'd been next to her. She'd been so relieved she hadn't even minded the way his big body had sprawled across the majority of the bed. She hadn't minded, but she'd still nudged him until he rolled over with an annoyed mutter, giving her more space. It was the principle, after all.

She'd contemplated leaving, but finally decided against it, marking another subtle shift in their relationship. They left together now, no one around in the predawn hour to catch them.

Livvy was no dummy. She knew what was coming. There was pain on the horizon.

She'd deal with it. It would be hard, and possibly bad, but this was worth it.

Her best friend bustled out of the kitchen and dropped a tray in front of her. Livvy eyed the tower of sandwiches and baked goods covered by cling wrap. "You weren't kidding. That's a lot of leftovers."

"Business was slow today." Sadia placed two plates in front of them and sank into the seat with a sigh. "Here, grab a bite before you leave."

Sadia looked as tidy and sensible as ever, in her jeans and T-shirt and sneakers, but there was an air of weariness about her. "You doing okay?" Livvy asked.

"Oh yes. Of course." Sadia nudged aside the plastic wrap, picked up a scone from the tray, and started to crumble it on her plate.

After careful deliberation, Livvy went with a cookie. She bit into it, chewed, and swallowed. "Huh. Did Rick change the recipe?"

"Why? Is something wrong?"

Livvy raised an eyebrow at the sharpness in the question. "No. It tastes a little different, is all."

Sadia cleared her throat. "I made that batch, actually."

Weird. Sadia was no baker. "Is Rick out sick?"

"No. He, um, retired."

"What?" That was huge news. Rick had been at the café for as long as she could remember. The menu he'd crafted was small but his emphasis on fresh ingredients had helped endear the place to locals.

Sadia continued crumbling the scone. "He wanted to spend more time with his grandkids."

"When did this happen?"

"Right about the time you got back."

"And you've been doing all the cooking since?"

Sadia shrugged.

If Sadia was playing chef as well as manager, that meant she was probably waking up before the sun to get into the kitchen. How was she even functioning? "Why didn't you tell us?"

"Mom and Aunt Maile know. I didn't think it was that big of a deal. You had so much on your plate."

"And you don't?" Guilt crawled through Livvy. "I'm the worst friend."

Sadia cocked her head. "How's that?"

"I should have known something was up with you. I think I did know, but I wanted to give you space."

"You're not psychic, and I do like space." Sadia's smile was faint. "Let's save some time and energy and agree not to feel bad about silly things. I know you love me."

Livvy bumped her knee against her friend's. "I do love you. I'd like to help."

"Have you been hiding your cooking skills all this time?" Sadia asked hopefully.

"Unless you count omelettes, no."

"Yeah. Me neither." Sadia looked down at her plate. Her best friend's shoulders slumped infinitesimally.

Which was basically a full-on wail of despair from anyone else. "Oh, Sadia."

She rubbed her forehead. "It's fine. I'll find someone soon. I can't afford not to."

"That sounds dire," Livvy said cautiously.

Sadia's exhale was loud. "When Paul died, I discovered he'd taken out a couple of loans."

"Big loans?"

"Big enough. Oh, we were fine while he was alive. I know it's not what he'd planned on doing with his life, but Paul was good at running the café. He knew the business and he had that magnetic personality, you know?" Sadia blinked, hard. "People wanted to be around him."

Livvy placed her hand on her sister-in-law's shoulder and handed her a napkin, her sinuses feeling a little tickle. Sadia was so stoic, it was easy to forget she'd lost her husband not too long ago. "He did. I'm sorry."

Sadia wiped her eyes. "I'm not Paul. I'm not a business genius or a magnetic person."

"I have savings—" Livvy began, but Sadia shook her head.

"I can't take money from you."

"I'm family, as you like to point out. And those are my brother's debts."

"And now they're mine," Sadia said quietly. "Mine to deal with. Just because I didn't know about them is no reason for you to have to hand over your life savings."

She thought about Nicholas's offer. Livvy hated feeling so useless. "What if I could get you more than market value for the café?"

For a second, Sadia looked tempted, but then she shook her head. "What would I do if I didn't have this place? I have a high school degree and no real skills. I can't move, and take Kareem away from your mom and my sisters and his cousins. My choices are limited."

"I want to help you."

"You are." Sadia pressed her hand over Livvy's and squeezed. "You're here."

"I'm going to leave soon." She said it more for herself than for Sadia.

"I know." Sadia lifted a shoulder. "I didn't mean you're here physically. Being able to see you like this, for a day or a week or a month, is great, but I meant you're here." She indicated her heart. "I'm always in your pocket and you're always in mine, aren't you?"

Livvy swallowed around the lump in her throat. "Always."

"Plus, I'm going to assume I'll see you more now, right?"

"Yes." She wouldn't be able to stay away for another decade, no matter what happened with Nicholas. She needed these connections far too much.

Sadia relaxed. "Good. You have much more to teach Kareem. I caught him explaining to his friend that his cool aunt Livvy is a *fucking tattoo artist*."

Livvy squeezed her eyes shut. "Oh no."

"Oh yes."

"I'm so sorry. I swear, I'll watch my mouth next time I babysit." The words fell from her lips so easily. *Next time.*

Sadia, thank God, looked more amused than annoyed. "Please. Now, tell me what you've been doing. I haven't seen you all week."

What am I doing, or who am I doing? Yeah, she wasn't quite ready to talk about Nico. "I saw Grandpa John," she said quietly.

Sadia pursed her lips in a soundless whistle. "Wow."

"Yes."

"What was that like?"

"Fantastic. Better than anything I could have imagined." She wrapped her arms around herself. "He hugged me."

"As he should. You're eminently huggable."

"He said he would have come to Paul's funeral, but he didn't want to upset us."

A shadow moved behind Sadia's eyes. "How kind of him."

"Nicholas said the same thing."

"Nicholas? You saw him again?"

Livvy bit her lip. Shit. "I mean, you know. He said it that time I told you about." It wasn't a lie. It wasn't the full truth either, but it wasn't a lie.

No one can know. They would hold firm on that part of their agreement. They could resolve whatever was between them without anyone else getting hurt.

Sadia's brow cleared. "Oh, right. Well, I know John tried to talk to Paul a couple of times, but Paul refused."

"I'm probably going to see John again soon. Maybe you and Kareem could come with me."

Sadia wrinkled her nose. "To be honest, Livvy, I'm not too eager to introduce Kareem to the whole Kane-Chandler dynamic. It messed Paul up. Being an heir to C&O was his whole identity, and once it was gone, he didn't know who he was."

"None of us knew who we were after it was gone. It's hard to go from feeling so certain about what your life is and then having it ripped away from you."

"I have no doubt. But you found yourself, Livvy."

Livvy raised an eyebrow. Had she?

"Paul . . ." Sadia frowned. "Paul didn't. Being a small-business owner and my husband and Kareem's father—any and all of those things could have defined him, but they came in second place to what he'd lost."

Though Livvy hadn't spoken to her brother for a long time, she could see that being the case. "I'm sorry."

"Don't be sorry. Paul was responsible for himself."

Livvy nodded slowly. On the list of things she needed to deal with from her past, her estrangement from Paul would have to be one that couldn't be resolved. Whatever regrets and sorrow she had about their relationship would be ones she carried. "Right."

"Don't get me wrong, though. I'm happy you saw John and I hope you can get some closure with him."

"Yes, well, that was the reason I went to see him. I needed it." She drank her coffee. "Jackson was right. It was unrealistic to think I could only confront tiny parts of my past." But he'd been wrong about those parts being unresolvable.

Sadia froze. "Wait. You talked to Jackson?"

"Not much. He saw me for about two minutes, then got on his bike to go to New York."

"You *saw* Jackson? He was in town?"

Oof. She hadn't thought about how Sadia would feel about that. "Yeah."

"What . . . but he didn't even come to Paul's funeral!"

"He said he couldn't." The bit about being in jail, Livvy would keep to herself. It wasn't that she was ashamed of her brother. She didn't know enough of the story to relate it to anyone.

"Yeah. Right." Sadia's lips thinned so much they practically disappeared.

"I'm sorry. I didn't mean to upset you."

"I'm not upset. I don't understand why he'd show

up now when he couldn't be bothered for anything else."

Sadia was totally upset. But Livvy wasn't about to rile her up further.

Her friend attacked the shreds of the scone. "Is he gone for good?"

"I got a text this morning saying he'd be back tomorrow." Livvy finished her cookie. "I can tell him to come see you."

"Whatever." Sadia tossed down the food she'd been playing with and came to her feet. "I haven't seen him in years. What do I care if he doesn't bother to see his sister-in-law and nephew? I don't care at all."

"Uh." It sounded like she cared an awful lot, but Livvy wasn't in a hurry to point that out. "Okay."

Sadia smiled, though it was nothing more than a fierce baring of her teeth. "Listen, I have to run. I want to check in on Kareem before my sister comes over to watch him while I'm at the bar."

Part of Livvy wanted to pursue this, but Sadia had said she liked space. Plus, she wasn't sure what else to say. Jackson was complicated. "That's fine." Livvy grabbed the food and said her goodbyes to Sadia. It wasn't until she checked her phone in the car that she realized she'd received a text.

Nicholas. Coordinates and a time, eleven o'clock.

His texts had come so often she'd stopped counting them, but she couldn't stop treasuring them. She ran her fingers over the numbers before checking her watch. She had plenty of time to eat dinner in front of the blaring television and try to engage her mother in conversation before she headed off.

The awful guilt threatened, and she pushed it aside. Nope. While what she was doing with Nicholas wasn't totally risk-free, he'd been right: it was far healthier than anything she'd done with the man in a decade.

She didn't realize she had a goofy smile on her face until it widened when she got another text.

Wear something nice.

Chapter 17

BEAUTIFUL.

Such a trite, overused word. Nicholas wished he could come up with something that better described the punch-to-the-gut feeling he got when he saw Livvy.

Nicholas leaned against a pillar. Livvy appeared utterly at home at the bar of the swanky hotel. She was wearing a red dress, short and strapless, with polka dots on it. A white petticoat was visible under the hem. Her hair was styled in some utterly complicated old-fashioned pouf that matched her pinup-girl dress. On another woman the outfit might have looked sweet and girlish, but she'd paired it with high-heeled wedges that had straps crisscrossing her ankles and calves. The vine on her shoulder peeked out from under the strands of her hair. The dragon was barely visible on the back of her calf, under the skirt, a flash of curling tail.

They'd had sex with the lights on now a couple of times, but he hadn't spent nearly long enough inspecting and licking every spot of ink on her. He

didn't know if there was a point where he'd be satisfied.

For the first time in his life, he'd consciously
stopped trying to compartmentalize his personal
life from his work and family, and it was an amazing experience. Yes, nothing was as orderly as he
was used to. Yes, he'd had to rely on his staff more.
Yes, sometimes he zoned out during business
meetings since half his attention was focused on
how many hours it would take to see her, text her,
talk to her again.

But he was happy.

Of course, he could see the problems looming
ahead of them. He was growing more and more
certain about his feelings for her; she was un-
derstandably skittish as hell. But for once he was
living in the present, not the past or the future. He
was living for himself, Nicholas the Man, not Nicholas the Son or Nicholas the Brother or Nicholas
the CEO.

A man sitting next to Livvy at the bar edged
closer, turning his head as if he were contemplating talking to her, and Nicholas stifled the growl in
his chest. He walked closer, until he could wedge
in between the two of them to lean on the bar.
"Hello there," he said quietly.

Livvy glanced his way, amusement dancing in
her dark eyes. The dim chandelier lighting in the
room caressed her golden skin. "Hello."

"Can I buy you a drink?"

Livvy tapped her martini glass. "I have a drink.
Can I buy you one?"

"I'd like that."

"What will you have?"

"Scotch."

She caught the bartender's eye and waved him over to place his order. They didn't speak until after the bartender poured his drink and moved away. The scotch was smoky and delicate, settling over his tongue and throat. "My name's Nicholas."

He could tell by the way her mouth puckered that she was biting her cheek. "Olivia."

"You don't look like an Olivia."

"You don't look like a Nicholas."

He shrugged. "Call me whatever you like, then."

"I'll do that, Nico."

She'd been sighing that in his ear for the past week. Those two syllables filled him with an unmatched sense of delight. "That'll do, Livvy."

She swiveled on her stool. "So, what brings you here tonight?"

"I'm looking for something."

"What?"

Solace. Relief. You. He wanted to grin but controlled his expression. "Not sure yet."

"You look like you have everything."

"Seems that way on paper."

She rolled her eyes. "Poor little rich boy."

"How do you know I'm rich?"

Her hand smoothed over his chest, stopping his heart. Would he ever be tired of her touch? He feared the answer was no. She tugged on his tie. "This. This costs more than some people's paychecks. That's how I know."

"You got me."

"What do you do?"

"Boring stuff."

"I bet it's something important."

"Not really. I take care of things."

"Things? Or people?"

Nicholas looked down at her. "Both, I suppose."

Her lashes fluttered. "Sounds important."

"I hope it is. What do you do?"

"I'm an artist."

"Ah." He took a sip of his scotch, barely tasting it. "What's your medium?"

"Skin."

"Hmm." Since she'd touched him, he dared to lift his fingers and trail them over the vine at her shoulder. "Did you design this?"

"I did."

"Where did you get it?"

"Boston."

"Nice."

He continued tracing the vine, feeling her shiver. "For a tattoo artist, you don't have many visible tattoos."

"There are few people I've been able to trust to execute the designs I want on me."

"I've been thinking of getting a tattoo."

"Have you? I can't see you with one." She cut her gaze away from him, telling him she was lying.

"Maybe a fairy," he ventured. "Or a mermaid?"

Her lips twitched, and she took a sip of the fruity drink she'd ordered. "If they're naked, I guess."

"Look how smart you are. Such a professional."

He followed the vine to the back of her shoulder. He knew exactly where it ended, curling over the delicate bump of her shoulder blade. "I welcome any other suggestions you have."

"I'll—I'll think on it," she murmured.

"Are you good at what you do?"

She didn't hesitate. "I'm the best. Are you good at what you do?"

"Taking care of people?"

"Yes."

"I—" He was about to downplay his accomplishments but instead took a cue from her easy confidence. "I am. Though sometimes I can't take care of everyone."

"No one can."

"You're right. I'm learning to prioritize."

"You should prioritize yourself first."

His smile was genuine. "I don't think you're wrong."

"Well." Livvy picked up the cherry from her glass by the stem and took a bite of the fruit, holding the stem between her white, even teeth. "What are two competent people like us supposed to do with their time?"

He smiled, though he didn't feel like smiling. His body was so hard it hurt, watching her slowly make love to that cherry. "I've got a room upstairs."

She put down the stem. "I'd have been disappointed if you didn't."

They didn't speak as they made their way upstairs to the room he'd reserved. This wasn't a comfortable silence, but the kind of silence that came from two people who didn't know each other that well.

Feeding the fantasy.

As the elevator rose, he slid his hand from the small of her back up to her shoulder, then down over her arm, scraping his calluses over the vine, until he could clasp their hands together. "The things I want to do to you," he murmured.

The look she cast him was sizzling. "What do you want to do to me?"

He took one step, then another, crowding her smaller body. He raised their joined hands and placed them against the wall of the elevator. "Strip you. Lick you. Fuck you."

Her legs fell open, giving him room to press against her. He couldn't stop himself from grinding his cock in the warm, wet space between her legs.

"That all sounds good," she breathed.

The elevator dinged, and he'd never been so grateful when the doors opened to reveal an empty hallway. If she hadn't easily matched his eager pace, he would have been dragging her. He inserted his keycard wrong at first, and he cursed impatiently when it flashed red, giving her a dark look when she laughed.

Finally they were inside. He didn't wait, pressing her up against the door, as he had in the elevator. With great care, he pushed her hair over her shoulders and looked down into her eyes. "I want you to tell me what you like."

"You know what I like."

"How, when we've never met before?"

Her lips quivered, but she didn't contradict him. Her small breasts pillowed over the neckline of her dress. He lowered his head and kissed the flesh, not breaking eye contact with her. "I need you to tell me. Is this okay?"

Her eyes darkened. "Yes."

He reached around her and found the zipper, pulling it down so he could properly trace her spine down to the dimples at her waist. He wanted to lick those dimples. He eased back and paused before lowering the dress. "Can I strip you naked?"

"Yes," she whispered.

With a shove, he had the dress on the floor. He took a second to admire her braless breasts, then dropped his hand to her panties. It was a scrap of fabric, tied at each hip with a tiny bow. He gave the strings a gentle tug. "Please, can I get these panties off you?"

She nodded. Two tugs at each bow, and the lace was on the floor, her body completely naked in front of him. He took a second to admire her smooth skin, decorated with ink. He knew this body so well, and yet at the same time he didn't know it at all. "Will you get on the bed?"

She bit her lip and sauntered past him, the muscles in her short, powerful legs clenching and releasing. She crawled onto the bed in a way he knew was designed to get his blood rushing to his cock. He swallowed, then slowly worked his tie free.

He dropped it onto the bed and quickly stripped off his shirt and pants, preening only a little when she ran her hungry gaze over him. He donned a condom and then grabbed the tie and crawled up her body, her smooth legs grazing his hairier ones. "Can I tie you up, Livvy?"

Her eyes widened. "Uh, with the tie?"

"Yes."

"Yes, yes, yes." She nodded for emphasis. "A million times yes."

Well, that confirmed his suspicion she had some sort of weird fetish with his ties. He bit the inside of his cheek as she flung her hands above her head. He looped the tie around both wrists. She tested the knot, her expression growing more heated as she realized she was caught. "Boy Scout."

He ran his lips down the inside of her arm, making her shiver. "Good with knots. Always prepared." She arched up, and he controlled her easily, placing a hand on her hip. "Be patient," he whispered.

"Patience is not my strong suit."

"That's too bad. It is mine." He licked his way over her breast, to her nipple. "I still need you to tell me what you like."

"Nico . . ."

Her breasts were fuller on top than the bottom, which meant he had to cup and lift them to get her nipples into his mouth. He plumped one up, then ran his mouth all around the tip and down the valley between her breasts. Her foot dragged up his leg and ass and back, exerting a steady pressure to get him closer and tighter.

He readjusted so her legs were caught under his,

and took in her glassy eyes and flushed skin. "Do you want me to stop?"

"No."

Very carefully, he ran his tongue around the areola of her nipple. She cried out, and he lifted his head. "What do you want?"

"Suck me."

He drew a bit of her skin on the curve of her breast into his mouth and sucked it softly. "Like this?"

"No. My nipples, damn it."

He pushed her breasts together and opened his mouth wide, his groan matching hers when he sucked in a mouthful of her pretty nipples. He drank in the sound of her sighs and moans like they were ambrosia. If he could, he'd consume her completely.

He played with her for a long moment, until she was writhing beneath him. He kissed his way over her body to the tattoo on the outside of her left breast. A heart, with parentheses around it.

"Where did you get this one?" he murmured, and traced the heart with his tongue.

"Los Angeles."

He nipped her skin, then moved lower, kissing over her clenched stomach. He nibbled her cute navel, then lower still, over her hipbones and the pot of gold there. Her first.

He spread her legs wider and traced his fingers over the intricate stylized dragon that ran up her leg, its head on her thigh. "What about this one?"

"D.C."

He frowned, something niggling at the back of his mind, but he shoved it aside, barely able to concentrate on breathing when her body was so wet and ready beneath his.

He ghosted his lips over the crease of her groin. "Livvy, can I fuck you with my tongue?"

She stifled a sob and pulled at her binding, but he really had been a Boy Scout. That was a solid knot. She wasn't going anywhere. "Yes. Yes, please."

"Do you know why I always wanted to go down on you?" He kissed her mound.

She inhaled. "The answer every woman wants to hear is because you love it."

"I do love it. I love your taste and scent and how you move under me. I love I can make you crazy for my touch. But also . . . I was always so grateful." He nuzzled his nose against the landing strip of hair there, breathing her in, allowing himself to pretend they were together for real and that this was his right and privilege at all times. "Whenever you contacted me, I wanted to get on my hands and knees and show you how grateful I was."

She stilled under him. "Most people send a card."

"I don't like writing." He spread her open with both fingers and touched his tongue to her hard clit, holding her still when she would have jumped. "I love licking you."

He settled in to feast, fucking her deep and hard with his mouth. The world around him vanished, his entire focus on the wetness on his tongue, her trembling thighs surrounding his head, the gasping cries she gave. He used his thumb to keep stimulating her clit, even after she started coming, sensing she wouldn't be satisfied with just one orgasm. He loved it when she hit multiple peaks. It didn't always happen, but when it did, he felt like a god.

When she was replete, a boneless heap beneath him, he stretched up her body and kissed her lax mouth. "Livvy, can I fuck you?" he whispered.

"Yes," she whispered, then gasped when he re-adjusted his body and sank inside her, her heat making his toes curl. With the exception of the time in the woods, he'd worn a condom. She might be on birth control, but he wasn't a man who took chances.

Except with her, he supposed. He should pull out and suit up but this was such perfection. Fucking her bare sent him back to when they'd been young and hot and committed to one another.

He pressed his lips against her ear. "I've never been naked like this with anyone but you." Her pussy contracted around him at the confession, and he had to swallow to keep speaking. "Just like no woman's gone down on me but you."

Her head snapped back, incredulity edging out the passion in her gaze. "Are you serious?"

The sense of vulnerability was overhelming. So was the freedom. "Extremely. I told you it had been a long time."

"But that long?"

"Yes." He worked his way deeper. "Those words are exactly what I want to hear when my cock is out, by the way. Say them with more excitement."

She huffed out a laugh, her breasts jiggling. She tugged at her bonds. "Let me touch you."

Fearing she might tweak a muscle, he complied and then entwined his hands with hers. He pressed them flat against the mattress as he withdrew and shafted back inside.

He grew selfish and greedy as he fucked her, shoving harder. He thought he could hold out longer, but then she turned her head, her teeth sinking into his shoulder, her orgasm tightening her pussy around him. He came with a strangled shout, his come spurting out of him in great spasms.

He returned to reality in slow degrees when she shifted her body under his and brought her hands to rest on his shoulders, her fingers caressing his skin. He turned his head and kissed her inner wrist, where three dots decorated her skin, so tiny one could miss them. She'd had them since she was twenty-one or so. He remembered the first time he'd noticed. "Where did you get this tattoo?"

"New York."

He nodded, closing his eyes, a nagging sensation still tugging at his consciousness. He would move in a second, once he could get his shit together, but right now this felt so fucking good, resting on top of her while she stroked his shoulders and hair. If he could, he would stay here forever.

Boston.

D.C.

Los Angeles.

New York.

He frowned, trying to shoo the wriggling thoughts as his brain struggled to piece together parts of a puzzle he hadn't been aware existed. He didn't need his head to ruin this perfect night.

He pulled out of her and took care of the condom, dropping it into the wastebasket by the bed. Then he ran his hand up her side, urging her onto her stomach.

Her lashes fluttered. "Wha—?"

"Let me rub your back," he murmured.

She complied, and he had her entire lovely back before him. He ran his hands over her shoulders and lower, rubbing the flesh, working out the knots there.

His fingers brushed over vibrant ink, so colorful it felt alive. She had a watercolor tattoo of a gold compass centered on her spine, splashes of soothing purple and blue and green behind it. He traced the script *N* above the arrow at the top. It stood for *north*, not *Nicholas*.

He drew a circle over the compass. She turned her head so her cheek rested against the pillow and sighed. He drew another circle. "A box," she murmured.

"What?"

"Draw a square, not a circle."

He didn't understand her request, but he changed the motion. Her eyes narrowed in pleasure.

"Do you like that more?"

"Yes."

"Why?"

She didn't answer for a moment. "It's something someone taught me. If I'm feeling overwhelmed or like my emotions are too big, I think of putting my feelings into a box. It helps calm me down."

How funny. She had to put her feelings in a box, while he'd only recently allowed his out.

He shifted to lay on his side, and continued the motion, finding it soothing to him as well. He moved to the N, boxing that. "Where did you get this tattoo?"

"Chicago," she murmured.

Boston.

D.C.

Los Angeles.

New York.

Chicago.

His mind whirred to life, fitting the cities into a pattern, alongside what he knew about those tattoos and when they'd appeared on her body.

What were the odds she would get a single tattoo in every city he'd met her in?

He ran his finger up to the vine that unfurled on her upper back, almost kissing a splatter of ink from the compass. The harsh lines of the vine were a sharp contrast to the dreamy blurriness of the compass. He drew a square there, around a prickly flower. "What does this mean?"

Her shoulders moved. "I told you. I thought it was pretty."

He nodded and slid his hand down her arm to her wrist. A box there. "And this?"

"It's an ellipsis."

"What does it mean?"

She rolled over on to her back and stared up at him. "Punctuation."

He bent and pressed a kiss on the side of her breast, where the heart lay. "What about this?"

"It's from a poem I liked."

"What poem?"

"What's with all the questions?" She moved, subtly edging away. She shoved the sheets and comforter down and crawled under them, wrapping the bedding around herself.

"I'm curious."

Boston.

D.C.

Los Angeles.

New York.

Chicago.

"What about your other ones?"

She yawned, her eyes closing. "Other what?"

"All your tattoos? Where did you get each one?"

Her lashes fluttered. "What's the big deal, Nico?"

That *Nico* wasn't a caressing endearment. It was a warning. His stomach churned.

Too bad he'd never been good at heeding warnings. "Did you get a tattoo in every city we met up in?"

She straightened, clutching the sheet to her chest. "Huh?"

"There's a pattern. Boston, D.C., L.A., New York, Chicago. I flew to all those places over the years. I'm betting you have other cities we met in on you, don't you? Atlanta? Minneapolis?"

"Uh, I was living in those places, of course I got ink there. And I got tattoos in places we never met up." She raised her arm and flashed the tiny velociraptor on her inner biceps. "That was in Denver."

Well used to her wily ways, he rested on his elbow and watched her. "I asked you if you got something in every city we met up in, not if you only got them in those places."

"So what if I did?"

He tensed. "That's interesting."

"Why is it interesting?" She rolled her eyes. "It just is."

His gaze dropped to the pot of gold on her hip. She'd gotten that one the day after her seventeenth birthday.

He might love patterns, but Livvy loved anniversaries. He had trouble swallowing. "It was the next day, wasn't it? Each time?"

"Jesus, what does it matter?" She sat up and threw her legs over the side of the bed, tugging the sheet so she could wrap it around her body toga-style.

She stood and stalked over to her dress, picking it up and shaking it out, the petticoat flaring.

He ran his hand over his face, suddenly, fiercely tired. "Livvy, I thought you wanted to resolve the stuff between us."

She dropped the sheet and stepped into her dress, quickly zipping it up before he could be distracted by her body. "That's what we're doing."

"We're not if you won't talk to me."

"This conversation is pointless. You're digging for something and I don't understand what."

"Were you punishing yourself? For sleeping with me?"

She drew back, a sneer on her lips. "No, dumbass. Tattoos are never punishment."

She'd skipped calling him Nicholas and gone straight to dumbass, but he didn't have the mental reserves to deal with that.

She smoothed her badly wrinkled skirt. "Why would you even think that?"

"Because I know you . . . hurt . . . after we broke up."

"Yeah, I told you that."

"I know . . ." He licked his lips, certain he should shut up, but unable to stop himself. "I know you were depressed. I know you said you wanted to die."

She went utterly still, every muscle frozen. It was like looking at a statue. Her lips barely moved when she spoke. "Who told you that?"

Aw shit. He had to keep going now. "Your brother paid me a visit."

Her head snapped around. "What? When?"

"Last week."

"Last week . . . when?"

"The day we went to my grandfather's."

Her gaze flickered, and her skin paled. "Oh God. The day you suddenly decided we needed to talk? Is that why . . . is that what this has been? You and me, this week? The sweetness, the talking, the fucking? Was this all out of, what? Pity?"

He came to his knees, uncaring of his nudity. "No, no."

She laughed half-hysterically. "We talked about

hate-fucks and guilt-fucks, but I suppose I should have brought up pity-fucks."

"That's not it. Damn it, Livvy."

Fury joined horror in her expression. Beyond listening, she grabbed her shoes from where she'd kicked them off. "That's what all the questions were about. Was I *punishing* myself for having sex with you? Because I was so heartbroken, I couldn't stay away from you, right?"

"That's not—"

"Yes. I was depressed after you broke things off with me, is that what you want to hear?" The tears trembling on her lashes broke something apart inside him. "I fell into the deepest, scariest pit of depression, so much I never thought I'd crawl my way out. I did want to die." She didn't bother to tie her sandals properly, simply wrapping the strings around her ankles in a large knot. "That first time I texted you, that first birthday, I felt so pathetic and lonely. After you left, I cried for days. But then the next year, I cried less. And even less the following. I built myself back up. And tonight? I'm not going to cry at all. So take your pity and go fuck yourself with it."

He scrambled out of bed, panic driving him. Wait, she couldn't leave. Where were his pants? He had to stop her. "Livvy, wait. You've misunderstood everything. It wasn't pity. It was never pity."

She stalked to the door and glanced over her shoulder. "Then what was it?"

Love. He opened his mouth, the answer there, on the tip of his tongue.

Say it.

The seconds ticked by as he struggled to do it, to strip that final protective layer off his heart. Cold moved through him, freezing all animation, the wind-up man going still.

Finally, she shook her head. Tears shimmered in her eyes, but they didn't fall. "Actually, I think I finally understand everything." The look she cast him was inscrutable and cool. "I think we're done now, Nicholas. I'm going to do my damnedest to forget your number. Don't ever text me again."

Chapter 18

Livvy'd lied. She cried all the way home.

With grim determination, she took ten minutes in her mother's driveway blowing her nose and using the tiny tube of concealer in her purse to cover the puffiness under her eyes. It was late, but it was entirely possible her aunt may still be awake.

She would not let anyone see what a mess she was inside.

Like an object of pity.

Don't think about it. Get upstairs, get to your room, and then you can fall apart.

When she entered the house and heard the murmur of a late-night talk show, Livvy was glad she'd taken the time to tidy up. She crept to the stairs, wincing over every creak. She was almost to the first step when her aunt's low voice came from the living room. "Livvy?"

She hastily ran her fingers through her hair, then walked to the arched opening, tugging on her wrinkled dress. Her aunt sat in her usual chair, her usual knitting in her hands. The only light in the room came from a small Tiffany lamp next to her chair and the T.V. Livvy stuck to the shadows right inside the door. "Hey, Aunt Maile." She was proud her voice wasn't tear-fogged and hoarse.

"You're home late." Maile looked at her, and her ready smile faded. She put down her knitting. "Are you okay?"

Livvy nodded, trying to control her lower lip. "Y-yes."

"Come here."

"I should go to bed."

"Come here."

Livvy didn't often hear that commanding tone from Maile. Her feet moved before her head could catch up.

She tried to straighten her shoulders as Maile surveyed her in the light. Head up, chin up, no tears. She was tough and strong, not some dumb girl screaming in her bedroom over a boy.

Maile's eyes softened, and she held out her hand. "Oh, my love. What did that man do to you?"

Her lip quivered, and the next thing she knew, she was on her knees next to her aunt's chair, her face buried in her lap as she sobbed. Maile's calloused hand swept over her hair, keeping it from her wet cheeks.

Livvy didn't know how long she wept there, her aunt stroking her, but eventually her sobs turned to silent tears. She turned her head to speak. "Does everyone know about me and Nicholas?"

"I don't know about everyone. I ran into Darrell's mother at bookclub, and she told me he saw the two of you together at the café."

Darrell. The cheerful kid behind the café counter.

Maile continued petting Livvy's head. "It was natural for you to want to see him again, honey."

"I slept with him."

"That's natural too." There was no judgment in her aunt's voice.

"I thought we could resolve what was between us."

"Is that really what you thought, my love?" Her voice was incredibly gentle. "Is that really why you saw him again? Or were you holding out some hope that this time it would all work out?"

Livvy started to say no, but her breath arrested.

It was never pity.

Then what was it?

She knew what she'd wanted him to say. "I'm so stupid." Counter thought. *I deserve compassion.*

"No, you're not."

"It could never work out."

"*Never* isn't a good word," Maile said. "It's complicated."

"I think I still love him." The words whispered into the dimly lit room, her worst truth fully revealed. "I can't stay away from him, even when I try. Even when I know it'll only hurt me. If that's not stupid, I don't know what is." *I deserve compassion.*

"That's love, not stupidity."

"It's irrational."

"If someone told you love is rational, they're a liar. Sometimes you can't stop loving someone."

There was such understanding in Maile's voice,

Livvy looked up. In her memory, her aunt had always been happily single, but there was a brooding sadness in her dark eyes that told Livvy she understood. "Did you love someone like that?"

"Yes. Her name was Jacinda." Maile's fingers separated Livvy's hair and started braiding. "We were young. My parents disapproved. Your father told me he would give me money to run away with her. Start over fresh somewhere new. But I was scared, so I broke things off."

"What happened to her?"

"I don't know. She left for New York City. She came back a few times. Until one day she didn't."

"You could find out where she is now."

"I don't know if I'm brave enough for that." Maile tugged on Livvy's crooked braid affectionately. "I'm not quite like you."

"I'm not brave at all." *I'm a good person. Please let me be compassionate to me.*

She just couldn't.

Fresh tears stung her eyes. "Nicholas found out how I reacted when we ended things last time." And she would be giving Jackson a piece of her mind. Later, when she could concentrate more on her justifiable anger instead of this deep, yawning despair.

"What do you mean?"

"About how depressed I was." She shied away from the word *suicidal*, though that was what she'd been. Her depression had been triggered by multiple events, that meeting in the woods the final push she'd needed. If Jackson hadn't hid everything that could have harmed her in the house that first night, she wasn't certain what she would have done.

"Good. He should know how much he hurt you."

Livvy lifted her head at the unexpectedly blood-thirsty relish in her aunt's voice. "I never wanted him to know. It makes me look so weak."

"Olivia."

Livvy straightened at her aunt's stern tone. "Yes?"

"You were hurt. It's not a weakness to love someone like that. It's not a weakness to be in pain when that love is ripped away from you."

"It's not exactly strength to fall apart when a man dumps you." And that was how Jackson, and probably Nicholas, had seen the episode.

"Says who?"

"Says everyone." Strength was soldiering on, with or without a man. Strength was being invulnerable.

"Oh, is that right?" Maile straightened, her nostrils flaring. "Who did the heavy lifting in yours and Nicholas's relationship, Livvy?"

"I don't know what you mean."

"I mean, you were the one who made sure his needs were being met."

"He met my needs too," she felt compelled to say.

"Yes, fine. But it was you who said 'I love you' first, I bet. You who coaxed him into asking you out. You who kept your sadness a secret from him at the end, partly out of pride, but probably also because you didn't want him to be hurt." Maile grimaced. "Society tells women that they have to be responsible for the emotional health of their relationships and then tells them they're weak for feeling emotions. What kind of message is that? Nicholas was part of your world, and up until the end was a good, dependable part of it. Why shouldn't you have grieved when you lost him?"

"Because . . ."

Maile tapped her under her chin. "Do you know what I remember during that time? I remember you curling up next to me at your father's funeral after I read his eulogy and holding my hand. I remember you getting out of bed when Jackson was arrested and helping me find an attorney for him. I remember you packing up your things in one duffel bag and leaving for a new city where you knew no one. If you fear you aren't strong, put those fears to rest."

She swallowed. "Some nights I cried so hard for Nico I physically hurt."

"So?" Maile made a dismissive noise. "Strength isn't about how much you cry or the bad nights you might have. Strength is here." She tapped Livvy's forehead. "And here." She poked a blunt finger into Livvy's chest. "You can be strong and have moments of incredible despair, when everything feels like it's collapsing in on you, and yes, when you feel like you want to die. Those moments are not weaknesses. They are simply moments. And they are not you."

Maile spoke with such certainty, the tiny, defenseless part of her bleating how she was dumb and silly was momentarily silenced. Livvy brushed at her cheeks. "Okay."

"Livvy, you are sweet and rebellious and talented and soft-hearted and mouthy. You have had to endure a number of tragedies in your short life, and you still put one foot in front of another. You have nothing to be ashamed of. Cut yourself some slack."

Her fingers trembled. *I deserve compassion.* "I'll try."

"Don't try. Do."

Livvy nodded. It was hard after so many years of berating herself for every emotion she'd ever had.

Maile was right. That needed to stop. "It's late," she finally managed. "We should go to bed."

"Go on, then." Maile gave her another sweet smile, her round cheeks creasing. "I have to finish this row, and then I'll be up."

Livvy headed for the stairs, but then made a detour around the corner to her mother's room. She was surprised to find a faint light coming from under the doorway. She hesitated for a second, then knocked. She pushed the door open after her mother's muffled acknowledgment. Tani sat in the armchair next to the bed, watching the large flat screen on the wall. "Mom? Why are you awake?"

"I couldn't sleep." Her mother's voice was gruff. "You're coming in late."

Livvy raised an eyebrow. Tani hadn't said anything before about when Livvy got home. Livvy ran her hand over the edge of the door. "Sorry."

"You don't have to apologize to me. You're an adult."

She wanted to have to apologize to her mother.

Perhaps you shouldn't come home for a few weeks and expect your relationship with your mother to be magically fixed.

Humans were complicated. Parents especially so. She glanced around the dark room. "How about tomorrow we go shopping for something to brighten this room up?"

Tani looked away from the T.V. She appeared especially small in the chair, her walker by her side. "You don't like the room?"

"I mean, it's not—" Livvy cut herself off, not eager to have any more emotional conversations tonight.

If her mother hadn't opened up to her about mental health before, she definitely wasn't going to do it now.

"Not what?" Tani asked.

"It's not what we used to have."

"What do you mean?"

"At our old house."

"Of course it's not." Tani stared at Livvy like she was a simpleton. "Because it's not the same house."

"I'm not talking about just the house. You decorated so nicely back then."

"Your father cared about all of that. Not me."

She raised an eyebrow, not only at the words, but also at her mother even bringing up her late father. "Dad made you do all of that?"

"He didn't make me. I wanted him to be happy," Tani said stiffly. "I enjoyed him enjoying it."

Livvy nodded, mildly disturbed. How much of her parental dynamics had she missed when she was young? "Oh. Well. I'll let you sleep."

Livvy turned to leave, but then she noted the sketchpad on her mother's nightstand. She was too far away to see what she'd drawn in it, but the pad was open, suggesting use. "Have you used the charcoal I got you?"

Her mother glanced at her hands. "I did."

"What other stuff do you like to use?" She made her tone brisk and matter-of-fact.

Her mother looked like she wasn't going to respond, but then she shrugged. "Watercolors."

"I'll get you some while I'm out tomorrow."

Tani pursed her lips. "That may be nice." She picked up the remote.

Livvy started to back out, but Tani continued speaking. "I heard you with Maile."

Livvy stopped, her blood freezing, and turned back to her mother.

Tani nodded. "I know why you think grieving a relationship is a weakness. Because you think I was weak, when your father died."

Livvy shook her head, numb.

"Yes. I'm not dumb. You, Paul, Jackson. You resent me for how I was then, and I cannot blame you. I was unresponsive to your needs for a long time, and then you were gone, and . . ." Tani's lips tightened. "And that was that."

Livvy found her voice. "I can't speak for Jackson and Paul. But if anyone in the world can understand a fraction of how you felt then, it's me. Especially in hindsight." Whether or not her mother dealt with depression too, Livvy would never say Tani was weak.

So why did you call yourself weak?

Because it was far easier to be kind to other people than it was to be kind to herself. *I deserve compassion.* Ugh. She did. She really did.

Tani fiddled with her collar.

Livvy scuffed her toes on the carpet, wishing she knew how to speak to her mother. "You know, it's funny you asked for watercolors. Watercolors are kind of my specialty, you know. I love the finished product, how it's supposed to look imperfect. How people celebrate its flaws and find beauty in it."

Her mother eyed her. "What on earth are you talking about?"

She bit her lip, regretting the silly words. "I don't know. Thinking about things we have in common, I guess."

Tani's eyes gleamed. "Do not see that boy."

Livvy stiffened. *Selfish, greedy bastards*, Paul whispered in her ear. If anyone had a beef with the Chandlers, it would be Tani. "I know you hate—"

Her mother spoke over her. "You said you can empathize with me. I can empathize with how crushed you felt then." Tani met her gaze. "The difference between you and me and how we lost our partners is Nicholas left you voluntarily."

Livvy had to stop herself from buckling under that harsh reminder. "Oh."

"I do not want to see you hurt like that ever again." Tani picked up her remote and refocused on the T.V. "Go to bed now."

Unable to compose any kind of response, Livvy dumbly left, closing the door behind her.

Her chest ached and her cheeks were dried out from too many tears. She'd probably weep more tonight, and curse Nicholas's name.

The darkness wasn't swallowing her whole, though. Maybe it would later. Maybe it would be triggered by something unrelated to Nicholas. And how he left her.

Why had her mother had to say that to her? It was so needlessly cruel and—

Think about what else she said.

Livvy stopped on the stairs.

I do not want to see you hurt like that ever again.

Livvy blinked. Her mother cared.

So did Maile, who would hug her and pet her. So did Sadia, who would feed and fuss and threaten to stab people for her.

A tiny kernel of contentment bloomed inside her. Connections. She may have gotten her heart batted around, but she'd found what she'd come here for.

Livvy continued up the stairs. She'd battle the darkness with whatever tools she could find.

Chapter 19

Nᴵᴄʜᴏʟᴀs ᴄʜᴀsᴇᴅ a tomato around his plate. His father and grandfather had escalated from quiet disapproval to outraged shouts twenty minutes ago. The prison-labor scandal was resolved as best it could be, but the men had started arguing over the scope and cost of the investigation.

His sister sat quietly across from him at the boardroom table. Eve had tried to talk to him before the meeting, but he hadn't been able to concentrate on the annual gala the foundation was throwing and what she needed from him.

He didn't much care about anything, to be honest.

It was never pity.

Then what was it?

I love you. I always have. I probably always will.

I love who you were, and I want to get to know you properly now so I can tell you how much I love you as the person you've become.

I am nothing without you. I live for the hours I can see you. Locked in stasis, waiting for you to turn the key.

Any of those would have been acceptable responses. How had he fumbled so badly?

Because you're an idiot. And now look what's happened. You've lost her. She's going to leave town, and all you'll be left with is—

"Nicholas."

"Nicholas!"

He jerked, his head swiveling between the two patriarchs. "Sorry?"

Brendan folded his arms over his chest and glared at him. "Seems you've been sorry a lot lately. What's going on with you?"

"I'm . . ." *Tired from trying to save a family and a business that doesn't care about saving me.* "Nothing."

"Then pay attention."

Nicholas looked around the table, taking stock of his grandfather and sister and their concerned faces. Past and present and future, they were seated here.

If he'd learned anything from spending time with Livvy it was that he couldn't change their past. He could regret it and learn from it, but their history would always exist.

He could change the present, though. He could take actionable steps to have some sort of future.

He'd feared every crank of emotion would ruin him, but instead it was like each one had made his life finally come into focus, like he was a camera with a clean lens.

Nicholas closed his eyes and opened them again, and this time, instead of noting the similarities between him and his father, he took stock of all the differences. They weren't the same.

He could break this, right now. He didn't need to be afraid.

He didn't have to stay cold.

He put down his fork. "I have something on my mind."

"Something more important than the business?" Brendan scoffed.

"Yes. Someone more important than the business."

"Nothing is more important than the business."

"You would say that," Eve snapped.

Nicholas wasn't sure which one of them was more stunned by Eve uttering the caustic words. His father shot her a fierce frown. Nicholas bet the man had forgotten Eve was there.

Since he couldn't look at the girl for longer than a few minutes, Brendan returned to Nicholas. "Well? What's on your mind then, that's so important?"

He glanced at his grandfather, who had straightened in his wheelchair, a hopeful glint in his eyes. "Livvy."

A gasp came from Eve, quickly muffled.

Brendan stilled.

Nicholas met his father's gaze. "Olivia Kane."

Nicholas had witnessed his father's rages. They were scary things, straight-up red-faced meltdowns. But this . . . this was new.

Brendan paled, his lips barely moving. "No."

"Yes."

"I told you to stay away from her."

John leaned forward. "You did what?"

Oddly enough, uttering Livvy's name had calmed him. It was done. His father knew, and all that was left to see was how the man would handle it.

He didn't care what Brendan did, though, because Nicholas knew what he was going to do.

Nicholas shoved his salad aside and perused the platter of dessert. No cannoli, but there were chocolate chip cookies. He picked up two and placed them on a napkin. He took a big bite of one, aware his entire family was watching him like hawks. "I told you, I'm not a child."

"You're my child."

"Your child, not your robot." This magical land of not giving a fuck was pretty cool.

"I will not tolerate you seeing a member of that family."

Another bite. "I don't care."

Brendan slammed his fist on the table. Eve jumped, but Nicholas didn't move. Nor did he usher her and his grandfather out of the room.

They were adults, and he couldn't protect them anymore. Let everyone see exactly who Brendan was.

"You know what they did to us!"

"They didn't do anything to us."

"They killed your mother."

"No. Robert was behind that wheel. It sucked. It was bad. It was a fucking tragedy. But that had nothing to do with the rest of them. You're the only one who wanted to punish the whole family for one man's mistake."

"One mistake? The fire—"

"The charges against Jackson were dropped," he said flatly. It didn't matter what he thought about the younger man.

It was too late for him to make peace with Paul. Regret slammed into him at the thought of his former best friend. Paul had been difficult and stubborn, no doubt, but Nicholas should have and could have tried harder to speak to the man instead of letting their friendship disappear.

Nicholas would have to carry that regret for the rest of his life. He could, however, make peace with the living Kane son.

"We all know he did it." Brendan thumped his fist on the table again. "I knew this would happen. You were always panting after her like a dog after a bitch. What's so special about her pussy, Nicholas?"

John barked out, "Watch it, Brendan," but Nicholas couldn't fully appreciate his grandfather scolding his father like a child.

He sat up straight, taking advantage of the few inches he had on his father. "Don't speak that way about her ever again."

The paleness in Brendan's cheeks had vanished, replaced by a red flush. "Because it's the truth?"

"Because if you want any place in my life, you'll be civil to her." Nicholas picked up his second cookie and bit into it, savoring the chocolate and brown sugar. It tasted like freedom. "You will not go near her, pay anyone to go near her, or do anything which could be seen in any way, shape, or form, as aggression." Cookie in one hand, he leaned forward, not breaking eye contact with his father. "Do you understand me?"

"If you date that woman, Nicholas . . ." Brendan shook his head. "I told you what would happen."

"You were bluffing."

"You think so?" Brendan looked at Eve. "Do you want to gamble on it?"

Nicholas couldn't help but cut his gaze to Eve. Their eyes met for a split second, and it was enough. Realization dawned on her face. "This is about me? He threatened you with something to do with me?"

No matter how much he wanted to, Nicholas couldn't keep every ugly thing away from Eve. Especially not now that she was an adult. "Yes."

Eve reached forward and grabbed her own cookie. "What was it?" She sounded only mildly curious, but that wasn't surprising. If the Chandlers did anything well, it was pretending everything was fine.

"He said he would disinherit you if I didn't stop seeing Livvy." The words rang with accusation in the silence of the room.

"Whoa. Disinherit an innocent child? Cold." Eve's eyes had hardened to obsidian chips.

"You didn't." John's voice rang out. Their grandfather was pale. "Brendan, tell me you didn't say that."

Brendan was silent. He rested his hands on the table, shoulders stooping.

Nicholas could almost pity him. For all his stomping around and machinations, Brendan wanted the world to think of him as perfect.

Eve and John eyeing him with disgust had to grate.

"If you ever disinherit either of these children, son, I will make you pay," John rasped.

Eve nibbled at her cookie. Nicholas wasn't fooled by her nonchalance. He'd seen that carefully controlled rage before. In his father, but in himself as well. "Nicholas, if that's what Dad was holding over your head all these years, consider the shoe fallen."

Brendan shifted, rallying. "I won't tolerate the president of Chandler's dating a Kane."

A rush of realization and resolve swirled within Nicholas. Focused. He was so focused. "Then I won't be the president of Chandler's anymore. I quit."

A crafty gleam entered his father's eyes. "You wouldn't sacrifice the company like that."

It would hurt, no doubt. It would be so awfully painful to walk away from this company that had been built by his hands and the hands of men before him. He thought of the list of people sitting on his desk, every extended family member who relied on the place for their livelihood.

But he'd done enough for it. More than enough.

"I would."

His grandfather's measured voice came from the end of the table. It was the first time in ten years Nicholas had heard that tone from his grandfather when speaking to his father. Normally, John met his son's coldness with impassioned heat. This time, a blast of pure frigidness came out of his mouth. "Enough, Brendan. The poor boy has suffered enough."

"Poor? Suffered?" Brendan scoffed. "He's had everything money can buy. He'll inherit a multimillion-dollar company."

"I've suffered," Nicholas admitted, and saying that, acknowledging the pain he'd experienced, felt better than anything he could remember. He didn't have to lock it up in a little box and soldier on. He could bring it out and let it grow inside him. It hurt, but it was the good kind of hurt that came with acceptance. Freedom. "I stopped seeing Livvy because I thought I had to. Because I was certain I needed to keep this company and this family together." His laugh was short. "Look at us. You and Granddad never talk to each other without fighting. You barely acknowledge your daughter and only speak to me when you want something."

Nicholas looked around the conference room. "Our only meals together happen in a boardroom, and we never discuss anything more than business. My initial motivation doesn't exist anymore. There's no family to keep together." His voice turned ragged. "And as much as I hate the thought of the employees suffering for your and Grandpa's temper, I can't let that control my life anymore. Go on. Splinter this family. Kill the company. I'm done with letting you and the past and your ridiculous anger and secrets dictate my life. I gave Livvy up once for this family, for the company. I won't again." He came to his feet, feeling like a ton of bricks had lifted off him.

Brendan sneered. "So fucking dramatic. Come on now, Nicholas, this isn't you. Be realistic."

"Realistic like you, you mean? Nah. I could never be like you," he murmured, certain of at least this much. He could never be like his father. He had too much of his mother and grandfather in him. "Besides, you weren't being realistic, then or now. You were being vindictive and selfish."

John cleared his throat. "Nicholas, I hear what you're saying, but I don't accept your resignation. What would you like us to do in order to ensure you stay?"

Nicholas raised an eyebrow while his father sputtered. He hadn't foreseen any part of this discussion, but he certainly hadn't anticipated bargaining his way through his resignation. He thought for a second. "Both of you need to stop squabbling like children. Since I don't think that's going to happen, I need you to establish an independent board of directors so I won't have to play this ridiculous balancing act between the two of you. Plus, Dad has to learn to treat Eve and Livvy with the respect they're owed. Or simply stay away from them, and me." He rose, the rest of his cookie still in hand. He'd eat it on the way to Livvy's. "You can think about it and let me know if those terms are acceptable. Now, if you'll excuse me, I have to go talk to Livvy."

He almost made it to the elevator before Eve hailed him. She ran up to him, huffing and out of breath. "Nicholas."

He turned, regret and sorrow hitting him. "Eve." He glanced around, grateful the hallway was empty. "Sweetheart, I never wanted you to—"

"I know," she interjected, and then wrapped her arms around his middle, hugging him tight. "You've always been so good to me, and I needed shielding when I was thirteen or fourteen or fifteen. I can't thank you enough for that. I'm an adult now, though, and if you'd just talked to me like an adult, we could have removed this obstacle for you long ago."

He returned her hug with no reservation, absorbing her love inside of him like sunshine. "You're right. I'm sorry. You know, I don't know if he would have honestly written you out—"

"There's that shielding again. You and I both know he would have done it." She patted his back, like she was offering him comfort. "And we both know why."

He exhaled, feeling her final words like a punch to the gut. Christ, so many secrets. He drew away and looked down at her, uncertain of what to say, unable to give voice to the suspicions he'd always harbored. Finally he settled on something unequivocally true. "I love you."

"I love you more. I don't think you should quit, by the way. I know mediating between those two isn't fun, but this place makes you happy."

"I don't think I have to. Once Dad and Grandpa calm down, they'll give me what I want. Who else is going to run this place?"

"Not me." Her smile didn't quite reach her eyes. "You couldn't pay me enough to do your job. Or work at the foundation, actually. I really do want to quit. I hate it there."

"Eve, you can do whatever the hell you want with your life, and I'll help you."

She blinked up at him like she'd expected more of an argument. "Okay."

He shoved his thumb at the elevator. "I have to go."

"Oh! Yes. Yes, go." She tucked her hair behind her ear. "I'm very happy Livvy makes you happy. If there's anything I can do to assist with that . . . well. I'd like to make up for my previous behavior in any way I can."

Nicholas had thought his father would be the big boss he fought at the end of the game, but now he knew Brendan wasn't the problem. The biggest struggle, getting Livvy to see how good they could be together, was ahead of him. "I'll let you know. For now, keep your fingers crossed."

She showed him her crossed fingers and he smiled tightly. If only it could be that easy. But when had Livvy ever made anything easy? No, she would be difficult and troublesome and contrary.

As the elevator doors closed, he popped the rest of the cookie into his mouth and brushed the crumbs from his hands, uncaring about the mess he was making. Luckily, he could be just as stubborn.

SOMETIMES THERE was a very thin line between dumb and romantic.

Nicholas eyed the trellis on the east side of Tani Kane's house. At her old home, Livvy had a tree right outside her bedroom window, a huge oak Nicholas had grown intimately familiar with. This trellis wasn't much different. Except he'd been a lean kid then, not a much bigger man with a creaky knee.

He pulled his phone out of his pocket and tried calling her again, cursing softly when it went right to voicemail. He'd sent texts too, for the past few hours. All of them had gone unanswered.

He glared up at the window. It was getting dark, so hopefully the neighbors wouldn't notice him casing the place and call the cops. Her car was in the driveway. Maybe if he could get her attention? He picked up a rock, then hesitated, staring at it. It was a big rock. What if he ended up breaking the window? He couldn't imagine that would endear him to Tani.

Knock on the door.

Wouldn't it be better to talk to Livvy before introducing the rest of their families into the mix? She wouldn't be concentrating on them if she was worried about everyone else. And damn it, for once he wanted them both to only be concerned with themselves.

He dropped the rock and stared grimly at the trellis before giving it a good shake. *Seems sturdy.*

Livvy's sardonic tone whispered in his ear. *Now you're a trellis structural engineer, huh?*

Nicholas grabbed ahold of the wood, grimacing at the dirt. He hoisted himself up, halting when the thing gave a fraction of an inch beneath his weight. Dying like this would be mortifying.

He placed his hand on the next rung carefully, trying to avoid the thorns there. He'd gotten about two feet off the ground when a throat cleared behind him. "Olivia isn't home."

He dropped his head for a second. Dying like this might have been less mortifying than being caught like this.

Not seeing any way past it, he crawled back down the trellis and hopped to the ground, surreptitiously wiping his hands on his pants legs before turning to speak to the small woman behind him.

He hadn't seen Tani since the night he'd rushed into his father's office to try to stop her from signing away the business. She'd been pale then, her eyes vacant, the skin below them bruised. She'd looked right through him.

She seemed smaller now, more fragile, and not only because of the cane she was leaning on. She'd always dressed in fashionably expensive dresses, but today she wore soft pink pajamas, tennis shoes on her feet.

Losing her hadn't created the hole in his life losing Paul or Livvy had, but it had been a loss nonetheless.

He straightened and met her dark gaze. "Hello, Tani."

"Nicholas." She shifted her weight. "One would think you would have learned to use a doorbell in the past ten years."

"Uh."

"It's been at least that long since I've seen you creeping into my daughter's room."

Busted. Busted from years ago, it seemed. Nicholas's smile was more of a grimace. "Uh."

Tani's lips curved, but her eyes were pitiless. "Each generation thinks it's far more clever than the generation before it, doesn't it?"

He tucked his hands in his pockets, trying not to feel like a chastened nineteen-year-old caught by his girlfriend's parent. "I'm sorry, Tani."

"Sorry for what? For disrespecting me and my husband by crawling into our daughter's bedroom when you were both young?"

He winced. "Ah, yes."

"Hmm." She pivoted, leaning heavily on the cane. "Follow me."

It wasn't an invitation, but an order. Her cane was sinking into the ground, so he tried to walk closer to her, in case she fell, but she seemed fairly surefooted.

They rounded the house, and he took in the modest backyard. As unfair as Nicholas had found the takeover, he'd taken some comfort in knowing the money she'd received from it and the estate was enough for her to live comfortably for the rest of her life, with proper investment.

She led him to a well-built back porch where a larger woman dressed in a blue dress, tights, and a matching fleece sat on the white wicker furniture. The other woman raised an eyebrow at spotting him. "That walk you took came with a souvenir, I see, Tani."

"I found him trying to break and enter."

He nodded at Maile, his face heating again. "Hello, Ms. Maile."

She settled back in her chair. "Boy."

Mentally, he resigned himself to an awkward delay in finding Livvy.

Tani gestured to a seat to the left of Maile, and then took her own seat to the right once he sat down. He glanced back and forth at the two women he was sandwiched between. They stared at him, but their faces gave nothing away.

Finally Maile spoke. "So. You're seeing Livvy again."

"Yes, ma'am. I'm sorry you had to find out this way—"

"We knew before you almost broke my trellis." Tani pursed her lips and poured a cup of coffee from the press in the center of the table.

Maile leaned to look around him. "How did you know?"

"Please. I know everything. Like I knew about this one sneaking into Livvy's room years ago."

Maile grinned. "I do like you, sister."

"You never said anything then," he said cautiously.

"If she'd been younger, I probably would have intervened. But the way you two looked at each other . . ." She shrugged. "I assumed if you weren't sneaking into my home, you'd be sneaking off together somewhere. I kept it from Robert. Livvy's father—" She cut herself off and cast him a wary glance.

He gestured for her to continue. "I'm fine. What about Robert?"

Her shoulders relaxed imperceptibly. "Robert would have killed you. Olivia was his baby girl."

"Thanks for not letting me die. I'm sorry we did what we did."

"Are you?"

"No," he admitted, with brutal honesty. "I'm sorry you knew, though."

Maile's laugh was deep. "You always were an honest boy."

He accepted the mug of coffee Tani shoved at him, though he didn't want it. "Thank you."

"That wasn't necessarily a compliment. It would have been nice if you'd been a little less honest sometimes."

The bite in the words didn't startle Nicholas. He welcomed them. "I hurt Livvy back then. I know that."

"One of the few things I remember about that time," Tani said quietly, "was walking past Livvy's bedroom and seeing Jackson holding her while she wailed on the floor. That was the day you ended your relationship, I believe."

His heart shredded, imagining his Livvy sobbing after leaving him in those woods, with only her twin to comfort her. *I don't care what that idiot burned down. I will owe you forever for that, Jackson.* "Tell me," he managed.

Maile shifted. "Tell you what?"

"Tell me how bad it was for her. I have to . . . I have to make up for every tear she shed."

"Because you pity her?"

He shook his head. "I only want to make up for my mistake."

"And what was your mistake, Nicholas?"

He turned back to Tani. "I gave up." Their path had been so open and easy before that. A crown prince and princess merrily walking hand-in-hand. The royal family, before the villain arrived and threw the realm into chaos.

"Do you think the outcome would have been different if you hadn't given up?"

"I don't know," he admitted. "But I want to try again."

"The obstacles are gone now?"

He thought of his father. "No. But I'm better prepared to handle them. Him."

"Your father doesn't approve," Tani guessed.

"Would you approve?" he hedged.

"No. I think you'll hurt her again."

Fair concern. "I won't."

"Have you told Brendan you've been seeing Livvy?"

"Yes," he responded.

She raised an eyebrow. "I can't imagine he was pleased," she replied with the kind of sardonic air that came from someone who knew Brendan well.

"He wasn't. My grandfather and sister gave their blessing, though."

Tani's hand jerked, tapping her mug. It jostled but didn't spill. "John?"

"Yes. He holds no ill will against any of you. He never has."

A yearning need filled Tani's eyes, and she took a sip of her coffee, her hand trembling. When she put the cup down, she looked away. He wanted to wait for her to compose herself, but the clock was ticking. He needed to find out where Livvy was and get to her before she had more time to dwell on all the reasons they couldn't be together.

"He didn't want my father to buy you out. Neither did I. That was a shitty deal Brendan gave you."

"It was." A smile played over Tani's lips, surprising him. "I don't resent you or your father for that deal."

"You weren't in the right state of mind to—"

"Don't tell me my own state of mind," she said, forestalling him with quiet dignity.

"Yes, ma'am." He shoved his mug away. "My grandfather would probably like to see you. He's not getting any younger."

Her sigh was deep and long. "None of us are."

He was well aware of that, acutely conscious of every second and minute and hour he had already lost with Livvy. "Can you please tell me where Livvy is?"

There was a long silence. Just when Nicholas was ready to get up, Maile spoke. "Her brother is in town."

Tani made a small sound, and Maile cast her a sympathetic look and named a hotel. "I assume she went to see him."

He nodded and pushed back his chair. "Thank you."

"It won't be easy," Maile warned.

"We can make it work."

"I mean getting her back."

A cold sensation ran down his spine. "I know.

I'm confident, though. I'll tell her how much she means to me. Then and now."

"And you think that's all she needs to hear?" Maile's words were cruel, but her tone was gentle, as if she were delivering a necessary stab wound. "That you decided you want to be with her, and she'll fall in your arms?"

He remained silent, and Tani picked up a sketch-pad and a pencil.

"Good luck," she said.

Nicholas wasn't sure if that sentiment was sincere or not, but it didn't matter. He'd take every well wish he could.

Chapter 20

"I'M GOING to kill you," Livvy growled when Jackson opened the door to his crappy hotel room.

Her twin studied her, then opened the door wider. "Want a beer first?"

So that was how they came to be seated side by side on his bed, nursing beers.

Livvy took a long sip of the alcohol. It was good beer, which didn't surprise her. Jackson had always insisted on drinking and eating the best. She rested the cold bottle on her stomach and stared straight ahead at the ugly, faded, rose wallpaper. The hotel had seen better days, but it wasn't as seedy as the place she and Nicholas had used. "It was a dick move you pulled, talking to Nicholas. Telling him about my episode back then. If I'd wanted to tell him, I would have."

Jackson set his jaw, and for a second, he looked eerily similar to Paul. "I'm not sorry. He's so goddamned self-satisfied and rich and confident. He needed to know what he did."

Her cheeks turned red, and she spoke through gritted teeth. "You had no right to do that."

Jackson closed his eyes, irritating her more. "It was my right as your brother."

"You haven't played my brother in years," she snapped back. "You can't roll in whenever you feel like and pick up the title."

He froze, mid-sip, then lowered the beer. "Fair enough. All I could think about was what he put you through. Guess my temper got ahold of me."

Livvy's lips twisted. "You understand that episode wasn't exclusively about the breakup right? It was everything. Like an avalanche of triggers, combined with my depression."

Jackson worried the label on the bottle. "I guess I didn't think of it like that. It was an avalanche of stuff for me, too, and then Nicholas fucked shit up. I know I'm not much of a brother now, but your hurt was mine then, remember?"

"I do." Two peas in a pod.

"It scared me," confessed her big, tough brother. "I couldn't lose you, too. I guess in my head it was easier to place all my anger on Nicholas."

At Jackson's stark admission of fear, Livvy deflated. While Paul drank in their father's study and their mother unraveled, Jackson had been the one to hold her on her bedroom floor. "I guess I haven't been much of a sister either. We've both been too busy running."

"Yeah." He looked out the crack in the drapes at the depressing parking lot. "You over him now?"

"Yup," she lied.

"He hurt you?"

She breathed out a low exhale but didn't respond. There was no easy answer. Of course he'd hurt her. He hurt her by existing because she knew they'd never be together.

"I told you not to stay here," Jackson said, when she didn't reply. His tone was infinitely gentle. "This place isn't good for you."

No.

No, that wasn't true. Her heart might feel like a herd of bison had trampled all over it, but she had made some gains. She had her family back, with John as a bonus. Plus, she figured she would now be able to successfully resist any texts from Nicholas. Partially because she'd blocked his number, but mostly because she was utterly conscious of the fact that her heart would simply crumble into a million pieces if she got back into bed with him anytime soon.

Whatever silly, romantic, lingering hope she'd had for them had been killed.

Yay, progress.

"I'm glad I stayed," she replied, and she believed every word. That darkness would never go away, but it was easier to beat darkness back when you had a secure base to fight from, when you had people willing to hold your purse while you lit the torch. "You said I couldn't pick and choose which parts of my past I resolved, and you're right. I think there's value in confronting stuff even if you end up acknowledging some parts can never be fixed."

Jackson was silent.

Livvy sipped her beer. "How was New York?"

"Fine."

"Why were you there?"

Nothing.

"Is it illegal, Jackson? Whatever you do?"

Out of the corner of her eye, she watched his head swing around, his scowl fierce. "Why would you ask that?"

"You're the one who told me about your prison stint in Paris."

His brown skin darkened with a flush. "That was an anomaly. And it was for a good reason."

"What was the reason?"

He mumbled something.

"What?"

"I was protesting, okay? It was bad luck I happened to be one of the ones caught."

"Protesting?" Her heart lifted. Okay. That wasn't awful. "Was it for a good cause?"

"Always," he murmured.

"Is that what you were doing in New York?" she persisted.

His sigh was weary. "No. I was working in New York. And yes, it's legal."

Aware of the we-are-done-talking-about-this tone in her twin's voice and what it meant, she subsided. "Okay."

They sat in silence and drank their beers for a while. Finally, he cleared his throat. "How's Mom?"

The question was torn out of him. "She's okay. Getting much better. She started using a cane."

Jackson grunted.

Livvy crossed her legs. She hadn't wanted to project her desire for family on him but screw it. "I know she's difficult, and I don't know everything that happened between the two of you, but it might be good for you to try to talk to her. Just once? Go see her."

Jackson ignored every word she said. "How's Aunt Maile?"

"As good as she was the last time you asked." She shifted. "And before you ask, Sadia's fine too."

Jackson nodded.

"You could see *her*, at least?"

"She doesn't want to see me."

"She does. She misses you."

"I'm sure she's fine."

Livvy thought of the sadness and anger on Sadia's face whenever Jackson's name had popped up. "She's not fine."

Jackson's frown was ferocious. "What's wrong?"

Ugh, Sadia was gonna turn her stabbing knife around on Livvy if she ever found out about this. But her sister-in-law needed friends, and Jackson had, once upon a time, been Sadia's best friend. "She could use a hand, is all. She could use you." When Jackson frowned, she pressed. "She always stood by you. You owe her, Jackson."

The knock on the door interrupted whatever Jackson's would have said in response. "You expecting someone?" she asked.

Jackson swung his legs over the side of the bed. "No."

It could be Maile. Livvy had told her aunt Jackson

was here, on the off chance her brother would agree to see the family. She set her beer on the side table.

Jackson opened the door and stopped. Then he moved aside, his eyebrow raised sardonically. "It's for you."

Livvy's knees were shaky as she came to her feet and met Nicholas's gaze. She wasn't accustomed to seeing Nicholas look so rumpled. His tie was loosened, his shirt unbuttoned with dirt covering it, his hands scratched up.

"What happened to you?" she asked, and took a step toward him. She halted at the warmth and tenderness in his expression.

"Nothing."

"Something's about to," Jackson remarked. Then he lifted his massive fist and slammed it into Nicholas's face.

Livvy squealed. To his credit, Nicholas only staggered back a step at the blow that would have probably felled a smaller man.

"Jesus, Jackson," she spat, and skirted around her brother to grab Nicholas's arm. Nicholas allowed her to lead him to the bed and set him down on it, and then she pried his hand away from his face, wincing at the blood trickling out of his nose. "What were you thinking?" she asked her brother, and grabbed a handful of tissues from the box on the bedside table.

"He hurt you. He knew the price he'd pay." Jackson cocked his head. He studied Nicholas like a scientist with a lab experiment. "I probably owe him a few more hits."

Nicholas straightened as she dabbed at the blood coming out of his nose. "That one was free. You won't be hitting me again."

She looked between the two men while the charged silence extended, then finally threw up her hands. "Enough of this shit. Jackson, out."

"It's my room," he pointed out mildly.

"Go," Livvy said briskly. If nothing else, she had to get Nicholas's blood cleaned up and find out what had him showing up here looking like a mess.

Jackson grunted. "Fine. I'll be in the lobby. Call me if you need me."

The door clicked softly, and Livvy bent over Nicholas, awkwardly dabbing at his face. She hadn't seen enough fights to know exactly how to take care of a bloody nose. "I don't think it's broken," she offered.

"That's a relief." Thankfully, he took over the doctoring and accepted the tissues from her, tilting his head back and pinching his nostrils closed. "I'll be fine."

She twisted her hands between her and sat next to him. "Sorry about that. I didn't know he'd punch you."

"He did warn me." He lowered the tissues and glanced at her. "And I did hurt you."

Livvy worried her lip. Nicholas shifted so he was angled toward her, and picked up her hand with the one that didn't hold bloody tissues. "I'm sorry, Livvy."

"It's not your fault," she mumbled, her heart breaking anew. "You can't help what you feel."

He paused. "How do you think I feel?"

She shrugged.

"Like I pity you?"

"Yeah." Restless, she pulled her hand from his and stood, pacing away from him, then back again.

"No. Livvy, I don't pity you. I love you."

The rushed words made her stop and stare at him. "What?"

"I love you." His shoulders lowered and he smiled up at her, the years falling away from his face, his younger self and the man he was now merging together.

She shook her head, feeling like someone had dunked it in a bucket of water. His words were coming from far away, too muffled and low for her to understand. "What?" she repeated.

He didn't look impatient, but amused. He came to his feet and walked over to her to hold her shoulders and look down at her. "I love you. I've always loved you. That's what I should have said when we were in that hotel room. I don't know why it was so hard. It feels pretty easy right now." He pulled her unresisting body closer.

She allowed it. She reveled in it. Livvy closed her eyes and absorbed every second of this moment—the way he smelled like an inexplicable combination of chocolate and earth, the strength of his arms around her, the words resonating in her ears, smoothing over the ragged edges of the wound she ripped open on an annual basis.

She drew it in and wrapped it around herself, because she knew it couldn't last. Committing everything to memory, she pulled away. "Thank you."

"Thank you?" His dark eyebrows met over his swollen nose. "Is that all you have to say?"

"I love you too. But you know that."

His smile destroyed her. Especially when it started to fade. "Why do you look like that?"

"Like what?"

"Like this is bad news?"

She'd opted for a simple button-down and leggings to come over here, and she was glad she had. She didn't need her usual armor of outrageous clothes when she was going to strip them off anyway.

Nicholas kept his gaze on her face as she removed her shirt and leggings, until she was standing in front of him in only a bra and panties. She pointed to the heart in the parenthesis on her breast. "It's an E. E. Cummings poem: 'i carry your heart with me(i carry it in my heart).'" She touched the dragon on her leg. "Because I need protection sometimes." She tapped her shoulder and the vine crawling over her flesh. "I didn't want to cling to you anymore."

She almost turned around to show him the compass, but that would be a step too far. She couldn't.

When his gaze met hers, she took a step back from the tenderness there. "Livvy."

"Nico. I can't."

He recoiled, the words seeming to hit him harder than her brother's fist. "What?"

"I can't accept your love." She licked her lips. "I

can imagine what Jackson told you, but my wanting to die after we broke up, that wasn't solely about you. I have depression."

He didn't move, simply watched her.

"Jackson was the only one who knew about it when we were young. I hid it, because I thought I had to. My family called me moody or temperamental, and I don't think it was so awful until I hit my late teens anyway." Livvy ran her hand through her hair. "When we broke up, that was a bad episode. Probably the worst I've ever had, though the time after Paul's death wasn't so great either."

Nicholas took a step closer to her, stopping when she backed up. "Let me finish. This is a part of me, and sometimes the darkness comes and goes for no reason. But there are definitely things that make it worse. Feeling alone, or overwhelmed." She swallowed. "Feeling like the people I surround myself with can't accept all of me."

He drew in a breath. "Livvy."

She spread her hands in front of her. "The reality is, you're always going to be inside me. On me." She gestured to her body. "In one way or another, you've influenced my life. But I only have so much skin left." She picked her shirt up, drew it around her shoulders, and buttoned it up.

"You don't trust me. I know what mistakes I made last time, and I won't repeat them. Give me a chance, Livvy."

"You can say that now, Nico. When our relationship comes out, what's going to happen the first time some obstacle gets thrown in our way?"

"You think I'll choose the company or my family over you? I wouldn't."

"It's happened before." Each word fell between them, damning him. "I believe you love me. I just don't know if you'll be able to stay with me. Out there, in the real world. And I—I deserve that." As she said the words, she felt them lifting her spirits and her self-confidence. "I deserve that," she repeated. "When shit goes down, storybook princes are unreliable. I need a man who's going to stand by my side in the cold light of day. I can't be someone's secret anymore. I can't carry the emotional load all by myself."

"What if—"

There came that word again, and she couldn't afford to be distracted. "Ifs belong in fairy tales." She shook her head and put every ounce of pleading in her voice. He wouldn't ignore her if she truly demanded something. "Please leave, Nicholas."

He stilled completely, and then he nodded, a dip of his head.

She didn't look up when he left, closing the door quietly behind him. She figured she had a little while before her brother came back. Plenty of time for her to crawl under the cheap comforter and sob.

She didn't budge until she felt big hands pulling her close. The motions were awkward, but not hesitant. Her brother arranged her so she was tucked in tight next to his larger body. "I'm going to kill him," he said, and it was one of the calmest, most alarming declarations she'd ever heard. Listening to that, a person could believe a more reckless Jackson had gone ahead and burned down a store to avenge his sister.

"You are not. You said you don't do illegal stuff."

"I'll make an exception." His hand ran up and down her back.

"He told me he loved me and he wants to try again," she said miserably.

He snorted. "No shit."

She leaned away. "You don't sound surprised."

"You know what the security code on his house is? Our birthday. Yeah, I believe he's still hung up on you."

She swiped at the wetness on her cheeks. "What? How do you know his security code?"

"Not important." He pressed her face back against his chest. "I'm guessing you don't want him."

"I don't know if he can love all of me. I can't do everything all over again and then pick up all the pieces when he quits."

"There's nothing wrong with all of you."

There's nothing wrong with you. You're going to be fine.

He meant well, but, ugh. She grit her teeth, unable to stop herself from saying something. "I always hated when you said that, you know. It made me feel pressured to pretend I was fine and I'm not fine."

Jackson stroked her hair for a while, his chest moving beneath her cheek. "I never meant for you to feel like that," he said finally. "I only meant to say you were perfect."

Perfect?

Jackson, who more than anyone, had seen her at her lowest, thought she was perfect? "I'm imperfect."

"Yeah, so's everyone." His voice dropped, fumbling. "But there's nothing bad about that."

Oh.

His voice grew stronger when she didn't respond. "You are who you are and I love you."

She drew each word close to her heart, using them as tiny torches to illuminate the scary loneliness.

She'd done the right thing, though it hurt. This. This was what she needed. People who could see all her imperfections and find beauty in them. It was possible.

I deserve compassion.

She rested her head against his chest.

I deserve love.

Chapter 21

"OLIVIA? OLIVIA."

Livvy blinked open her crusty eyes, jerking when she found her mother hovering over her. "What?"

Her mom held out her cell phone. "Sadia. She says she tried to call you and that it's important."

She rose on her elbow. "I'll call her back later," she whispered.

"Did you not hear her say it's important?" Sadia snapped with uncharacteristic impatience.

Damn it. Livvy'd forgotten about her mother's fondness for speakerphone.

With a sigh, she accepted the phone. Her mother silently hobbled out of the room.

"Hello," she said, her raspy voice startling even her.

"My God, where have you been?"

Livvy sat up and scrubbed at the goop that had sealed her eyes shut. She'd come home yesterday in a daze, barely acknowledged her mother and Maile sitting on the sofa in the living room, and made her way upstairs only to engage in more of the same crying she'd done in her brother's hotel room. She'd tried to tell herself there was value to discovering all this stuff with Nicholas and someday she'd look back on this as a period of massive growth as a human, but all of that was really hard to swallow when she was hurting so fucking much. "What's up?"

"Listen, you need to get down here."

"Down where?"

"To Chandler's."

The word drove a knife in her already fragile soul. She groaned and fell to her back. "Not now, Sadia."

"No, you really need to."

"I can't go to Chandler's."

"Livvy. I really think you'll want to."

"Why?"

"It's closed, and there's a sign on the entrance with your name on it."

"Wait." She sat up with a jerk and swung her legs over the side of the bed. "What?"

"You heard me. It's giant. Like, A-plus signage." Sadia paused. "At some point, you and I are going to have a long talk about what's been happening with you and Nicholas and why you wouldn't confide in your best friend about it."

Oof. Livvy winced at the frostiness layering Sadia's words. "Because you would want to shiv him?" she ventured.

"Only if he was hurting you."

He'll always hurt me.

"Get down here, Livvy. I really don't know what

to make of this, but the man clearly wants to talk to you." The phone went dead.

The silent line galvanized her into moving, like Sadia's urgency had been transferred to her. Livvy pulled on her leggings from the night before and ran a brush through her hair, forgoing makeup in favor of running out the door. She was aware she looked like a mess, but she didn't have time to don her usual armor.

It wasn't until she tried to start her car that she remembered Ruthie wasn't doing so hot. The poor girl sputtered and died. As preoccupied as Livvy was, a spurt of sadness coursed through her and she stroked the car's steering wheel. Silly to feel sentimental over a car, but her parents had given Ruthie to her. She'd seen Livvy through everything.

A horn cut through her sadness, and she glanced out her window to find Maile and her mom sitting next to her in their little Kia. Livvy got out of Ruthie and Maile rolled down her window. "We'll give you a ride."

"How did you . . . ?" Oh. Speakerphone. The invention of the devil. "Guys, actually, I can drive myself."

"For crying out loud, Olivia, get in the car," Tani said, with great impatience. "And don't frown so much. You're already getting wrinkles."

Do not get sidetracked by that beautiful blunt criticism.

Maile drove like a bat out of hell, but Livvy was too distracted to so much as clutch at the armrest in the back. When they were within eyesight of the store, she gasped.

"Well," Tani murmured.

Maile drove closer. Multiple young men stood at each entrance of the parking lot, turning cars away. Would they be allowed in?

"Turn here," she told her aunt.

When Maile pulled into the lot, the teenager there bent over, peered into the car, caught sight of her and smiled widely. He waved them in.

Maile parked in the spot closest to the entrance. Livvy fumbled with her belt and tumbled out. She was so focused on the sign, she barely noticed her mother and Maile also getting out of the car.

NICO + LIVVY = 4EVER

Holy shit. Holy shit.

A-plus signage indeed.

The white banner was humongous, covering the Chandler's name entirely. It could probably be seen from the sky. She dragged the back of her hand over her mouth.

"What was he thinking?" she whispered.

"Livvy."

Livvy's attention darted to the entrance. Eve stood there, a folder in hand, looking poised and polished in a sensible business suit. Unable to resist getting to the bottom of Nicholas's apparent break with his senses and reality, Livvy staggered to Eve. "What's going on? What is this?"

Eve handed her a sealed envelope. "My brother asked me to give this to you."

Livvy turned the envelope over. She wanted to

rip it open and read the contents almost as much as she was terrified to.

Eve's gaze went past Livvy. "Mrs. Kane."

Envelope forgotten for a second, Livvy stiffened. Whatever issues she had with her mother, she was not about to let this Baby Chandler snap at her the way she had Livvy.

Tani drew even with them. "Evangeline." Her voice was caressing. "What a beautiful young woman you've grown up into. Your mother would be so proud."

Sharp sorrow and pleasure moved behind Eve's eyes. "Thank you, ma'am."

Livvy relaxed. Her thumb tucked under the folded flap of the envelope. Ever so slowly, she eased it open.

There was a paper inside, but she couldn't quite bring herself to pull it out. Too many eyes were on her. Tani, Maile, and Eve, and hell, probably the kids tasked with turning away poor shoppers who just wanted to pick up a cake or a rotisserie chicken.

"Can I show you something inside?" Eve asked quietly. "I think it may help."

Grateful for the reprieve, Livvy nodded. Though Eve had spoken to her, Tani and Maile followed them in.

The three of them halted inside the entrance. Tani was the first one to move, and she stepped closer to the framed photograph of John and Sam that Livvy had last seen in John's home. "I thought this burned," she whispered.

"It did," Eve replied. "That's a reprint. Nicholas ordered it restored yesterday."

"Brendan must have shit a brick," her mother said softly, and Livvy did a double take at the foul language.

Eve's laugh was quickly disguised as a cough. She cleared her throat. "My father wasn't happy, but Nicholas was adamant." She looked at Livvy. "This isn't what I wanted to show you, though."

Tani was utterly still, staring up at her father's young face. Maile placed an arm around her sister-in-law's shoulder, and drew the smaller woman into her side. "Go on," Maile told Livvy. "I'll wait right here with your mother."

Livvy followed Eve into the store, tapping the envelope against her thigh. The place was cool and dark. "How much money are you losing, closing for the day?"

"We were ordered to take the sign down and open after you arrived, so luckily, not too much, since you came early. Though Nicholas is still paying all the employees."

Livvy licked her lips. So, a lot.

They wound through the deli and produce section, each step taking her back to her past, the sight of the floral section and the yellow roses there forcing her to avert her eyes. The store had essentially been rebuilt as a perfect replica of the C&O that had burned down. The tiles were the same, the fixtures upgraded, but familiar. Though she'd had no interest in the running of this business, she knew this store intimately.

Eve stopped in front of the bakery and pointed to something behind the glass. It took Livvy a second to understand. When she read the sign perched in front of the desserts, she inhaled deeply.

Olivia's Cannoli, the tiny sign read.

He'd teasingly brought her here when they were dating to show her the sign he'd had the bakers make. It wasn't uncommon—John had a cookie in here with his name on it. Their families wouldn't have noticed in corporate, or if they had, would have only rolled their eyes.

It's my favorite dessert, Nicholas had whispered.

The envelope burned in her hand. She looked down and pulled out the sheet of paper inside. Coordinates, printed at the top, ones she recognized instantly.

And underneath: *All your nights. Everyone can know.*

Tears burned. That asshole. That beautiful asshole.

When footsteps approached her, she swiped her hand over her eyes. It wouldn't do to actively sob in front of Eve.

The other woman held out a white bakery box. "For the two of you."

Livvy automatically accepted the box. "You're really okay with this?" she demanded. "With him and me? Even knowing what a shit storm this is going to unleash?"

"I am."

"It wasn't so long ago you hated me."

"I didn't hate you."

"You sounded like you did."

"I'm . . ." Eve looked down at her hands. "I was mad at you."

"Yeah, I know."

"Not because of your father." She glanced up, her face red. "I'm not proud of this. I was mad you left."

"You mean after the accident?"

"Yes. You left. After that night, it was like everyone left, except Nicholas. And even he changed. I felt like I lost everyone. My mother, my father, my brother and . . . you. My sister."

"Oh, Eve."

Her dark eyes glinted. "I missed you until I got mad at you. I told you, I'm not proud of my behavior. I'm sorry."

Livvy bit her lip. "I'm sorry too. I should have . . ." What? Friended Eve on Facebook? Texted her? She'd had no idea if the girl would welcome or hate her.

"No. There was nothing you could have done. Don't feel bad." Eve wrinkled her nose. "I'm a grown woman. I should be able to separate childish abandonment issues from reality. It was my fault, and it won't happen again."

"I thought about you quite a bit over the years." Out of necessity, she'd had to eventually stop wondering how Eve was. She hadn't very well been able to ask Nicholas about Eve when she saw him annually. Googling her—which she'd done, a time or two—had resulted in more than a few public records but nothing of note.

Another casualty to the feud.

Eve nodded slowly. "That makes me feel really good."

Livvy tucked the card under the flap of the bakery box. "Even if you're okay with us, I bet your father won't be."

A faint smile played over Eve's lips. "Just a guess, Livvy, but going by the small fortune my brother spent to hang a giant announcement outside and close this store, I don't think Nicholas cares. And you don't seem like the type to care either."

"He might—"

"Look, I have no horse in this race." Eve shrugged. "But Nicholas is tougher than you think. Tougher than he used to be."

But was Livvy tough enough to take a gamble on him?

"Of course, the question is," Eve remarked, "whether or not you believe that."

She trembled. She wanted to, so badly. She wanted to believe that this time, everything would work out. But that didn't happen outside of fairy tales. Right?

Chapter 22

SITTING AROUND doing nothing wasn't really Nicholas's thing, but he was far too committed to this scheme now. If he had to hang out nearly naked in these woods for the whole day, he would, damn it. Even if that meant most of that time was spent battling every doubt under the sun.

She wouldn't show up.

She'd show up and be pissed.

She'd already left town.

When he heard footsteps crunching over twigs and grass, he exhaled long and low and opened his eyes. She walked into the clearing, taking his breath away. "You look beautiful," he said huskily, forgetting the speech he'd prepared.

Livvy placed her hands on her hips. She wore the same clothes from yesterday, her hair was uncombed, and there wasn't a trace of makeup on her face.

Beautiful. As always.

"What the fuck are you doing, Nico?"

So beautiful.

Aware he had a dopey smile on his face, he shrugged. "I wanted to get your attention."

"Well, you got it. What were you thinking?" She stomped over and dropped the box she carried in his lap.

He opened the flaps, smiling when he saw the cannoli inside. "You saw the sign in the bakery?"

"Yes."

"'i carry your heart with me(i carry it in my heart).' I read the poem. Pretty. You're not the only one who's been carrying someone's heart with you. I may not have put you on my skin, but you've always been close at hand." Pretending not to see the tremble of her lips, he reached inside and picked up a cannoli, taking a bite of the sweet, cream-filled dessert. He offered her the other one and she shook her head.

He finished the whole thing in a greedy couple of gulps and dusted his hands off, putting the box aside. He'd feed the second one to her later. In his bed. "Thanks for coming."

"I didn't think you'd be naked. Presumptuous, aren't you?"

He was, technically, not totally naked—he still wore his boxer briefs, but since he was covered by a quilt as a nod to the weather, she could be forgiven for thinking that. "I wanted to give you easy access." He held out a Sharpie. "You still haven't shown me what tattoo you're gonna give me."

She stared at the Sharpie. "You're kidding me."

"You want to talk to me? Give me a tattoo." He

was no fool. He liked having her touching him, but more importantly, drawing calmed her.

With shaking hands, she accepted the permanent marker. She looked down at him, and then knelt next to him on the blanket he'd spread out under their tree. "Turn over."

Obligingly, he rolled over onto his stomach. "Is this going to be another nude?"

"No. I know what I want to put on you." The tip of the marker touched his shoulder. The sensation tickled, but he held still.

He closed his eyes and pillowed his head on his arms. The fall air was chilly, but the sun was shining. Anyway, he couldn't help but feel hot when Livvy had her hands on his body.

"Honestly, what the hell were you thinking with that big display?"

"The sign?"

"Yes, the sign."

He gestured at the tree. "You made it sound like a joke when we were kids, how you wished I'd woo you. It wasn't a joke. You thought a grand gesture of love was romantic. I wanted to give you one."

The marker paused. "Oh Nico."

"I see who you are, Livvy."

Her breathing came faster. "I don't know—"

"What was our agreement?"

"Which one?"

"The original one. All those years ago, when you sent me that first message."

"One night." She swallowed, audibly. "No one will know."

"That agreement, you were right, it wasn't healthy for us. And yet, there were some years of my life when that night with you was the highlight of twelve months."

She was silent above him. He was barely clothed, and every word stripped him down further. He welcomed the vulnerability. Like the pain of confronting his father, it felt productive. "When Eve was sick, I didn't leave her side for a night, except for those ten hours with you. You gave me the strength to go back to the hospital and sleep on that couch in the pediatric ward for weeks."

"I did?"

"You did." He breathed deeply, releasing the protective mechanisms he'd carried all his life. "You're not my secret anymore. My love for you is bigger than anyone who might try to tear us apart." He paused. "I won't leave you, Livvy. You don't have to trust me completely right now, but watch me. Watch me fight for you this time."

A drop of wetness fell on his back. Since she was still drawing, he didn't turn around, though he hated the thought of her weeping. "Your family—"

"My father knows. He knew before I came to you yesterday. He's the only one who would disapprove of us, and I am done living my life so it revolves around him. You're my family. You always have been. I promise you won't have to carry the emotional load this time."

She didn't speak, but the marker lifted from his skin. "I'm done."

He tried to crane his neck around, but the drawing was out of his range of eyesight. "I can't see. My phone's over there. Can you take a picture?"

She stretched over him to grab his phone from where it sat on his neatly folded clothes. "What's your password?"

His first instinct was to tell her he would enter it, but he swallowed the urge down. Quietly, he rattled the numbers off.

The phone slipped out of her hands. "How long has that been your password?"

"Always," he admitted. He used different passwords or combinations for various other stuff, but the things that were personal—his phone, his home—they were all protected by some variation of Livvy's birthday.

"Jackson said it was your home security system code. I didn't fully believe him."

"It was." He'd changed it after Jackson had broken in, and resented the younger man every time he had to type in the new randomly generated code. "Now take a picture."

She picked up the phone, fumbling as she entered the numbers. "I probably don't want to know why Jackson knows the code to your home, do I?"

"Maybe not right now," he conceded.

Livvy snapped a picture of his back and avoided his eyes when she handed the phone to him. "It's a sketch," she said defensively, like he would judge her.

It took him a second to understand what he was looking at. The drawing was rough, but even in the quick lines, he could see the beauty of the design.

It was a compass, similar to the one on her back, though hers was dreamy and paint-splattered and colorful.

A crown capped the N at the top of the *north* arrow. He used his fingers to zoom in on that crown. The outline of it consisted of precisely printed numbers. He had to tilt the phone to understand the significance. "It's this place," he said, with a sense of wonder. "The coordinates. You just came up with this on the fly? Like the mermaid or the fairy?"

She concentrated on capping the marker like it was imperative that the thing not dry out. "No. I thought of it a few years ago."

He looked at her sharply. "It's similar to yours."

IF SHE'D tattooed him for real, he'd see how closely it matched hers. Livvy wouldn't do his in watercolor. It would be sharp neat lines. The intricacy of the compass, though, that would be the same. "I don't have a crown." She'd left it off, finding it far too painful to put the numbers designating their special place on her skin.

"I love it. I want it done properly."

She snorted. "You're ridiculous."

"It's not ridiculous for me to put some literal skin in this game." He sat up, his abdomen muscles clenching and releasing. Not like she was noticing things like his muscles or his lovely smooth olive-toned skin or the trail of hair on his belly.

She averted her eyes from the bulge at his lap under the blanket. Nope. Not noticing at all.

"Come here," he murmured, and she allowed herself to be tugged forward, because she wanted nothing more in the world than to keep touching him.

He arranged her so she sat astride him. "What's holding you back?"

Fear and anxiety swirled inside her. "You know."

"You think I can't love you because of the depression?"

Her lips trembled. "It's a chronic condition. I can manage it, and I'm in a good place now, but I can't be cured."

"I wouldn't try to cure you."

"You haven't seen me during an episode. I kept those away from you before."

"I haven't." He hesitated, looking out into the distance. When he met her gaze again, she could read his resolve and pain. "There are things you don't know about me, too."

"Like what?"

"My . . ." His Adam's apple bobbed. "My father is awful."

She made a face. "I know."

"No, you don't. No one does."

"What do you mean?"

He ran his hand over his head. "The only ones who saw what he was truly like were my mother and me, and I guess Eve, though I tried to protect her from it."

A chill ran down her spine at the dark, lost look in his eyes. "Did he hurt you?" The words were sharper than she intended, but she couldn't help herself. The Chandlers and Kanes might have been close, but it was easy enough to miss all the dynamics in your own family, let alone someone else's.

She felt sick, imagining all the ways Brendan could have hurt his son. She'd borrow Sadia's knife, and cut the bastard.

"Not physically. He'd yell, throw things. Belittle, manipulate."

"Emotional abuse. Mental." Still totally stab-able offenses.

Livvy unclenched her fists, trying to focus past her anger. Nico needed her now. Later. Later she'd hunt Brendan down and start cutting.

"Whatever it was, it's left its mark on me." His smile was tight and humorless. "I know I'm not good at expressing my emotions. I'm rigid and I have control issues. I want to do better by you, and I will, but I'll probably slip up now and again. I'm not perfect either, whatever perfect even means. You'll have to love all of me, just like I'll love all of you."

She ran her hands down his arms to his hands, capturing them in hers. They were strong hands, the fingers long and capable.

You can be strong and have moments of incredible despair. Those moments are not weaknesses. They are simply moments. And they are not you.

He interlaced his fingers with hers, squeezing tight. "I'm not a prince. This is not a fairy tale. This is reality, with all its problems and hassles and issues and absurd family dynamics, and I want you with me. Honestly."

I deserve compassion.

She was standing on a precipice. There was beautiful water below, the color of Nico's eyes. Rocks, too, though, hidden underneath. "I'm scared."

"So am I. Let's be scared together." He dipped his head to brush his lips over hers, a delicate ghost of a caress.

"You like predictability and order. I'll mess your world up."

He smiled. "Order's overrated. I don't care if you leave your clothes all over our bedroom or dishes in the sink or you run off somewhere on a whim for a week. Those are superficial things. The most predictable, dependable thing in my life was always you."

If she wanted to throw up more road blocks, she didn't have to look far. "Living here could be a challenge. We have so much history." Good, bad, and in-between, this town held their past.

"We'll move."

Her eyebrows shot up. "Uh, what?"

"If you didn't want to live here, we could move. I'm sure I can figure out something for work."

He'd walk away from his home and this place for her? Just like that?

She was silent for so long his expectant look turned to concern. "I wouldn't be happy without you, Livvy. Would you?"

She hadn't expected him to so casually propose moving away. Livvy compressed her lips. "You'll fight for us?"

He nodded. "I'll fight for us," he vowed.

What if he doesn't? What if he quits?

Then she'd hurt, and weep. She'd lean on the support systems she'd fought so hard to reclaim and she'd get through it, like she'd gotten through so much in her life already. "There will be problems. There'll be pain."

"Every relationship has peaks and valleys. We'll work through them."

She took a deep breath, and took the leap. "I want a steady supply of cunnilingus. Not because you feel grateful, but because you actually enjoy it." She reflected. "Actually, you can feel a little grateful."

His muscles went taut. Stunned hope flitted across his face. She wanted to weep at the sight of it.

Cool and controlled. Or hot. For a decade, those were the only emotions he'd allowed her to see.

This was beautiful. She'd treasure every feeling he trusted her with, collect them with her own in invisible containers.

"I'll start now," he said, his voice hoarse.

She twined her arms around his neck. "Okay."

He cocked his head. "Okay what? Okay you want oral sex, or okay you'll give us a shot?"

"Yes. To both of those."

The brilliant smile that spread across his face had her grinning in return.

With a twist of his body, he had her on her back. He lowered himself on top of her, making a place for himself between her legs like he was home. "You can't just say okay. Not after I poured my heart out."

"You want a speech or something?"

"You're not the only one who needs to be wooed."

Livvy scraped her nails over the back of his neck. "I love you. I've always loved you. That grand gesture was silly and expensive, but you're right, I adored it. There were times that one night with you got me through every other day of the year. You're under my skin—literally. We'll get those matching tattoos, but not today, not next week, not when we're running high on endorphins, but after we've actually faced some problems and come out on top, because we're motherfucking adults now, not dumb kids." She paused. "Did I miss anything?"

He rubbed his nose against hers. "Instead of the *N* for north on my tattoo, can you make it an *L*?"

She had to clear her throat twice before she could speak. "I think so."

"Also, I would like to try that whole blowjob thing some more."

Tenderness ran through her at his deliberately light tone. "We can definitely work on that."

With his thumb, he carefully stroked a strand of hair away from her cheek. "You make me happy. We deserve to be happy."

I deserve compassion. "Yes."

He shifted and traced his finger over the ellipsis on her wrist, making a perfect box shape around the three dots. She had to bite back the purr of pleasure in her throat. "You never told me what this one meant," he said.

"It's to remind myself my story isn't over, even if it feels like life is paused or like I'm wandering."

He rested his forehead against hers, and for a few brief moments, the only noise was the sound of his breath and hers and the rustle of leaves. Between the layers of clothes and blanket, his cock was thick and heavy against her leg, but he was in no hurry. Neither was she.

They had time.

"Let me be a part of your story," he finally said.

She released a shaky laugh. "You always have been."

"Good." He pressed a perfect, intimate, chaste, life-changing kiss on her cheek. "You'll always be a part of mine."

Don't miss the next
Forbidden Hearts novel!

WRONG TO NEED YOU

COMING WINTER 2017!